FORBIDDEN PUCK

BOSTON BRAWLERS BOOK 1

JUNE WINTERS

1

TOO MUCH
ELLA COUTURE

The stop-and-go chaos of New York City traffic was an ever-present hum through the open window. Brakes squealed, cars honked, and even from up here on the fiftieth floor, I heard someone yell at the top of his lungs in a comically thick Brooklyn accent—*"fuck you, ya fuckin' jagoff!"*

I rifled through my wardrobe, excitedly planning what to wear in advance. I couldn't *wait* to go somewhere else for a change.

My boyfriend, Matthew, watched me from the bed. "I can't believe you're seriously packing your bag three weeks early."

"I can't help it. I'm so excited. *Key West!*" I sang. "A *real* vacation. Do you have any idea how long it's been since I've had a vacation? Or heck, how long it's been since I've taken a day off?"

Matthew didn't answer. I peeked over my shoulder and saw he was multi-tasking with his phone, fingers busily tapping and swiping away at the glowing screen. I'd come to accept his constant phone use as one of the hazards of dating a lawyer—the poor guy never could get away from the office. But hey, I could relate! At least I don't have an office I need to be at ... I'm self-employed, so *my* office is always changing.

I think we'd make a good husband and wife duo: the lawyer and the interior decorator, both successful in our respective fields and enjoying a luxurious life together. If anything, this trip to Key West was just a taste of our lavish years to come.

While Matthew was distracted with his phone, I saw opportunity. Nervously, I clenched my fist around the racy lingerie set. With clumsy hands, I quickly stuffed the lingerie into my suitcase. Fearing I'd been too obvious, I glanced over my shoulder— but Matthew never even looked up from his phone.

I'd gotten away with it. *Whee!* It's always the small thrills that get your heart pumping, isn't it?

I'd bought the lingerie specifically for our trip together and I wanted it to be a surprise. Not just the lingerie, but—well, the fact that I was finally *ready*. I could picture it so well—watching the sunset on the beach, a romantic candle-lit dinner, the two of us going back to our hotel, my hand in his, butterflies in my stomach as I knew the magic moment was about to happen. Then the look on his face, of true love and pure *desire*, when he took off my little black dress and saw my white lingerie for the first time.

The poor guy had already waited almost four months. Which was a lot longer than most other guys I've dated were willing to wait. There's a funny thing about being a virgin: every guy you date thinks it's *insanely* hot at first that you're 'pure.' But that's only because he assumes that *he'll* be the guy with the magic touch that makes your panties smolder and, after a date or two, you'll be begging and screaming for his cock.

But the first time his hand starts to wander up your legs, and you clasp your thighs shut and tell him no, the realization smacks his face like a brick wall: he'll actually have to work for this. And that is the *precise* moment when they stand up, mumble a few niceties, and run for the hills.

Don't get me wrong. I'm not waiting for marriage or anything like that. I never even *meant* to be a virgin. It just sort of happened, or I guess it *didn't* happen, and here I am—still carrying a v-card around at age twenty-two. But since I've waited this long, I feel like there's no point in rushing to lose it. The first time might as well be special, right?

All I'm looking for is a decent guy who can prove that he's willing to work for it. Most importantly, I want a guy who can be honest with me—because honesty is the most important thing in the world to me. But those two things are *way* too much to ask in this day and age, apparently.

Until I met Matthew.

Matthew. A thirty-two year old lawyer with his life together. Matthew is a big kid at heart and if you looked at the two of us together, you'd never know he was a decade older than me. Truth be told, I'm surprised his firm never lectures him about his messily-tousled hair or his suits that look like they could use a serious ironing ...

Oh well—the point is, Matthew is taking me to Key West for a week. Just the two of us. Which was a big step in our four-month relationship. He's not yet ready to make us Facebook official, but hey, he wants to take me to Key West. Which is a pretty big deal, in my opinion. Some people are just weird about social media, right? So what if he doesn't want all his friends and family on FB to know we're an item. That's not something I should be concerned about ... right?

But if I won't sleep with Matthew—what am I waiting for anymore? Do I even *know* anymore? What if I miss out on a real, quality guy?

I finished packing my bag, zipped it up and let out an accomplished and musical sigh. Matthew was still texting when I jumped on the bed next to him and curled up to him.

"Hey, who are you texting?" I flirted, rubbing my hand on his burgeoning tummy. With all the time he spent in the office and eating fast food for lunch, he was nurturing a cute little potbelly.

"Oh, uh, just some work emails." Matthew hurriedly shut his screen off so I wouldn't see it.

... *Hm.* Something about that maneuver I didn't like.

"Must be some awfully sensitive work emails," I teased.

"Well yeah, attorney-client privilege is pretty important—"

I wedged my fingers into his armpits and dug, giving him a good tickle. "You're not screwing around on me now, are you, Matthew?"

He fought me off and swore under his breath. "Fuck, Ella! How many times do I have to tell you? I'm super ticklish and I hate it when you do that."

I backed down. "Sorry. We just haven't talked at all since you showed up. You've been on that thing all night."

He laid his phone at his side. "Well. Here I am. So, what do you wanna talk about?"

"Hm. You could ask me how my day at work went."

He took a deep breath. I could tell he was still annoyed about the tickling. "So, Ella, how was your day at work?" he asked, slightly strained.

Happily, I began to tell him about the latest kitchen remodeling project I'd just finished in an apartment in Cobble Hill. It was an apartment that had languished in the décor of the boring, blasé 90's. Appliances that had once tried to look futuristic, now looked plain dated. The orange wood cabinetry and matching island hadn't aged so gracefully, either. The laminate countertops looked unacceptably cheap, and the white tile floor looked uninspired.

But as of today, I was happy to report that the project was finished. New cabinets, a new island, new appliances and lighting and a beautiful tile backsplash and hardwood floor and farmhouse sink, to just name a few of the upgrades, *and* the client had absolutely loved it all, and …

Matthew nodded while I told him all this, injecting perfectly placed *uh huh*'s or *right*'s whenever necessary. But the whole time, his phone, lying on the mattress between us, buzzed incessantly. One *bzzt* after another *bzzt* and I could see it in his eyes: he wasn't listening to me. His mind was on those text messages.

"Someone sure enjoys their attorney-client privilege," I said. "Who's texting you, anyway?"

He patted me on the head as I were his puppy. "I don't know. Probably one of my partners at the office."

"Don't lie to me, Matthew," I said lowly. "You know lying is a deal breaker to me."

"Yeah, yeah, of course." He was quick to change the subject. "Well hey, I'm glad to hear your little work thing turned out."

Little work thing?

"So, how's Lance doing?" he asked. "Spoken to him lately?"

Really? He's asking about my brother again?

"I dunno, why?"

"He's on a goal scoring tear lately. Lance and his winger, Ryan Ryder, have some *serious* chemistry together. Ryder is like a wrecking ball out on the ice, crushing guys left and right and clearing space for Lance. It lets your brother focus on scoring goals, while Ryder does all the dirty work. They've got a good thing going. It's a really exciting brand of hockey they're playing right now, honestly. Everyone's talking about them."

"Oh." I gave a small shrug of my shoulder. "I wouldn't know. I don't really watch his games all that closely. Or at all."

"Yeah. I know. You're crazy." Matthew chuckled. "If *I* had a brother in the NHL, I wouldn't miss a single game."

"So you've said," I said with a sigh.

"Ella," Matthew said, sounding suddenly serious. He took my hand in his and gently squeezed. "Can I ask you something?"

"Um, sure."

His eyes probed deeply into mine.

"When do you think I'll get to meet Lance?" he asked at last.

Why did I feel like Matthew would be happier taking *my brother* to Key West ...?

"I don't introduce guys to my family unless we're serious," I answered at last.

Hint, hint.

"This again?" Matthew smiled, but it wasn't a happy one. He let go of my hand. "Holy shit, Ella. That's a hell of a thing to say to a guy who's taking you to Key West in three weeks. How paranoid are you? How many times do I have tell you that I'm not dating anybody else? I mean, seriously, what more do you want from me?"

My eyes searched skyward for guidance. On one hand, I hated to make demands. On the other hand, he *was* asking, wasn't he?

"You could make our relationship Facebook official, for one."

"Facebook official," he scoffed. "I don't subscribe to all that social media bullshit, okay. If you wanna obsess over it, that's *your* problem, not mine."

Says the guy constantly on his phone.

I shrugged. "Alright. Sorry."

"Hell." He blew out a heavy exhale and pulled me closer. "I'm sorry, too, Ella. I just get so stressed out and anxious before a vacation, you know? But don't worry, I'll be able to relax once we're on the beach ... just you and me ... some drinks ... you know?"

"Yeah. I'm excited," I said.

"Me too."

He smiled at me, stroked my face, and moved in for a kiss. I kissed him back, even if I didn't really want to. But then Matthew cupped my breast, and his hand began the quick descent down my side, over my hips and between my thighs ...

"Matthew," I said, and I pushed his hand away as gently as I could. "Not now."

He threw his arms into the mattress with a *thud.* "Alright—alright. *Nope.* Can't do this."

I sat up. "What?"

"I thought I could, but I can't."

"Can't do *what?*"

"I'm not going to Key West with a girl that refuses to put out."

"*Excuse* me?"

"You're just so much to deal with, Ella. You're so demanding and overbearing and *ugh*. It's a lot of shit to put up with—all for a girl that doesn't even wanna fuck."

My stomach twisted into sickening knots. I could not believe this was truly happening. "Are you for real right now?"

"I'm dead-ass, babe. You wanna know the truth? You wanna know the *whole* truth, like you're always asking for?"

He snatched up his cell phone and showed me what his 'business emails' really were: girls that he was busily messaging on Tinder.

"These aren't work emails. These are the sluts that I'm going to meet as soon as I leave your place tonight."

My jaw dropped.

"Surprised? You shouldn't be. I'm a *lawyer*, Ella. I'm single, I'm young, and I live in a fan*tastic* apartment in Park Slope. I don't *have* to wait for pussy. Pussy comes to me. Pussy is *dying* to fuck me. Get it?"

My face soured. The stench suddenly emanating from him was unbearable.

"Wow. So this is the real you, huh? You are *literally* repulsive.

Those girls can have you, for all I care. You might be a lawyer, but you look and dress like a middle-school boy—and you talk about sex like one, too. It's time to grow up, Matthew, you're not getting any younger."

"And what about you?" he taunted.

"What about me?"

"Did you really believe that I was going to wait around for you? You're a seven at best. And that's if I'm feeling charitable."

My blood boiled and my fists clenched. My infamous temper began to rise and it took all the restraint I had left not to hit this idiot square on the nose …

"Then why the hell would you waste my time? Why even offer to take me to Key West, if that's how you feel about me?"

"Because." He gave an arrogant chuckle. "I told all the boys on my beer league team that I'm banging Lance Couture's little sister." He punctuated the barb with a grotesque sneer. "Figured I should probably hit it at least *once* to cosmically justify all my bragging, or something—but fuck it. I'm cutting bait. Right now."

He stood up and put his shoes on.

"Wow, you're an asshole," I snarled. "For your information, I was actually planning on making the colossal mistake of fucking you in Key West. Thanks you for shooting yourself in the foot, moron."

"Oh, I'm *sure* you were, Ella." He rolled his eyes. "And as soon as we got on the beach, I was going to drop to one knee, pull out a ring, and *finally* pop the question."

"Whatever. Get out of my apartment already, you heartless douche-bag."

He headed for the door, but stopped to get one last word in. "You know. You were right about one thing. *Damn,* it feels good to tell the truth."

With that, he left.

I shoved my suitcase off the bed, crawled under the sheets, curled into a ball and told myself I wouldn't cry.

So much for Key West. Guess I'll just spend the week working like usual ...

2

THE CODE

RYAN 'RADAR' RYDER

At thirty-four thousand feet in the air, the Boston Brawlers had left Denver and were finally heading home.

Four of us sat in the team plane's lounge, crammed into the restaurant-style booth.

On my left was Lance Couture. At twenty-four years old, Lance is our all-star. He's all speed, flash and skill, and supreme confidence in his talent. He's also my best bud and roommate. At the start of this season, we moved into a sweet condo together downtown.

Across the table, captain Shea Ellis. At thirty-six, Shea is still the Brawlers' undisputed #1 defenseman. He's not the fastest d-man anymore, but there's no substitute for the years of experience that the crafty vet has accumulated over his career.

To Shea's side sat goalie Ilya Zarkov, a fierce competitor who didn't speak a word of English when he arrived in the States to play hockey at age twenty. Ilya still speaks with a thick (and sometimes hilarious) Russian accent—but his English has really improved since he first joined the league. We all love Ilya, even if we think he's completely nuts.

Anytime we flew home after a road trip, the four of us had a tradition of getting together for a cut-throat game of poker. And we were feeling the heat: our suit jackets had come off, neck-ties loosened, and shirt sleeves rolled up to the elbow.

I laid my cards on the table with a sigh. "I'm out. I got nothing."

"Same," Ilya muttered.

Now the hand was between Shea and Lance.

"Long road trip, eh, boys?" Shea said, pushing a small stack of $500 chips into the pile with a clattering, plastic *clink*. He lifted a salt-and-pepper eyebrow and cast wry a glance at Lance.

"It was only a week on the road," Lance said, clutching a bag of ice to his purple and swollen eye. "You feeling it in your bones, old man?"

Shea didn't react. "Waiting on you, youngblood."

"I've played enough poker with you to know that you *love* small talk when you're bluffing," Lance said, pushing a stack of chips into the pile.

Suddenly looking ten years younger, Shea revealed his cards.

"Aw, *fuck!*" Lance swore while Shea lunged forward and greedily scooped up the entire pot with a snicker.

"You've got a lot to learn, kid. You don't realize I'm setting traps for you every time we play."

"Oh, that was a trap, was it? Yeah, right, you gambled and you got *lucky.*"

Ilya, always amused and always laughing, chuckled heartily. "That, that was not luck. You walked right into that, Lance. Everyone could see that coming!"

"Just like everyone knew Hunter Rockwell was going top cheddar on you tonight, right Ilya?" Lance shot back.

Someone in the row ahead of us overheard the insult. "*Damn!*"

Rockwell had scored the only goal of the game for Colorado

with a laser of a wrist-shot that he fired over Ilya's shoulder and into the roof of the net—AKA, *top cheddar.*

Ilya grinned. "Yes. Same way *you* saw Beau Bradford's right hook coming right for your eye."

The boys in the row ahead of us went "*ooooh!*"

"Can't stand that Bradford prick," Lance said as he repositioned his ice bag. "Can you fuckin' believe he sucker-punched me?"

I chuckled. "What did you expect? You were cracking jokes about sleeping with his wife. You gotta expect a response like that from a guy like him. You joke about a guy's family, the code says he has a right to lash out."

Lance patted my shoulder. "Well, thanks for standing up for me anyway, Radar. I can always count on you."

After Bradford sucker punched Lance, I rushed in and grabbed a hold of him. The two of us squared off and threw bombs at each other. Beau's a big kid and a tough customer, but I'm no pushover, either. We fought to a draw until the refs broke the fight up.

That's my role out on the ice—police the code of the game. When things get too heated on the ice, I step in to calm the tensions—and sometimes, I have to let my fists do the talking. But most importantly, I have to make sure that no one takes any liberties on Lance. Because you have to protect your star if you want to go far in this league.

"Just doing my job, bud," I replied.

Shea made small talk while he dealt another hand. "So it'll be nice to be back home, eh boys? Anyone got plans?"

He was met by a few grunts and grumbles.

"Nobody?" Shea asked with a shrug. The cards kept coming. "Hey Radar, Lance, how's that new condo of yours?"

"It's nice," I said. "We're in Charlestown, right on the water, and close to all the bars downtown."

"So when are you two gonna have the team over for a little housewarming party?"

I shot Lance a look. "Actually, we should have the boys over soon. But the place is still so empty. We need to hire someone to furnish it or something."

"Yeah." Lance agreed with a frown. But then something dawned on him. "Wait a minute—Ella—my little sister! She's an interior decorator and she *loves* fashion and design and furniture and all that bullshit. I'll ask her right now." He whipped out his phone and started tapping away. "And hey, I put her through college, so I figure she owes me one."

"As long as you gents are getting along at home," Shea said as an aside. "That's all I care about. Because the last thing this team needs is to be torn apart by *dissues*."

"Dissues?" Ilya asked. "What is this word?"

"It's a slang word. It means 'dish issues,' " Shea told the Russian. "Like when someone leaves their dishes in the sink without washing them." He lowered his voice. "And I'm betting Lance is the slob."

Lance rolled his eyes. "Yeah, I'm a slob, so what? Radar wakes me up in the middle of the night, so it all evens out in the end."

Ilya joked with his infamous shit-eating grin, "Don't you hate it when you wake up freezing, only to look over and see your lover has stolen all the bed sheets from you?"

He earned a few snickers from around the plane.

"Don't go bringing your sick wank fantasies into this, Ilya," Lance countered. "Anyway, *no,* Radar didn't steal the comforter from me ... but maybe that's what his lady friends are always screaming about!"

My teammates' heads suddenly popped into every aisle of the airplane, and every last set of eyeballs was focused right on me.

Oh, for God's sake. Ever since Lance and I moved in, he's been spoiling these guys with the details of my love life. I felt an embarrassed heat rising in my cheeks.

"*Another notch in the belt, eh Radar?*" someone called from the front of the plane.

"*Notch in the belt? Don't you mean, pair of panties for the panty-box?*" someone else replied.

And then everyone exploded into laughter with that last one.

"Shutup," I roared back at them. And then I mumbled quietly to the poker table, "I never should've told them about that."

"You didn't tell them about your panty collection," Lance said with a glint in his eye. "*I* did."

"Right. Thanks for reminding me, dickhead."

Lance knew he had the attention of everyone on the plane. He spoke loudly, addressing the team.

"So, it was the night before we left Boston for this road trip. At three in the morning, I wake up to this guys' headboard crashing against the wall—*bang bang bang*! And a girl starts screaming, '*No! No ... don't ... no—nooo! Ohhh, yesssss!*' I swear, it went on for hours! So if you were wondering why I played like shit in that first game in Ottawa, there's your answer."

More hysterical laughter over Lance's orgasmic dramatization.

I gave Lance a shove. "At least I *am* getting laid. When are you gonna figure out that your lovely Instagram butt model just wants to see how severe a case of blue balls she can give a pro athlete?"

Lance smirked. "Thanks, but I'll pass on the dating advice from the guy with the panty collection."

Josh Stone, a rookie sitting across the aisle, leaned over. "Wait, I'm confused. You said Radar's girl was screaming *no*?"

"I don't get it either," Lance said. "In Radar's defense, she sounded like she was having a good time. She came a *lot* more than once. Trust me. It was super hot."

Ilya's body shook with a silent laugh. "Sounds like you enjoyed listening."

"Honestly? Yeah, okay, I got hard." Lance gave a shrug. "Hey, why's everyone laughing? At least I'm man enough to admit it. And yeah, I'll admit it, I rubbed out a quick one, too."

"*Ugh,*" everyone groaned. Lance had taken it too far, as he always does, and now all the heads disappeared from the aisle, ear-buds were stuffed back into ear canals, and everyone went back to minding their own business.

The look of amused horror on Ilya's face said it all. "And only a minute ago, you said *I* had weird wank fantasies."

I threw down a chip. "That really is fuckin' sick, Lance. I never want to think of you, one door down the hall, jerking it to the soundtrack of my sex life."

"Then next time you're nailing some dumb broad, keep it down! And I won't have to!"

"Fine."

Long-in-the-tooth Shea wore a rare and wily smile. The old man was loving this whole exchange. "So what were her panties like, Radar?"

You know the roast is bad when even old Shea wants to get in on the action.

"Pretty standard," I said, resigned. "Black thong."

"Oh, so a black thong is the standard, is it? Not a unique collector's item then?" Shea replied.

"Guess not."

"And how the hell do you even *get* their panties in the first place? Do you steal them when they go to the bathroom or what? Don't they notice they aren't wearing any panties when they get dressed?"

"Jesus, Shea. I'm not some creeper rifling through a girl's shit and stealing her panties. I don't even have to ask. They know to give them to me."

"They *know* to give their panties to you," Shea repeated, and then he *really* looked mind-blown. "How the hell does that work?"

I sighed. "Can someone else explain to Father Time how dating works in the modern era?"

"No, no no no." Shea shook his head. "That's not dating. I don't know what it is you kids do today, but it is *not* dating, lemme tell ya."

Groans arose all around us. The team feared a history lesson on what dating was like back in Shea's day.

Someone shouted, "Thanks Grandpa, but it's time for a nap!"

Shea ignored the comment and pressed further. "So what're you going to do when you fill that panty box up, Radar? Is that when you'll know it's time to settle down and get married or something?"

"Get a bigger box, obviously." I slammed another chip down on the table. "Are we going to play this hand or what?"

"Uh oh. I think we made him mad." Lance put his arm around my shoulder and gave me a squeeze. "Don't go all unhinged psycho on us now, Radar. We're just fucking with you, big guy."

Lance's phone beeped. Quickly, he picked it up and read the message. "Oh. Hey. *Perfect*, dude. Turns out my little sister is free to visit for the weekend. She said she had some plans but they fell through. You mind if she stays with us, Radar?"

"Not at all." I paused. "But didn't you say your sister was nuts?"

"Oh, she's *completely* insane. She has this idea in her head that lies are the worst thing ever. If you lie to her and she finds out, she flies off the fucking handle. Just be warned."

I laughed. "Well, whatever. She'll be your problem, not mine."

"Visiting sister, eh?" someone in the row ahead of us wisecracked. "You *know* Radar will be dying to add some 'hot sister panties' to his collection, right, Lance?"

Laughs came from all over, but Lance slowly turned his head to shoot me an enraged stare. The idea that I might do something improper with his sister—crazy as it was—was enough to fill my best friend's eyes with a seething rage that I'd never seen before. Not on the ice or off it, either.

"He better fucking *not*," Lance snarled.

I pat him on the shoulder. "Relax. He's just being stupid. Family is off-limits and everyone knows that."

That put Lance at ease. Because if there was anything you could say about me, it was that I lived by the code. And *everyone* knows that there's no bigger sin than sleeping with one of the boys' family members. Wives, girlfriends, sisters, moms, aunts, *whoever*—just don't.

Don't even look at them.

Because there's no faster way to tear a team apart and get your ass traded than to get involved with a teammate's sister.

3
___

WEEKEND PLANS
ELLA

I sat in front of my drafting table, the bright light from my work lamp focused on the layout in front of me. My workspace was, and always is, an organized chaos: hundreds of overlapping photographs of the client's rooms. Floor plans. Fabric swatches and samples. Clippings from fashion magazines for reference and inspiration.

This table might look like a mess to an outsider, but to me, it's a puzzle in progress. Each piece has been carefully arranged and *belongs* exactly where it is, forming a picture and a plan in my mind.

Tonight, though, no matter how much I stared at my project, I couldn't see the next move.

I sipped from my glass of wine and sighed. Another Friday night with no plans. Work can take the place of a healthy social life and actual friends for only so long. Soon, you'll start to feel spent, and your work will suffer. And then you *have* to take a break.

I flicked off my lamp and forced myself away from my studio. Into the living room, I threw myself face-first on my couch. My cat, Eucalyptus—so named because of his adorable, koala-like visage, if you're wondering—saw an opportunity to assert his feline dominance and leaped into action. He jumped onto the sofa and planted his front paws into my back, as if he were a soldier stabbing a flagpole into foreign soil. Eucalyptus loudly purred as he stood triumphantly over me, the conquered enemy.

"Oh, yeah," I groaned into the sofa cushions as the cat kneaded the tight muscles between my shoulders with his paws. "That feels great. Can you do that a little harder?"

Sensing that I was actually *enjoying* this, Eucalyptus chuffed, jumped down from the couch and trotted away with his head held snootily high.

"Well, that figures."

It was, after all, the selfish behavior I'd come to expect from a male. Then again, a cat can be one selfish little asshole, but at least he can't lie to you.

Speaking of. It'd been three weeks to the day since Matthew revealed his true and revolting colors. And what made this Friday night particularly depressing was the constant reminder that, had Matthew been the guy I thought he was, the two of us would've been en route to Key West at this *very* moment.

It was all so disappointing. Not because I missed him, because I didn't at all—everything he'd said was more than enough to taint any good memories I might've had—but rather because he turned out to be *such* a goon.

What was most disappointing was the fact that I had to start over, again, and I still had no idea where to find any good men. And I still carried that awful v-card with me, which seemed to have only one true purpose in life: to scare men off.

Especially the men in New York.

It seems like every man in the city is only interested in one thing: trying to get between a girl's legs. And he'll say and do *any*thing to get there. Every man you meet, you can just *tell,* is immediately calculating his odds and mentally plotting his strategy to get you into bed. It's gross and lame, and what more can I say? Maybe if I wasn't a virgin, I wouldn't find it so gross and off-putting. Maybe I'd just accept it as the *reality* of modern dating.

Maybe it's true, what other girls sometimes say: all the good guys were snatched up long ago, and now they're married and raising kids.

And if they're not taken, I have *no* idea where they're at or what the heck they're doing with their lives.

Of course, it doesn't help that I spend all my time working. Back when I was in school, I couldn't wait to get out and go into business for myself. Don't get me wrong: it really *is* amazing, being my own boss. And I do very well for myself. But lately, I find myself wondering—what's the point? What's the point of all this work if I can't actually enjoy the fruits of my labor? How did I get to this point where, every time my friends call wanting to hang out, I feel like I have to blow them off because I can't take a break from my work?

Keep treating your friends like that, and soon they'll stop calling. *Ask me how I know!*

Just then, my private pity party was interrupted by a buzzing; the *bzzt-bzzt* of an iPhone on glass. I snatched my phone from the coffee table, praying that my guardian angels had heard my laments and delivered some evening plans for the night ...!

But I groaned when I saw it was a text from my brother Lance instead.

I opened it and read.

"Sup Honey Badger?"

Honey badger: that's my nickname in the family. I don't love it, but I don't hate it, either. (If you've seen that popular YouTube video about the honey badger, you'll understand. If not, well, don't worry—I'll explain more later.)

I tapped out a reply to Lance. "Just being super cool and hanging out by myself on a Friday night. What's up with you?"

"*LOL, loser. Hey, what are you up to this weekend? I moved into a new condo in Boston this season with Radar. You should come visit! I'll be home for a week, so you can stay as long as you like!*"

Red flags started going off in my head immediately.

"And why do you want me there?" I replied.

"*Uhhh, because you're my sister? And I love you?*"

That only made me *more* suspicious.

I replied, "Uh huh."

"*Look, do you wanna come or not?*"

I started tapping out my reply: "I'd love to, but I have to work." But before I hit send, I stared at those words. The same words that I was *just* complaining about, because they cost me my social life.

Then again: spending a week with my *brother?* Surrounded by his hockey friends, who were *just* as bad as he was, if not worse? Was that really my idea of fun these days?

Oh, what the hell, Ella, I thought to myself. *Why not? It'll help you forget about Key West and you haven't seen your brother in a while. Just do it.*

Besides, my bag was already packed. After the blowup with Matthew, I never had the heart to unpack it.

I texted him back: "Short notice, isn't it? And who the heck is 'Radar,' anyway?"

"*My teammate. Look, I need a yes or a no, Ella.*"

"Gosh, you sure are persuasive. But yeah, I can come for a few days. I actually had plans for a vacation, but they fell through. Womp womp, sadface."

"*Holy shit. You sure? You're not gonna change your mind at the last minute like you always do, right?*"

"Yes, I'm sure. Don't make a big deal out of it. So which flight should I take?"

"Check your email inbox."

Just as he sent that text, my phone chimed to announce a new email. I opened it and saw the itinerary, a first-class ticket to Boston departing tomorrow evening, bought and paid for.

"You didn't have to do that," I texted Lance. "I've got money. I can pay for my own stuff."

"Hey, don't mention it, you don't have to thank me at all," he replied, and I could just *hear* him saying that in his sarcastic-as-hell tone of voice.

"... Thanks," I sheepishly texted back.

"I'll send a car to pick you up at Logan Airport. By the way, if you got any hot roommates, I'll buy them a ticket too." Insert creepy, super-happy-winky-face emoji.

I groaned and said aloud to Eucalyptus, "Really? Lance thinks that's funny, even after the thing with Quinn?"

I texted him back a message that simply said, "NOPE."

Eucalyptus sat in the corner with a suspicious look on his cat face, as if he were regarding this entire development with skepticism.

"I don't blame you, Euc," I said aloud. "I don't trust him, either."

But hey, I had *plans.*

4

MEET HONEY BADGER

RADAR

After a long road trip, there's nothing quite like waking up in your own bed and realizing you've got the next few days off. Sure, your body is still fatigued from all the travel and a week's worth of hockey wear-and-tear ...

But damn, it's good to be home.

I was still in bed, my thoughts wandering, when there was a knock on my bedroom door.

"Come in."

The door opened. Lance stepped in and leaned against the door-frame. "Hey, Radar."

Besides the black eye, he looked good, dressed up and ready to go somewhere.

"Hey, Lance. You heading out somewhere?"

"Yup. Lindsay wants to meet up." He smiled boyishly, eagerly.

Lindsay—she's the girl that Lance is currently obsessed with. The Instagram booty model. Which is just what it sounds like: she takes pictures of her butt, from various angles and in various outfits. How this makes her money, or *if* it actually does at all, I don't really know or understand. All I know is that, as soon as we're home, Lance wants to spend all his time with her. He's started saying he loves her, even though he still hasn't gotten with her yet ...

"Meeting Lindsay now? Kinda early, isn't it?" I asked.

He tapped his gold watch. "Early? It's almost 11, man. Prime brunch time."

I looked at the alarm clock and grunted. "Oh. Damn."

"Anyway, I just wanted to remind you that Honey Badger arrives tonight. I'll be back here before she makes it in—which, for your sake, is a good thing. Because trust me, you would *not* want to be left alone with her for any length of time."

I blinked at him. "Did you say Honey Badger?"

"Oh, er, sorry. I meant Ella. My sister."

"I get that, but—*Honey Badger*?" I repeated with a laugh.

He shrugged. "It's her nickname. You'll understand when you meet her."

"Well, alright."

"How 'bout you? Plans for today?"

"Gonna get up and hit the gym," I said. "Ilya wanted to grab a bite, too."

"And what about tonight?" Lance pointed at the snake-skin treasure chest that rests on top of my dresser. "You gonna add to the collection?"

"We'll see."

"Alright, bud. Catch ya later."

"Later, Lance. Tell the butt model I said hi."

He raised both middle fingers at me as he walked out of the room.

Yeah, it's true, I give Lance a hard time over Lindsay. Part of it is because I miss my wingman. Lance and I used to have a lot of fun at the clubs. And that's what I thought us living together would be like ... instead, he's always spending his time with Lindsay.

But the bigger part of it is that I don't get how a guy in our situation can get all hung up over *one* specific girl. All we have to do is walk into any club in Boston, and everyone knows who we are. Girls start giving us the look—these big, inviting eyes—practically pleading with us to come over and talk to them. Hell, they'll do that even if they're at the club with their boyfriends. You'll see her boyfriend just turn absolutely white with insecurity, and he'll jealously wrap his arm around her and try to rush her out the door to some other bar. It must suck, knowing a girl would throw all your history aside that quick, just for one night with a famous athlete. And that's no exaggeration. Some girls absolutely will cheat on their boyfriends if it means a single night with one of us.

So that being said, how could a guy like us fall for just one chick? I truly don't get it. How would he ever know that she was actually into him, the *person,* and not just the hockey player? What makes Lance so sure that Lindsay is actually into him personally, and isn't just trying to further her modeling career?

I got out of bed and walked over to my treasure chest. I ran my fingers over the smooth, snake-skin leather before I popped open the latches. They clicked free with a solid and satisfying *thunk.* I lifted the heavy lid and peeked in.

I could've settled down with any one of these girls if I wanted to. The hell would be the point?

I shut the lid and closed the latches.

———

I made it home later that evening, after dinner with Ilya and his girlfriend. I walked in, expecting to find Lance and his sister, but the place was dark and no one was home.

Huh. Wonder when she's supposed to get here? He didn't say.

I was still in the shower when I heard a banging at the front door. I shut the water off and jumped out of the shower, running to my room to quickly dress.

"One minute!" I yelled as I sprinted past the door and hurried to my room.

I jumped into a pair of boxer-briefs and threw on a well-worn pair of jeans. But the knocking on the door did not stop.

"I'm comin', I'm comin'!"

I raced out of the bedroom before I had a chance to put on a shirt.

I swung the door open and was greeted by a new face. I didn't need long to solve the mystery. She wasn't anywhere near as tall as Lance, but it was clear she shared the Couture DNA—from the lithe athletic build to the fiery tint in her curly, golden locks. She didn't look like Lance in the face, though—thank God, for her sake!

"You must be Honey Badger," I said warmly.

"Oh, lord," she said with an emphatic eye roll. "I *guess* you can call me that. But my name is Ella."

"Ella it is, then. Can I grab your bag for you?"

"Would you?"

"Of course." I hoisted her bag over my shoulder and followed her in. She moved like a long, slinky cat on the prowl. She wore a snugly fitting pair of denim jeans, a simple spaghetti-strap tank-top, and ballet flats.

She stepped into our condo, wide-eyed, seemingly inspecting and appraising every surface and detail. And for a moment, it seemed as if she was aware of nothing else.

I cleared my throat, and just like that, she shot me a surprised look and remembered that I existed again.

"Oh, sorry, where are my manners? Lance said your name was—er ... what was it? Sonar?" Her nose scrunched up while she tried to remember. "Metal Detector?"

"Metal Detector, yeah, exactly," I said, grinning. "That's me."

"I *know* you're lying!" she squealed in a tone that was partly playful but partly serious.

"I'm just joking. It's Radar. Or Ryan, whichever."

"Radar it is, then."

We shook hands for the first time, but it struck me that I already knew her somehow. I guess that always happened when you met your best bud's family; there was a familiarity as soon as you set your eyes on them.

Ella had a heart-shaped face. Although her individual features were soft, when taken together, there was a certain hardness to her face. She looked, I dunno—*tough*? Capable? Independent? Something like that. She wasn't the type of *tee-hee I'm-so-impressed-by-you* girly-girl that I'd been so used to meeting ever since I went pro, tell you that much. Instead, her whole essence seemed to pose a challenge: '*are you ready for this?*'

I had to admit, she was cute—for being related to Lance, I mean. Not that it made any difference whatsoever.

"So, where's Lance?" she asked.

"He's out with his girlfriend."

Somehow, Ella didn't look like she believed me. "Lance has a girlfriend?"

"I'm not really sure what they are. Anyway, he said he'd be back by the time you were here. Maybe you should give him a call?"

She dismissed the idea with a wave of her hand. "I'm sure he's on his way."

I offered to get her a drink. She asked for a glass of wine, and while I poured it for her, I asked about her flight. I half-listened while she described the frustrations of air travel that I knew *far* too well:

"... *And then the TSA made me go back through security again, and do the whole thing over again, all because I had a pair of nail clippers ...*"

The other half of me studied her and her mannerisms while she talked.

Her tank-top revealed strong, athletic shoulders, and an ample set of perfect breasts that I was *not* going to steal a single glimpse at, under any circumstances, out of respect to Lance, and out of respect to our living situation, and out of respect to our team, and—really, I could keep listing reasons why it's a bad idea to glance at the tits of your best friend and teammate's sister, but you get the idea, right?

But then *her* eyes darted down and she stole a peek at my chest. I looked down at myself and suddenly realized I was standing shirtless in front of Lance's sister.

"By the way, do you always walk around topless?" she asked with a grin that was both innocent *and* devilish at the same time. She stole another look at my pecs and slyly bit her lip. "Because if so, this could be a fun couple of days."

Oh no. I hoped Lance's cute sister wasn't a flirt ... or else this would *not* be a fun couple of days for me.

"Sorry. I forgot to put one on," I said as I immediately booked it for my bedroom. "I was still in the shower when you knocked."

"Sure, Radar, sure," she teased.

I shut myself in my bedroom, threw on a shirt, and took a deep breath. When I returned, Ella was looking around the condo, glass of wine in hand.

"What do you think of our place?" I asked her.

"It's lovely. Just a gorgeous place. I bet you two bring a lot of girls back here, hm?"

She gave me a knowing smile, which I laughed off.

"But ... it's so empty!" She pointed at the living room, where we had two fold-out lawn chairs sitting in front of the huge, flat screen TV. "I mean, my God, your TV sits on the floor, and you don't even have a sofa? How do you two live like this? It looks like no one lives here."

"Yeah, it's a sad sight right now. We moved in right before training camp started, so we haven't had a chance to furnish it yet or anything." I paused. "So, I guess you've got your work cut out for you, huh?"

She whipped around to face me with a bewildered expression. "What'd you just say?"

"Um—I said—you've got your work cut out for you?"

"And what do you mean by that?"

"Didn't Lance tell you?"

"Tell me what, Radar?"

"That, uh, he wants you to furnish the place? Since you're an interior decorator and all?"

She was silent for a moment or two.

Then she started to laugh.

Then her laugh tapered off into a long, frustrated sigh.

"No. Lance didn't tell me that, actually. But it explains a lot."

Oh boy. Here we go.

I frowned. "Look, I'm sorry, can you forget I said anything? I don't know what Lance told you. And I don't want to cause any trouble between you guys."

She neared and touched her hand to my forearm. "Oh, no, Radar. This is not your fault. Don't worry. This is *so* like Lance."

I swallowed, whipped out my cell phone, and fired off an SOS text message to Lance.

"Dude, where are you? Your sister's here and I think I just got you busted. You didn't tell her you wanted her to decorate?! WTF, man? You better get over here quick before I make this situation any worse."

She noticed.

"And now you're texting him so he can get his story straight," she said with a giggle.

I was too stunned to deny it, but she must've read the guilt on my face anyway.

"It's okay. I know how you guys are," she said.

" 'You guys'?" I asked, my throat tightening on me as I spoke.

Come on Lance! Where the hell are you? You said you'd be here by now!

"Hockey players," she said.

"Oh ... um ..." I didn't know what to do or say. I figured, *fuck it,* the only move was to throw all my cards on the table. I waved my phone in the air as if were a white flag of surrender. "Yeah, I just told him that I might have gotten him busted. That's all. I really don't want to get between you guys."

She smiled at me. A big, genuine smile. She looked really happy in that moment, but I didn't know why. "Thank you for telling me the truth."

That's right. Lance said not to lie to her.

"You're welcome," I croaked.

"Why don't you give me the full tour?" Ella asked.

"Sure."

5

THE TOUR
ELLA

My knees were already weak after the scenic waterfront drive to the Port of Boston, with the city skyline looming just over the water. Lance lived on the top floor of an eleven-story brick building, and the lobby was nothing but class —it was modern, and very *tastefully* modern, with nothing tackily overdone.

A quick ride up the elevator delivered me to the top floor. I knocked and waited for someone to answer. When the condo door finally opened, I nearly drooled at the work of art standing before me.

I'm talking, of course, about Lance's *condo*.

High, vaulted ceilings. Hardwood floors. A *wall* of windows, floor to ceiling, that offered a breath-taking view of the harbor and Boston skyline. The kitchen sparkled with granite counter-tops and stainless steel appliances and an expansive center island. The condo also boasted an open living space.

A *very* open living space, actually.

Because as nice as this place was? Somehow, these two athletes had failed to furnish it with anything at all. Their condo looked more like a hillbilly's backyard with fold-out chairs and a way-too-enormous TV resting right on the floor. All that was missing from this scene was the rusted-out husk of some old muscle car.

Boys. Sigh. So clueless.

I guess I should mention Lance's roommate, too, shouldn't I?

Lance didn't tell me he lived with a *hottie.* But uh, guys are weird about that sort of thing, so I guess he wouldn't tell me that. But, yes, Radar was a handsome babe. A six-foot-something, imposing and muscle-bound babe.

Within seconds of meeting him, I felt like I knew him. He commanded a quiet but strong presence. He was almost painfully macho in the way he carried himself—so upright and strong. He had dark, clean-cut hair and a five o'clock shadow. Oh, and the best part? He'd opened the door wearing *nothing* but a mouth-watering pair of blue jeans that were so tight, they were practically painted on his round ass and thick thighs.

Sure, I was a little disappointed to say goodbye to his sizzling bare chest. That was the price I had to pay, once he caught me staring at his abs—*oh, to run my fingers through that chiseled six-pack*—but I knew it was probably for the best.

But then he returned in a crisp white t-shirt. It was a fit so perfect that his shirt was just as distracting as his bare chest, with biceps bulging from the sleeves and rounded pecs jutting upward and pushing his shirt high into the air.

Yow.

This Radar guy was seriously smoking hot.

But. *But!* Before you get carried away thinking I might have a crush on this guy, I don't. Like I told Radar, I grew up surrounded by these hockey playing dopes, thanks to Lance. I know hockey players. I understand the way they think. Sure, they might be hot, they might be cute or charming, and they might even *seem* innocent, but you should never trust one of these guys any further than you can throw them.

Those were some of the thoughts that ran through my mind when Radar accidentally let it slip: "So, I guess you've got your work cut out for you, huh?"

I knew immediately what he meant, I just couldn't believe it.

Lance! I cursed my brother's name internally. *So that's why you invited me out here?!*

He wanted me to decorate his place. And instead of just *asking* me to do it (and I gladly would have, by the way!), he had to manipulate the situation to get what he wanted.

My brother is just *awful!*

Radar, though? He seemed like an honest guy. For one, the way his handsome face got all flushed and nervous after he realized he'd slipped up was *ultra* cute. Poor guy. But it wasn't his fault. It was Lance's.

Second, I appreciated the way that Radar didn't ogle me or leer at me like the rest of Lance's teammates always did. That was an especially bad problem if I was ever left alone with one of those creeps ... ugh. Hockey players always talked a big game about how family was 'off-limits,' but as soon as they were alone with me, forget about it. You know they'd do something if they thought they could get away with it.

But Radar seemed like a good friend, a *true* friend. I wasn't mad at him, not at all.

In fact, I sort of liked Radar, more and more, with each passing second. Was I seriously flirting with him? No ... not exactly ... but I did enjoy the way he got so flustered when I *pretended* like I was flirting with him.

"Why don't you give me the full tour?" I asked.

"Sure," he answered, his Adam's apple nervously plunging down his muscular neck.

Oh, he's too cute.

———

Radar gave me a brief tour of the rest of the house, starting with the bathroom, which had an elegant stone tile shower. It was surprisingly clean, especially for a boy's bathroom, and it smelled nice, thanks to a grapefruit-scented candle that flickered on top of the vanity.

Lance's bedroom was our next stop. It was precisely the disgusting pig-sty I'd expected, with dirty laundry strewn ankle-deep around the floor.

"Gross," I muttered. "I just had a flashback. I shared a bedroom with him all throughout school, you know. This mess used to be my life."

And a big reason why I never even tried to bring any boys home …

Radar laughed. "Sorry to hear it."

And then Radar showed me his room—or rather gave me a glimpse into it from the doorway, as if he were afraid to let me in. His room was neat and simple, without much (or any) decoration, and only the necessities: a bed, a nightstand, a dresser. His bed was neatly made. Unlike Lance, he picked up after himself.

I looked up at him. "I guess you're the one who does all the cleaning around here then, mm?"

His chuckle confirmed my suspicions.

Then my eye was drawn to a beautiful box that sat atop his dresser. "Ooh, what's that lovely chest?" I asked, hoping he'd let me take a closer look at it.

"Oh, um, nothing," he mumbled shyly. And with that, he shut his bedroom door. "Anyway. That's our place."

Well, that was weird, but I guess it's none of my business.

"What about the rest of the building?" I asked.

"You want to see that, too?"

"Sure!"

After Radar put on his shoes, we left the condo and took the elevator down to the second floor. We stepped off the elevator, and he pushed through the glass double-doors and we stepped into a gargantuan fitness center with all sorts of machinery and equipment and free weights.

I tried not to laugh. It was adorable, in that dorky jock kind of way, that the first thing he'd think to show me was the friggin' *fitness center.*

"This is where I spend most of my free time," he said, proudly.

"It shows," I said quietly, unsure if I'd meant it as a compliment or a gentle poke at his ego.

"Did you bring your workout clothes?" he asked.

"I did, actually. If I don't exercise regularly, I go insane." I added, "More insane than normal, that is."

He chuckled, and his eyes darted down to my arms. "I was going to say, you've got some guns, girl."

"Yeah. Lance taught me how to work out." I flexed my bicep for him, and his lips cinched into an impressed o-ring. "Wanna feel?"

Radar wrapped his hand around my arm. His enormous hand made my bicep look minuscule. Gently, he gave a couple squeezes.

"*Damn,*" he said, wearing a handsome smile. "So Lance was good for something after all."

I snickered. "You know, I think I like you, Radar."

He whisked me out of the fitness center and down the hall, to the building's indoor swimming pool. They also had a private room with a hot tub.

"Did you bring your swimsuit?" he asked.

"I did. I was actually all packed up to go to Key West."

"Key West? Oh, that's right, Lance mentioned you had plans that fell through—"

"Yeah. Don't ask. It's a long story."

Radar bobbed his head with understanding. "Ah. Well. That's pretty much it for the tour. I guess there's also a rooftop—"

"Show me!"

He laughed. "Alright, alright. Let's go."

————

The rooftop had a full lounge, complete with a bar and seating area. And, of course, a wonderful view of the wharf and the not-so-distant downtown skyline.

"Can I buy you a drink?" I asked him as I pulled my wallet from my bag.

He looked a little surprised. "I was going to offer you."

"No, let me buy. You gave me a tour like I asked, *and* you're putting me up for a few days. Let me buy you a drink, Radar."

He chuckled and agreed. "Well, alright, sure. Next one is on me, though."

We took our drinks to the ledge of the rooftop and watched the Boston marina traffic.

"Those are water taxis," he told me. "On game days, Lance and I take one across the harbor to get to the arena."

"Oh, that must be fun! We have those in New York, too."

"How do you like living in New York?" he asked.

"It's nice. Hectic, but nice."

Radar smiled at me. "Yeah. Any time we visit New York, I'm amazed at how busy it is—everywhere you look, all you can see is people, cars, and buildings. Boston's a big city but it doesn't really *feel* big, you know?"

"Mm. Yes. I know what you mean. I don't see myself living in New York forever. But as long I'm building a name for myself, I have to."

"How's business, anyway?" he asked with a genuine interest.

"Good, good. I don't take much time off because I'm always busy. But I'm doing well, so at least there's that." I paused. "I'm not doing as well as you and Lance, of course, but hey."

"Hey, *I'm* not doing nearly as well as Lance, either." He laughed and bumped my shoulder with his. "He's the superstar, making the big bucks. I'm just eating the table-scraps."

"Lance. Superstar." Playfully, I rolled my eyes. "Somehow, I don't think I'll ever be able to reconcile that word with the idea of my brother."

Amused, his big blue eyes sparkled at me. "Must be weird," he said.

"It sure is."

We sipped our drinks and quietly watched the boats motoring by, to and fro. The waves rose and fell in the boats' wake, lapping at the harbor.

"I don't watch much hockey," I said. "Correction, I don't watch any hockey. But an ex-boyfriend once told me that you and Lance have a good thing going out on the ice. That you're a sort of—what'd he say—oh yeah, that you're a *wrecking ball* on the ice, hitting guys left and right."

Radar smiled at me bashfully. "Yeah."

I cocked my head at him. "But you seem too nice—too humble—to be this violent guy."

He shrugged. "It's nothing personal. I just have a job to do."

"Which is?"

"Create space for your brother. And protect him."

"He needs protecting?"

"I'm not sure if you realize how good he is, but he's our best player, Ella. If anything happens to him, the team is pretty much screwed. That puts a target on his back, because guys want to hurt him to take him out of the game."

"How grotesque."

"I guess. Of course, he brings a lot of it on himself. I'm always trying to teach him *not* to run his mouth out on the ice ... but he has a habit of talking shit to these huge guys. And then I have to step in and fight them."

I giggled. "Now *that* sounds more like my brother."

Radar gave a careless shrug. "Anyway, like I said, it's my job. I bounced around the league for years, from one team to the next, before I ended up here in Boston."

"Bounced around the league? You mean, you were being traded?"

"Traded, or waived, or demoted to the AHL, or not offered a contract renewal ... you name it."

"Huh. Why? If you play with Lance, you have to be pretty good, right?"

"Sure, I'm good. Just like the other 800-some players in the NHL. The elite are head and shoulders above the rest, but everyone else is very, very evenly matched. Every one of those guys can skate and shoot. But to keep a job in this league, you have to stand out. You have to have one skill you excel at."

"And your one special skill is ...?"

"Missing," he answered with a wide and infectious grin— and that's when I realized he was also *missing* a tooth.

"Aw, just like your tooth!" I said, smiling back at him.

"Oops." His hand shot up to cover his mouth. "Sorry. Yeah. I ate a slapshot four years ago. I've got a magnetic implant-thingy that I wear when I'm out in public."

Normally I found missing teeth a serious turn-off, but on Radar, it was cute in a genuine, folksy sort of way. I grabbed him by his meaty forearm and pulled his hand away from his mouth.

"Don't cover it up. I promise you, I don't mind it," I told him. "Anyway, sorry, I interrupted you. You were saying that your one special skill is missing."

"Right. Until I had a try-out with the Brawlers and played with Lance. The coaches weren't sure about me, since they knew

I hadn't stuck in the league so far. But Lance? He liked playing with me so much, he went to the front office and personally vouched for me. He basically told management to offer me a contract. He's the star of the show, you know. He gets what he wants."

"And now you're like his bodyguard," I teased.

He chuckled. "Sort of. I do more than that, but yeah, I guess that's fair."

"What if something happened to Lance out on the ice?"

He pondered that question gravely. "I dunno. Wouldn't be good for me, though."

We finished our drinks. Radar bought the second round, like he promised. But the evening had grown brisk and, with a bone-chilling breeze coming off the water, I shivered.

Radar must've noticed. "You're cold. Want to head back inside?" he asked.

"Yeah, let's go."

6

THE CRAZY NASTYASS HONEY BADGER
RADAR

Drinks in hand, the two of us burst through the door, laughing and acting more than a little tipsy.

"Lance?" Ella called. "Laaance?"

He still wasn't home yet. But after spending a little bit of time with Ella, I wasn't nearly as worried as I had been earlier. She was a cool chick, and not nearly as crazy as Lance had made her out to be.

Actually, deep down, some twisted part of me might even have been happy that Lance wasn't back yet—at least for a little longer. I liked being alone with her, getting to know her.

"I can't believe he's not home yet," she said. "Where the heck is he?"

"Yeah, I dunno. He's been spending a lot of time with Lindsay lately."

"Lindsay? That's his girlfriend?"

She sat in one of the living room lawn chairs. She patted the seat of the other one to summon me. When I neared, she quickly yanked the seat so it sat even closer to her.

Sneaky, I thought with an amused grin.

"Girlfriend, or something. I'm not sure what they are," I said, as I sat next to her.

"Okay, Radar. Spill it. Tell me everything you know about her."

"I hope I don't get in trouble by showing you this." I pulled up Lindsay's Instagram page and passed my phone to Ella. "But here she is."

"Oh ... My ... *God!*" Ella scrolled through one photo after another. "Every single picture! They're all of her ass!"

Her finger swiped down, again and again, marching through the butt parade until she got the point. She handed the phone back to me.

"Well, I certainly see what Lance likes about her," she said. "I can't really blame her, though. Girl's got a great butt and she clearly works for it. In half the pictures, she's doing squats at the gym. Rock it, girl, rock that ass."

I laughed, and so did she, and then a silence came over us. Not an uncomfortable one—not at all. She kicked off her ballet flats and crossed her legs, took a sip of her drink, and so did I. And then I noticed that she'd touched her tiny foot to my leg. Her foot was so light, I almost didn't feel it against me. Her touch was so soft, I went on pretending I didn't notice it there.

"So how'd you get the nickname Radar?" she asked suddenly, quietly.

"My name is Ryan Ryder. So it sounds similar, I guess. But a coach in Junior started calling me Radar and it stuck."

"Yeah, but why Radar? Is there a reason behind it?"

"Er—well, yeah, but it's kind of lame."

Her green eyes beamed at me. "Remember, you're talking to *Honey Badger*."

I wagged my finger at her. "I want to hear the story behind that, by the way."

"Sure. After you tell me yours."

"Deal. Basically—and this is in my old coach's words, not mine—once someone gets my attention, I lock onto them and don't let them go. A heat-seeking missile on ice, on a mission to destroy."

She covered her mouth and tittered.

"What?" I asked.

"You're right. That *is* lame."

"Hey, what the hell?" I growled, and I stuck my finger into her shoulder and gave her a tiny shove.

"Sorry! It is. But it's not your fault that your coach came up with it."

"Yeah, yeah. Anyway, it's your turn. What's the story on 'Honey Badger'?"

She gestured for my phone again. I gave it to her and she loaded up a YouTube video titled, *The Crazy Nastyass Honey Badger.*

I raised an eyebrow at her. "The *what?*"

"I know," she said. "Just watch."

I watched as a weasel-looking animal, long-bodied and short-legged, came trotting on screen. The top of the animal, from its head to its tail, was covered with a band of white fur—but the sides down to its legs were all black fur.

"Is this a nature video?" I asked.

"Just watch!"

"*This is the honey badger,*" the video narrator said in a goofy voice. "*Watch it run in slow motion. It's pretty badass.*"

I busted up with sudden laughter. "What the hell is this?"

"Keep watching!" she giggled.

She huddled closer, so she could watch over my shoulder. I scooted over and made room for her on the chair. She sat on the edge of my chair and our thighs touched.

The two of us watched as the honey badger climbed a tree to eat a snake, chased a jackal, and ignored the stingers of thousands of bees as it terrorized their hive. Ella and I howled with laughter.

"*Honey badger don't give a shit, it just takes what it wants!*" The narrator continued, "*The honey badger has been referred to as the most fearless animal in all the animal kingdom. It really doesn't give a shit.*"

She had such a cute laugh, where her whole body shook, and her laugh climbed higher and higher until she reached this lovely, carefree crescendo ... like she was experiencing pure joy and letting it flow right through her.

I didn't know why the sound of her laugh resonated in me so much. All I knew was that I loved it and I wanted to hear more of it.

But why I had such strange thoughts about a girl's laugh, I couldn't possibly tell you.

The video ended. We were still sharing my fold-out chair, the two of us side by side. She was so close, I smelled her, her scent alluring and sweet like vanilla. Was it her hair? Her perfume? Her skin? I didn't know, but the smell made me want to pull her closer, brush the golden lock of hair from her face, and kiss her.

Of course, *holy shit,* I couldn't ever do that, and even thinking it was a bad idea ...

Still, she locked her eyes on mine. Bright and shining, her green eyes were flecked with radial streaks of a brilliant amber. Her eyes offered me an invitation, and if this were any other girl I might have taken her up on that invite, but—I knew I couldn't, of course.

"And, so, that video ought to explain it," Ella said quietly, her eyes still glittering and fixed on mine.

"What?" I laughed. "That didn't explain a thing. In fact, I'm more confused about your nickname than I was before."

Gently, she pounded her fist square against my chest. "C'mon! You don't see it?"

I leaned back to appraise her from head-to-toe. Of course she didn't *actually* look like a honey badger. But like I said earlier —the girl was athletically built and, hell, she just seemed *tough*, even if she wrapped all that toughness in a cutesy package.

"Okay—I'll say this," I began. "You've got a certain swagger."

"Ah-ha! So you *do* see it."

"Are you proud to be like that animal?"

"I used to hate it. Because Lance first started calling me Honey Badger as an insult. Then, one day, I showed the video to my mom to tattle on Lance. But when she saw it, she couldn't hold back her laughter. She said, '*I'm so sorry, sweetie, but Lance is right. You really are a honey badger.*' I couldn't believe it! I was *beyond* pissed, but that only made the problem worse. Soon, the entire family was calling me Honey Badger. At a certain point, I stopped fighting and embraced it instead."

I chuckled and quoted the video: "*Honey Badger don't give a shit.*"

She smiled at me, looking deep into my eyes, and I smiled back at her.

"*Honey Badger just takes what it wants,*" she quoted back at me.

I looked at her lips, so pink and full, and she looked at mine. I had a terrible feeling I knew what was going to happen next ... that I wasn't strong enough to stop it ...

But a conflicted voice inside me screamed, *You guys have been drinking! Do not do anything stupid! This is Lance's sister, you moron!*

But she was so close, I felt the warm, gentle puffs of her breath against my face. Her scent, her pheromones, whatever it was, smothered that screaming voice and lured me closer.

I *had* to taste her lips ...

I reached my hand for her cheek, when a sound made me freeze.

Kthunk!

It was the sound of a key inserted into a lock.

For a second, I froze. Deer in the headlights. We both paused, face-to-face, eyes huge, as if to say to each other, *is this really happening?*

Then we heard the sound of the key turning, and the dead-bolt popping free—*cli-thunk.*

Ella jumped out of my lap, and I hurried across to the far side of the room.

Like my life depended on it.

Because, well, it kinda did.

———

Lance never had a chance to suspect anything. The second he stepped through the door, Ella was already half-way across the room and advancing on her brother like a lion about to ambush its prey.

"Uh, hey, Ella," he said nervously. He was carrying a large plastic shopping bag from the sports store. "How are you?"

"You *lied* to me, Lance!"

He played dumb. "What do you mean?"

"You only invited me out here to decorate your place! You know you could've just *asked* me to, right? I would've done it! I would've been happy to do it! But *no*, all because . . ."

I watched, wide-eyed, as Ella berated her brother and jammed an angry finger into his sternum again and again. The tops of her breasts jiggled in her tank-top. No—I still wasn't looking, and I wasn't ever going to. But it'd be impossible not to notice that they were there.

In fact, after our close call, I vowed *never* to look at Ella like that or be alone with her again. *Shit,* we'd come so close to making such a huge mistake. If I'd actually gone ahead and kissed that girl? If Lance walked in on us kissing? It could very well be the end of my hockey career.

I couldn't believe how close I'd come to betraying not only Lance, but also myself. Was that really all it took? A couple drinks, a few laughs, a little closeness? I'd throw my whole life away that easily?

The hell's wrong with me?

Meanwhile, the brother and sister feud continued. Lance pleaded his case, but he didn't sound very convincing.

"That's not the *only* reason I invited you. You're my sister! And uh, I love you! I told you, it's been way too long since we've hung out!"

"Oh, bullshit, Lance. You lied about this just like you lie about everything else."

"I didn't lie about anything!"

"Yes you did. Lying by omission is *still* a lie," Ella griped at her brother, her voice like a honeyed growl. She might have been his little sister, but there certainly wasn't anything fragile about her.

"Oh, come on! Now you're expanding the definition of a lie to include things I *haven't* said?" Lance complained.

"What if I had to cancel plans with friends to come out here?"

"Friends? *You?* Yeah, right!"

I smacked my forehead. *Yeah, that's not how you defuse this situation, bud.*

"*Asshole!*" Ella slugged Lance on the shoulder with a hard right.

"*Ow!*" Lance yelped, rubbing his shoulder. "Besides, I thought you'd be happy to do it. You're always telling me how much you love your job, right? And to be honest with you, I think you *owe* me this. I put you through school, after all—and a pretty pricey one at that! Not that I ever get any thanks for it ..."

"I have too thanked you! I thanked you every time you paid my tuition! I wrote a huge letter when I graduated about how thankful I was! You want me to thank you again? *Thank you, Lance! Thank you!* Now how about you thank me for all the sacrifices *I* had to make for your hockey career?"

"*You* made sacrifices for *me*? Oh, do tell, Honey Badger! Please, enlighten me about the life-crushing burdens you've taken on for my career!"

"Oh, I don't know, having to move every couple years to make sure you got to play for the best teams, maybe? Which meant changing schools and always leaving my friends behind? Or the fact that we were always on the road for your travel games? Or the fact that my life, my needs, always came in second place behind yours?"

Damn, I thought. *Get me the hell outta here. I can't be in the middle of this.*

I started to slink away, thankful that they hadn't noticed me. They could sit there and fight all day for all I cared, but I needed out now.

Lance flailed his arms above his head in a big, sarcastic show. "Ohh, I'm *so* sorry, Ella! I'm so sorry you had to move schools and now your brother is a multi-millionaire who generously paid your way through college. You've had it *so* tough in life."

Ella rolled her eyes; no, she rolled her *whole body* away from him.

And that's when she saw me trying to sneak out. She ran up and grabbed my arm and pulled me back into the room. I must've looked white as a ghost as she dragged me back.

"By the way, Lance, you should really thank Radar. He was a *wonderful* host to me, while *you* didn't even care enough to be home to greet me."

Lance held up the shopping bag. "I wasn't home because I was out buying you a sleeping bag!"

Her jaw dropped. "After everything, you seriously expect me to sleep in a *sleeping bag*?"

"Well ... er ... we still don't have a couch, and—"

Ella shook her head. "Nope. Tonight, *you* sleep in the sleeping bag, and I'll sleep in your bed."

Lance dropped his shoulders in defeat. "Fine. Jesus. I'll sleep in the damn bag. It's not the end of the world."

Ella stamped out of the room and locked herself up in Lance's room.

Holy hell.

"The Honey Badger has arrived," Lance muttered to me.

"I think I understand the nickname a little better," I muttered back.

"Hey man, I'm really sorry you had to put up with her. I lost track of time with Lindsay, and then I remembered I had to buy that sleeping bag ... anyway, I hope Honey Badger didn't give you too much trouble."

If only you knew how much trouble we almost got in.

"No, man, not at all," I said. "Sorry I slipped up with her in the first place. I had no idea you didn't tell her that you wanted her to decorate."

"Dude. Don't worry. If we didn't fight about this, we would've fought about something else. It was bound to happen." Lance shook his head as he rolled out the new sleeping bag in the middle of the living room floor. "Right now, I'm kinda regretting inviting her out here, to be honest with you. Could've hired *any* interior designer in Boston, any other Joe Schmo, who wouldn't make my life miserable. Man, if I start playing like shit because I'm sleeping on the fucking floor, I'm gonna be pissed at her."

I slapped his back. "It'll be alright, bud. Just a few days."

"Yeah, yeah." He paused, looking suddenly serious. "Radar.

Listen. Be careful around her. Whatever you do, don't get caught lying to her. Because God help you if you lie to her, or if she *thinks* you've lied to her. She has an honesty policy and she's serious about it."

I gulped. "I think—I think I'll just give you both a lot of space this week."

He slapped my back. "Good man."

Through the window, the lights from Boston's skyline dotted the night. I said goodnight to Lance, and thought about Ella as I walked past her room, Lance's words echoing in my head.

Be careful around her.

I knew I had to, but for entirely different reasons than Lance meant.

This girl could get me in trouble.

7

———

SILLY REVENGE FANTASY

ELLA

I woke up with the late-morning sun hot on my face and a thin layer of dew on my skin.

I blinked, trying to make sense of the lumpy mass that laid on the floor at the side of my bed. I blinked again and again until the blur in my vision began to clear, and at last I could make sense of what I was looking at: a pile of inside-out boxers and dirty socks; a pizza box full of half-eaten crusts and crumbs; several empty tubs of protein powder.

"*Euch*," I mumbled, sitting up in the bed that clearly wasn't mine.

That's right. I'm not home. I'm in Boston, at Lance's.

Last night was a haze. I hadn't meant to get drunk, but I'd gotten wasted in a hurry. Flying always does that to me though, doesn't it? Come to think of it, I never ate dinner last night.

That's how I got drunk so fast.

My stomach, pissed at how I'd treated it last night, gurgled emptily at me.

And I'd had, what, three drinks? Yeah, because Radar poured me a glass of wine, then I had two more on the rooftop with Radar before we went back to the condo together—

Oh no.

Terror washed over me as I had a flashback to the two of us together. I cringed as the memories played out: how stupidly giggly I was with him, how I couldn't keep my hands (or feet!) off of him, how I nearly jumped into his lap to watch that ridiculous honey badger video with him ...

And, *ugh,* how I'd come *so* close to kissing him.

I smacked my forehead, and a loud *clap* echoed off Lance's empty bedroom walls.

Did I seriously almost have a drunken moment with Lance's teammate? How embarrassing. He must think I'm a complete nut. Or a wasted slut or something.

Yes, I absolutely wanted to flirt with Radar during my stay in Boston—but *only* if Lance was around to witness and get pissed off by it. But last night? I was way, way out of line. I wondered if Radar would tell Lance about how I acted? I hoped not.

There was a knock at the door.

"Ella?" It was Lance's voice. "You awake in there? I hear you moving around."

"I'm awake."

"C'mon then, get up. I ordered breakfast and we've got a long day ahead of us."

Mm. Right. Shopping for Lance.

"I'll be out in a minute."

After I dressed, I headed to the kitchen. What I saw made me gasp with delight.

If Lance wanted to make things up to me, ordering in some of my favorite breakfast foodstuffs was a *very* good way to start. On the center-island sat a fruit and cheese dish, waffles, bagels with cream-cheese and lox, scrambled eggs, hot coffee and more.

"G'morning," Lance said. He stood by his peace offering

awkwardly, one hand on the center-island, the other hand nervously scratching the back of his head. "Hope you like it?"

"Aw, Lance!" I said, leaping into my brother with a flying hug. "I love it."

"Alright, alright," he mumbled. He hugged me back with a limp arm. "Don't freak out over it. I just want you to be well-fed and thinking clearly while we're out on our shopping spree."

I piled food onto my plate. "I've always wondered: do you *purposely* say the wrong thing, or are you just helpless?"

"Whatever. Listen, the point is, maybe you were right. Maybe I should've told you that I wanted you to decorate in the first place."

"Not maybe—you definitely should have told me."

"You're right," he said with a note of surrender. "So, yeah. Like I said. I'm sorry."

"Apology accepted." I nodded triumphantly and took a bite of my bagel and lox. "Mm. That's good."

"So you won't mind helping me pick things out for the condo?"

"Are you kidding? I *love* decorating, Lance."

"Even though our place is empty?"

"Even better. For an interior decorator, an empty space is like a blank canvas to paint on. What's your budget?"

"Budget?" He laughed the concept off as if it was totally absurd. "You *know* how much I make, right?"

I rolled my eyes. "It's a standard question I ask every single client. I'm not asking how much money you make, I'm asking how much you're willing to spend. Besides, I dunno, maybe you're responsible with your money?"

"Hell naw," he said.

I sighed. "Okay, the budget is apparently unlimited. Is there a specific aesthetic you're hoping to achieve?"

"A specific *what* now?"

"A specific look, or style or theme—" I cut myself off. Lance's face showed only confusion and we weren't getting anywhere like this. "I'll just take that as a no."

"Well, there *is* one thing I know I want."

"Which is?"

"A big leather couch. Like, *big,* so I can comfortably sleep on it. Oh, and I want it to be red, too."

"Easy enough. Anything else?"

"Nope. Other than that, it's all up to you. You know *way* more about this stuff than I do, Ella. I trust your judgment. The only thing is, someday soon, we want to have the team over for a party. And the boys will bring over their wives and girlfriends and stuff. So I'd prefer that our place looks like—er, I dunno ..."

"Like two classy professionals live here, and not two degenerate twenty-something bachelors that sit around in lawn chairs staring at a TV on the floor?"

Lance's face lit up. "Yes! *Exactly.* So yeah. You're the expert. Whatever you wanna do, it's your vision."

I pinched his cheek. "Aaaaw, Lance! You finally trust me?"

He batted my hand away. "Well, I noticed you haven't cashed any of the checks I've been mailing you. So I guess you really *are* supporting yourself with your job out in New York."

"Does that fact just eat you up inside?" I asked him with a grin.

"My accountant sure hates it. He's always griping about how my ledger's out of whack thanks to those checks." He shook his head. "But no. It doesn't bother me at all. I'm proud of you, sis. Haven't I told you that?"

"No. You haven't."

"Well ... it's true."

"Thanks, Lance."

With that, we hugged, and chowed down on our pre-shopping-spree breakfast.

———

After seven and a half hours of shopping all over Boston, and several thousands of dollars rung up on Lance's credit card, my brother was slowing down. We'd found almost everything *but* the perfect giant red leather couch.

"How do you *do* this for a living?" Lance griped as he parked his Lamborghini outside the tenth stop of the day. His bright-red Lambo wasn't the most practical car for our mission, and we'd stuffed it to the gills with any of our purchases that would fit. The other assorted large things were slated to be delivered later tomorrow.

Lance rested his forehead against the steering wheel. "We've been to like, eighty different stores and antique shops. This is worse than a bag-skate. Yet you're *still* going strong."

"It energizes me, really." I shrugged. For me, the quest of searching for that perfect rug or tile or fabric or piece of furniture was a stronger boost than any cup of coffee I'd ever drank. "But if you're exhausted, this can be our last stop of the day."

He let out a whimper of relief. "Really? Last one, you swear?"

"Yup." Reaching over the pile of shopping bags and fabrics and table lamps and other random things stuffed between us, I patted his shoulder. "Anyway, we're going to find your giant leather couch in this store."

"How the hell would you know that?"

"Intuition, of course! You learn a few things on the job."

I opened the door of his exotic sports car—it was the kind of door that opened upwards—and hopped out. Lance climbed out slowly, like a stiff old man, and shuffled to catch up with me. The door-bells of the furniture shop jangled we entered. I let out a breath of awe—this place was *huge.*

Lance groaned. "This is going to take forever …"

"Shh. We'll go fast. Come." I grabbed him by the arm and we began weaving our way down the crowded aisles. "So what do you want to do tonight, brother?"

"Why don't I take you out to Boston's most hoppin' clubs?"

"Ooh, that sounds fun. What's Radar doing tonight?"

"Uh, I think he said he's doing his own thing."

"We should invite him out with us anyway!"

"Yeah, sure," Lance said skeptically, and I could tell he was a bit jealous. It always amused me that Lance was allowed to hit on my friends constantly, but if I ever said *hi* to any of his friends in the wrong tone of voice? He went into a jealous rage.

I decided to throw a little fuel on the fire.

"Radar's just such a *hunk,*" I said dramatically.

Right on cue, Lance shook his head at me, looking all gruff and serious. "Don't even joke about that, Ella."

"What? Am I not supposed to notice that your teammate is hot? He's so tall and muscular and good-looking. I really think we hit it off last night. Since his name is Ryan Ryder, does anyone call him RyRy? No? I should call him RyRy. It's a cute name. Cute, just like him."

Lance was steaming. "I *know* you're just trying to piss me off right now. It's not funny though, okay? My protective older brother instinct starts kicking in and shit and I don't like it."

"Wait, you're implying that you actually have an instinct to protect me?" I laughed.

"From *him?* Yeah. I will if I have to."

"What's so bad about RyRy?" I asked innocently.

Of course, I didn't have to ask. Radar seemed like a nice enough guy, but let's be real. All the money and fame that comes from playing a sport professionally goes *straight* to these guys' heads. So yeah, if you're into vain, self-obsessed guys with room-temperature IQs, who can barely hold a conversation unless it's about hockey, who will cheat on you the first time some big-boobed, starry-eyed bimbo gives him the look ... then go ahead, knock yourself out, try to date a hockey player. Me? I wouldn't even bother. Even if he seemed like a decent guy, I was sure that Radar had *something* fucked up about him.

"Let's not get into it," Lance said. "I'll just say this: *RyRy* runs through women. So don't even pretend you think he's cute. I don't want to have to worry about—*ugh*—anything happening."

I rolled my eyes. *Nothing* was going to happen in the first place, and I couldn't believe Lance even entertained the idea that he had something to worry about.

"You really have no idea why I'm acting like I have a crush on Radar, do you?" I asked as we sampled one couch after another.

He tilted his head at me inquisitively. "Hm?"

"Quinn?" I asked simply, trying to jog his memory.

His eyes searched upward as he searched his memory bank. "Should that name mean something to me?"

I tutted loudly. "Uh, yeah. It should."

"Remind me."

"Last time I visited you, two years ago, when you were living by yourself? I brought Quinn, my best friend and roommate, to visit. And after you started blatantly hitting on her, I pleaded with you *both* not to do anything. But you wouldn't listen—because '*pussy*'—and she was too blinded by the novelty of sleeping with a pro athlete. That trip was a train wreck for me and I'm still mad about it, honestly."

"Ooooh," Lance nodded gravely. "*Crazy Quinn.* Yeah. I remember her."

"You call her *Crazy Quinn*?!" I punched him on the arm. "You dickhead!"

"Uh, *yeah*, I do! You should've the barrage of texts she sent me every day. I was afraid to reply to a single one, 'cause that would only encourage her to send me more."

"Lance, she sent you texts because you told her you loved her and then you ghosted her. That'd make any girl go crazy ..."

"I never said I loved her, Ella, that's bullshit."

"Oh, how I wish I could believe you."

"I only knew her for what, three days? A man can't fall in love with a woman in three days."

I tutted. "I wouldn't be mad if you *actually* fell in love with her. I'd be mad if you told my best friend you loved her just so you could fuck her."

"Whatever. I guess it's my word versus hers, isn't it?"

"*Anyway,*" I continued, "now we're not even friends anymore, because she can't stand the sight of me. In her mind, *I'm* the one who let her get taken advantage of by my heartless, asshole brother. I lost a good friend, all thanks to you."

"So what—you want to fuck Radar to get back at me? Is that what you're telling me?"

"God, no." I rolled my eyes. "I don't care about him. Besides, I've got enough bad luck with shitty men in my life. The last thing I need to do is go scraping at the bottom of the barrel with some hockey playing meathead who can't keep his dick in his pants. All I'm trying to do is teach you a lesson: you shouldn't sleep with your sibling's best friend."

"Whew. That's a relief." Lance paused. "You really had me going for a minute there. I really believed it when you said you thought he was hot."

"Well, I *do* think he's hot."

"Hey, what the hell?!"

"You know I can't lie, Lance! He's a total babe."

"Oh, God, here we go with that again ... you *could* just lie for my sake, but no ..."

"Relax. I don't go for hockey players. And besides, I'm not the kind of girl that would bone my brother's best friend." I paused. "That's the big difference between you and me."

"Oh. Okay. Thanks, uh, I think." Lance scratched the back of his head. "By the way, I'm a changed man now. I don't sleep around like I used to."

"Really?"

"Yep. I'm sort of seeing a girl right now. Lindsay."

"Oh—Lindsay the butt model!" I squealed.

His nostrils flared. "Radar told you about her?"

"You left us alone forever last night! Of course you came up. What'd you think we'd talk about?"

Just then, I saw it. I gasped and grabbed my brother's arm. "*Lance!*"

"Yeah?"

I pointed it out. A giant brick-red leather couch.

"Hey! That's it! The perfect color, too!" Relief filled Lance's face. "We can finally be done shopping!"

Lance paid for the item, and the shop owner told him they could actually deliver it today, which was perfect. We climbed back into Lance's sports car and headed home.

On the drive back to the condo, I quietly watched as the streets of Boston rolled by my window. I was thinking about last night.

I'm not the kind of girl that would bone my brother's best friend.

If that was true, then why did I feel guilty when I said it?

I wouldn't *actually* have kissed him, right? Even if I did, it would've been a drunken mistake ... but nothing else would've happened.

I snagged my lip between my teeth.

Normally, hearing a guy was a womanizer was a total turn-off. But with Radar, there was something appealing about losing my v-card to a rugged, experienced man, who'd just *take it* from me without a thought or the pretense of wanting something more. And then the whole thing would finally be over and done with and wouldn't torment me any longer or get in the way of any decent men I met in the future.

Listen to yourself. That's nothing more than a silly revenge fantasy.

8

PUCK BUNNIES
RADAR

I was still in the shower when I heard a huge commotion out in the living room. I was sure it was Lance and Ella, but what were they doing? How were they making so much racket?

Hope they're getting along, I thought to myself. *I don't know how much more of their fighting I can take.*

Last night had been on my mind all day. I realized how weak I'd been in the moment last night—how Ella's big, expressive eyes had captured mine, how her sweet smell had intoxicated me and made me *almost* do something really, really dumb. I still didn't know what the hell came over me. Was I really that close to kissing her? Or was I just drunk and not thinking clearly?

Man. Talk about a dangerous situation. Don't get me wrong, I wouldn't touch Ella. Not in a million years. It'd be bad enough, since she's my roommate's sister—but the sister of my best friend *and* teammate? Nope. You can't get any more off-limits than that. If I went anywhere *near* her, I'd create a firestorm on the team.

Hell, I've heard rumors of locker rooms that were split over less. I'd heard of guys getting shipped out of town because he boned a teammate's distant cousin. I wasn't about to invite *any* of that drama onto the Brawlers.

And besides—not to sound like a dick, but Ella wasn't the type of girl I went for. I liked girls who gave me that star-struck look. Girls who were easily entertained, and easily kept at a healthy distance. Ella? Something told me I'd never dealt with a girl like her before. That she wasn't quite so impressed by the fact that I was an athlete—that she wanted me to be something *more* than that.

Why the hell are you even thinking about her like that? I thought to myself as I shut the shower off. *You're losing your mind. Cut it out.*

I wrapped the towel around my waist and headed back to my room. That's when I saw what had made all that noise earlier— Lance and Ella had managed to bring home a big, red leather couch.

I tried to hurry past without stopping. "Hey guys. Sweet couch."

"Oh, there he is! Hi RyRy!" Ella sang. She jumped off the sofa, hooked her arm through mine and pulled me to a stop.

RyRy? The hell?

"We were just talking about you," Ella said with mischief in her eyes—eyes that stole a glance at my bare chest. "So what do you think of the new couch?!"

"Looks great. It's huge."

She smiled. "Yeah. We must've looked at eighty different red leather couches today, but they weren't big enough for Lance. I know how much you athletes love furniture made for giants."

"It's true."

She pulled on my arm, tugging me towards the couch. "Don't you wanna sit and test it out?"

Lance groaned. "He's wearing a *bath towel,* Ella."

"Yeah, maybe later," I said.

"So what'd you do today, Radar?" Lance asked.

"I hung out with Ilya and his girlfriend."

"Cool." Lance added to Ella, "Ilya's our goalie. He's Russian. So's his girlfriend. She's actually a star in women's tennis—maybe you've heard of her? Natalya Anasenko."

"Neat," Ella said, pretending to be impressed when she clearly wasn't.

"How about you guys? How'd the shopping go?" I asked, pretending that it was totally normal to be wearing nothing but a sopping-wet bath towel while my teammate's sister clung to my forearm and discreetly ran the pads of her fingers over my muscle.

This is insane.

"Good," Ella said. "We brought home what we could. The rest of the big things are getting delivered tomorrow."

"Cool," I croaked. "Thanks for making our place nice."

The smoothness of Ella's nails, lightly dragging along my warm and freshly showered skin, was a dangerously seductive sensation. I had to get away from her, and I had to get away from her *now,* because a carnal pulse began to pump between my legs, whether I wanted it to or not.

And I was *not* about to pitch a tent in my bath towel.

I put a foot or two of space between us. I couldn't help but notice that Lance made the smallest of approving smiles.

If Ella felt rejected, she didn't show it. She hopped right back to her spot on the couch. "Well, anyway, Lance and I are going out tonight and we were wondering if you wanted to come with us?"

"Nope. I've got plans. Thanks, though."

"Aw, c'mon," she said with a frown.

"You heard the man," Lance said, and now he was *really* smiling. "He's got plans."

"What kind of plans?" Ella wanted to know.

"It's none of your business, Ella! Leave Radar alone! Can't you see the poor guy is still dripping wet from his shower?"

On cue, her eyes swept down my bare upper torso.

"The last thing the team needs is this guy coming down with a cold! We've got a *game* tomorrow!"

Lance was carving out my escape path for me, and I'd be a fool not to take it. With that, I excused myself and retreated for my room.

Ella whined to her brother. "If you two have a game tomorrow, then why are you going out tonight at *all*? We should stay in and play cards or something, just the three of us. ... you know, that could be fun ..."

I shut the bedroom door behind me, and their bickering stopped. Or at least I couldn't hear it anymore.

I dropped my towel and rolled my eyes at myself—sure as hell, I'd grown half-hard out there. I hoped they hadn't noticed. What was she thinking, touching me like that?

———

Having escaped those two, I could breathe a little easier. Eager to take my mind off Ella, I got dressed, jumped into bed and fired up my tablet. I loaded the *MeatMarket* app and opened the first few messages I'd gotten in the past couple hours:

"Hi Radar! Plans tonight?"

"Ryyyyyyyyyyyyyyan. Ur so hot."

On my *MeatMarket* profile, I don't openly advertise who I am. Some guys do, some don't. I'm more of the private type of guy. No revealing bio information whatsoever. There's only two pictures of me: the first is me, shirtless at the beach, posing with two good friends of mine from back home. But the camera is far enough away that even the casual fan Brawlers wouldn't know it was me if they happened to see it.

The other photo was taken in a dimly lit bar, and I'm wearing a ball-cap. Again, most hockey fans wouldn't know the man in the photo was me if they saw it. The most revealing thing about me in that photo is the Brawlers logo on the cap—along with my signature smile.

It doesn't matter that the casual hockey fan wouldn't spot me in my profile pictures, because my profile isn't for them. It's for a specific group of girls. They're called puck bunnies, and they're hockey's version of jersey-chasers. They know my smile by heart —and that smile, along with the hat, all but confirms my identity. And they know that the sparsity of information in my profile is another big clue.

The puck bunnies have internet communities and forums dedicated to trading information about us players. What our favorite bars and clubs are and when we're likely to be there; the links to our private social media accounts; whether we have girlfriends or not. When a puck bunny finds a player, she posts the link to his profile so all the other bunnies can find him, too. They'll discuss things like what we're like outside of the rink. They'll share their intimate knowledge of us, too. Our likes, dislikes. Turn-ons, turn-offs.

What do they know about me? That I'm discreet. That I never text the same girl twice. That, just like on the ice, I've got a motor that won't quit.

And oh yeah. There's one other thing—one secret about me that the puck bunnies *won't* share so openly, but only give to other girls they trust.

I thumbed over to the next message, from *Brawlersbabe90,* and opened it. Her name was Kara. She'd sent a selfie. She was posing in front of a mirror. She'd unzipped her jeans and tugged them down just enough to give a scandalous glimpse at her lacy pink panties, with a little bow over the crotch.

I rumbled with a hungry growl.

"*How do you like my panties, Radar?*" her message read.

"Very nice," I texted back.

I went back to studying her selfie. Brawlersbabe90 was a babe alright, a petite blonde with a hard body. She was wearing a shirt with my name and number 90. A nice detail. One that appealed to my most base, possessive desires. Made me feel like she belonged to me before I'd even met her.

Kara texted me back. "*Think they'd look good in your collection?*"

"Club Regret. Midnight."

"*See you then. xoxo*"

Don't tell old man Shea, but that's how it's done. That's how a guy in my profession has all the no-strings-attached hookups he could ever want.

And that's how I'm gonna forget all about Ella, too.

9

———

NIGHT OUT

ELLA

Lance paced back and forth through the hallway, hanging around the bathroom door like an anxious cloud, while I carefully applied mascara.

He stepped into the doorway and let out another pained groan. "Hurry up, Ella! You take so long to get ready."

"I'm almost ready. But please stop pacing around like that. You're putting me on edge."

Lance's cell phone rang and he retreated into his bedroom to answer it. I breathed a sigh of relief—now I could put on my finishing touches in peace.

Lance was on the phone for a good half-hour, tittering in his bedroom like a schoolgirl, which proved to be quite a blessing in disguise—because I'd decided that I hated the floral print dress I was wearing, and now I wanted to change into another one. I could just *hear* the bitching and moaning Lance would've made if I'd wanted to change dresses while he was trying to hurry me out the door.

But alas, his phone call gave me the opportunity. I changed into a cuter, more flirtatious cocktail dress—something playful, but still sexy enough for the club.

Just when I was truly ready, Lance emerged from his bedroom.

"Oh, hey Ella," he said. He wore a dopey, almost love-struck smile. Dear God—he looked *happy*. It was disturbing.

"Gross," I muttered, "what's gotten into you?"

"That was Lindsay," he said.

"Oh? The butt model wanted to chat?"

"She does *more* than just model her butt, okay? Someday, she'll be a real model. Everyone has to start somewhere, you know?"

"True enough. Well anyway, I'm ready to go."

Lance frowned with the weight of some bad news.

"Sorry, sis. I have to cancel on tonight."

"*What*?"

"Lindsay wants to meet up."

"You're really bailing on me?"

"I told her you were visiting and we were going out tonight, and I asked her if she wanted to come with us. But she said what she *really* wants is me to head over and hang out with her. She said she had a long day and she wants to stay in."

"She had a long day of modeling her butt?"

"Don't be a dick, Ella. Honestly, I'm super exhausted from shopping all day, too. A night in actually sounds kinda nice."

"You didn't think it sounded nice when I suggested it over an hour ago," I quipped.

"Ella ..."

"Nevermind." I blew out a heavy breath. "I'm just a little annoyed. But whatever. I'll get over it. You obviously like her, so you should go be with her, I guess. I'll find a way to entertain myself."

My oaf brother wrapped his troll arms around me and squeezed. I gave him a half-hearted squeeze back.

"Thanks for understanding," he said.

"Yep."

And with that, Lance grabbed his things and rushed out the door.

Welp. This just figures.

I sighed, poured myself a glass of wine, and threw myself on the new, gargantuan leather couch fit for the Nephilim. I pulled out my phone and did what I'd do any other night—I read work emails and checked out the latest in industry-related blogs and forums. My other hand, operating on pure muscle memory, instinctively went to stroke the cat that would normally be sitting in my lap.

"Aw, man," I groaned. "I miss Eucalyptus."

This was just like a typical weekend night at my place. Except this was somehow more pathetic. I'd flown out to Boston to escape my sad life, only to be reminded of exactly how lonely I was in the end.

"Welp."

I took a long gulp from my wine.

And then I heard a sound down the hallway: a bedroom door opening. Then the crisp, satisfying clap of leather soles on hardwood floor.

Radar? He's still here?

I sat up in a hurry and tried to shake the lonely desperation from my aura.

———

Radar passed through the living room with purpose—that is, until he saw me. He stopped in his tracks, and the look he gave me said it all. He twisted and pointed a finger down the hallway, towards Lance's bedroom—a dumb-founded gesture that seemed to ask, *'why aren't you with your brother?'*

I shook my head. "Lance left."

"I thought you guys were going out tonight?"

"We were. But Lance had a last minute change of plans."

He gave a sympathetic frown.

"It's okay though," I said unconvincingly. "I don't mind." I must've been a sorry sight, looking all sad and frumpy on the couch.

Radar, on the other hand, was dressed to impress in an expensive slate-gray suit and a smart white-and-blue checked shirt. The top two buttons of his dress shirt were left undone, showing off his large and protruding collarbones and the tops of his round, muscular pecs.

But the fit of every item he wore was impeccable. The jacket accentuated his tall, broad-shouldered frame, and the pants hinted at his impressively-built leg muscles. My eyes momentarily wandered over the satisfying lines, mounds and bulges that swelled in *all* the right places.

Radar can dress himself, alright.

He stood straight as a board, not moving from that spot, just observing me in all my pity. My cheeks began to grow warm—was it from the wine, or the embarrassment and shame? Who knew. All I knew was that Radar stood there, feeling sorry for me, and I wanted to shout—*just go away already! Leave me!*

I took a self-conscious sip of wine. "You don't have to feel sorry for me, you know."

"Who said I feel sorry for you?"

"It's obvious you do. You're standing there, looking at me like I'm this pathetic puppy. I can fend for myself. Spending the night by myself isn't the worst thing ever."

And it's not like it's anything new to me.

"Did Lance say where he was going?"

I nodded. "Lindsay had a bad day and so she wants him all to herself tonight."

He laid his giant hand across his face and rubbed his eyes. "That sounds like Lance and Lindsay, alright."

"Oh well. That's okay." I flashed a polite smile. "Have a good time tonight, Radar."

"Yeah. Yeah, thanks."

His body leaned in the direction of the door, but something seemed to stop his feet from actually moving. He looked like he had something to say, but he struggled to find the words.

"You're not leaving." I sighed. "What's wrong?"

"I shouldn't say."

"You'll feel better if you get it off your chest," I said, matter-of-factly. "That's something I live by."

"That's right. Lance mentioned that you have an honesty policy."

"I do. So? Care to get it off your chest?"

Radar sighed. "Okay. You're all dressed up, you look nice, and you're ready to go—yet you're staying in. I feel bad. I feel like I should invite you out with me, at least."

"So why don't you?" I blurted out. Blame it on the wine. Or blame Lance for stranding me here in the first place.

But Radar let out a labored laugh, as if it were an impossibility.

"Ah. I get it." I gave an understanding, if not cynical, bob of my head. "Because you're going out to meet a girl, and I'd be the third wheel."

"How'd you figure that?" he asked.

"Oh, please. I know how you hockey players are."

He smiled with a hint of embarrassment.

"Besides, Lance told me that you're a real player off the ice."

"Did he?" He neared and lowered himself into the couch cushion next to me. Not too close—but close enough that the velvet richness of his woodsy cologne snuck into my personal space and hijacked my senses.

He smells so nice. I wish he didn't have to leave.

"Well, if we're going by your honesty policy, then I guess I have to admit to that," Radar said. "And yeah, I am going out to meet a girl."

"That's cute. What's her name?"

"Umm—" Radar squeezed his eyes shut as he tried to remember. "Fuck, I forgot." He pulled out his phone, checked something, then stuffed it back in his pocket. "That's right. Kara."

"So you and Kara have been going steady for a while now, I take it," I teased.

He gave a coy smile and an uncomfortable little laugh at the knowledge that his sleaziness was on full-display. That was also when I noticed his smile was a perfect row of piano-key teeth.

"Oh! Look! You even put your false tooth in for Kara."

"Yeah, the missing tooth look tends to scare women away."

"That's too bad. I thought you looked kinda cute without it."

He looked away. "You're the first, then."

"And where are you meeting Kara?"

"A club called Regret."

I nearly spit a mouthful of wine right out. "A club called Regret?!"

"Yeah. It's an odd name, isn't it."

"It's a very honest name for a club, if you ask me. It's right in your face. Destination? Regret." I giggled, amused. "It's like they're telling you, 'whoever you meet here, and whatever trouble you end up in, you're gonna regret it, and you'll have no one to blame but yourself.' "

"It's a good club, though. I've never had a bad time there."

"Are there any other clubs where you like to meet girls? Club 'Bad Mistake'? Club 'Walk of Shame'?"

Ryan rolled his eyes. "Oh, *ha ha.*"

"I'm just kidding you." I put my hand on his back and gave

him a gentle push designed to budge him off the couch and spur him away to that one-night stand that he was going to regret. "Don't worry about me, I'll be fine."

But Radar didn't move.

I looked at him and laughed. "You're still not moving. Are you just going to sit there and pity me all night?"

"I'm not pitying you."

"Then what's your problem?"

"Honestly? You really want to know?" he asked.

"Sure."

"I'd be more than happy to take you out and show you around Boston. But I don't think I should. See, you have an honesty policy you live by, but I live by the code."

My eyes narrowed. "Code? What code?"

"The guy code, I mean."

"The guy code! That's real? I mean, you guys actually take that seriously?"

"Us hockey players have to take it pretty seriously."

"And how is the code stopping you right now?"

"Because you're the sister of my best friend. Not just my best friend, but my teammate and roommate, too."

"And so you're telling me that taking your friend's sister out to the club would be against the rules of this fabled 'guy code'? Even though you just told me that you're meeting some random girl that you're going to fuck, and I'm just bored and want to come along for the ride?"

Growing uncomfortable, Radar tugged at his collar. "Well— when you put it like *that* it sounds ridiculous, sure, but—"

"How else could it sound?" I asked.

Radar's features darkened and he didn't answer.

"Oh my God, are you actually afraid that something could happen between us?" I gave his shoulder a slap. "Radar! Get your mind out of the gutter!"

"Of course I'm not thinking that," he growled, indignant. "Because nothing could *ever* happen between us."

"I agree," I told him cheerfully. "Because, no offense, but you're really not my type."

Radar's brow creased. "Yeah? Well, you're not my type, either."

He looked so cute and mad in that moment.

"Good! Then what's the problem?"

"It'd just look bad if I took you out, okay? I don't want to give Lance any reason to suspect us of anything, because it could blow up in my face in a bad way. That's all."

I shrugged. "Fair enough, dude. I've been telling you to go and leave me alone for the past five minutes, but you keep sitting here arguing with me over it. I don't know what else you want me to say."

Radar stared at me, his eyes burning like red-hot embers. I wasn't sure what was going through his mind, but I had to laugh.

But then my stomach butted into the conversation with a loud gurgle. I cradled my tummy and waited for it to stop.

"You haven't even eaten," he said, almost sounding annoyed by that fact.

I whimpered lamely. "I ate lunch."

He checked his watch. "Lunch was, what, nine hours ago?"

"So what? I'll order some food in. Besides, I'm sure the code says something about how wrong it is to feed starving women, too."

Radar bolted off the couch and extended his hand to me.

"C'mon. I'll take you to MacAllister's. It's a sports bar and grill, right across the harbor downtown. *Hardly* the kind of place you take a girl you want to impress. We can go our separate ways after."

I didn't say a word. I just stared at his hand and smiled. I understood now that Radar was only trying to convince *himself* that he was justified in taking me out. He needed a reason, that was all. But did I really want to go? He had a point, after all; Lance might get pissed at us. *Especially* after I made him all paranoid earlier ...

"Just come with me," Radar urged. "We're obviously not going to do anything stupid. We'll grab a bite to eat and then we'll split ways. I'm going to meet a chick and we just admitted that we're not interested in each other. Lance would *have* to understand."

"Are you sure? I don't want you to get into any trouble ..."

"If your brother asks, we'll tell him the truth. We've got nothing to hide."

"Well, I *would* like to get out of the house," I said.

He urged me to take his hand again. "Then come with me."

I gave him my hand. Radar pulled me from the couch, and I marveled at how my tiny hand had totally disappeared in the fighter's ridiculously rugged hands ...

10

———

HER RESCUE

RADAR

I knew something was wrong when I saw Ella sitting on that couch by herself.

She looked ready for a night out on the town in a stunning jade-green dress and taupe T-strap heels. But the look on her face told a different story—like her night had already ended.

When she told me Lance had bailed on her, my heart sank to my stomach. It's a sad thing when a girl gets herself all excited and made up and ready to go out and have a good time only to have her plans fall apart at the last minute.

I wanted to come to her rescue. But I couldn't just *forget* about yesterday. How I nearly did something very stupid—and how I came so close to getting caught by Lance.

But that *couldn't* happen again. Right? A single moment of weakness fueled by alcohol. That's all last night was. It's not like there was an actual connection between us.

Besides, she just told me that I wasn't her type. That kinda sucked to hear her say aloud, but okay. And, yeah, I guess she wasn't really my type, either. She was too smart, too ambitious, too much of a challenge.

And Lance couldn't *really* get pissed at me if I took Ella out to MacAllister's, right? Because I obviously wasn't trying to score with Ella if I took her to a noisy sports bar and grill. *And* I told her that I was meeting that girl from a hookup app. It was truly a win-win for both of us. I got to be the hero, and Ella got to be rescued, and Lance had nothing to worry about.

The smile on her face when she took my hand, and I hoisted her off the couch, made it all worth it for me. She glowed again, and she surprised me by jumping into my arms and giving me a hug. A knot in my throat tightened when she squeezed herself against me and I felt her breasts pressing against my chest.

Okay, fine—the truth was, yeah, this girl's beautiful, alright. And her dress was stunning, like I said. I knew I'd have to mind my manners all night and *not* check her out, no matter how much I was tempted. I don't mind admitting all that to myself— in fact, I think it's only healthy to be able to admit it. It just proves that I can think she's attractive without needing to act on that attraction.

We rode the elevator down and stepped outside. It was a beautiful night, the air cool and crisp, but smelling toasty and burnt in that way that only fall nights can. We took one look at the clear night sky and decided we *had* to take the water taxi to Boston.

"You sure you won't be cold?" I asked. "It's not too late to go back and grab a jacket."

"It's the perfect temperature," she said.

"It really is. But it'll be colder out on the water."

"I'll be fine. I'm tough."

I chuckled. "Okay."

Her heels clicked and clacked on the pavement as we walked. She moved with a natural grace, a hip-swaying swagger, with a cute wiggle in her butt.

We caught the water taxi just before it left the dock. Once on board, the two of us stood side-by-side. We clung to the railing and watched as our boat chugged through the dark waters of the harbor. The air over the water was cold, and I kept glancing over at Ella's toned arms, her athletic shoulders, expecting to find goosebumps, but they weren't there.

"Huh. You're really *not* cold."

"I told you, I'm tough."

I inched a little closer, so she could hear me better over the droning of the boat's motor and the splashing of the water.

"So tell me a little bit more about this honesty policy thing of yours. When did it start?"

"Short answer? One day, as a teenager, I realized that the world would be so much better if people didn't lie to each other. And so I vowed that I wouldn't live a life that required me to lie to anybody."

"And what's the long answer?"

She patted my forearm. "That's a story for another day."

"But aren't you obligated to tell me if I ask you, since you don't lie?"

She laughed. "No. Doesn't quite work like that, but nice try."

"Oh." I paused. "So how does it work?"

"It's just a core value of mine, you know? I try to be as honest as I can with myself and with other people. I'm not perfect and it's harder than it sounds."

"I bet. I wouldn't last a day."

"First, you have to know yourself. Which, as it turns out, is one of those ancient philosophical questions that humanity has struggled to understand throughout history: *who am I, really?*"

Sensing a sudden gulf widening between us, I gulped. "You're really smart, Ella."

She giggled. "No. I can promise you I'm really not."

"Ah-ha—there—you just lied."

Shy, or flattered, she dropped her gaze to her feet. "Oh, stop it."

"Seriously. You are smart. I never did well at school, but I could teach you anything you wanted to know about hockey. Besides that, I'm as dumb as rocks. Thank God this hockey thing is working out for me, or I'd be screwed."

"You're not dumb, Radar." She smiled at me, a bright, genuine smile that warmed my heart. "For a hockey player, that is. And you can take my word on that, because I've met Lance's other friends."

I let out a startled laugh and gave her a probing stare. "You know, for someone who doesn't lie, you sure are sarcastic."

"I can deal with giving up lying, but don't make me give up my sarcasm. I don't want to talk like a boring robot who only spits out factual information." She added in a robot voice, "*Beep boop.*"

I laughed. *This chick is kind of adorably nuts.*

She hooked her arm around mine and brought herself closer. "But I was only kidding, by the way, about the hockey player thing. You seem reasonably, no, *perfectly* intelligent."

"Anyone ever tell you that you've got a lot of personality?" I asked her.

"Oh, yes. They've also told me that I'm loud, that I'm too much to handle, and that I'm too demanding. That's the abridged list of my personality flaws, but I'm sure you could find more." She smiled. "What are yours?"

"I ..." I stalled.

I couldn't think of a good answer, and I quickly grew anxious. That treasure chest of mine flashed into my mind but I forced the thought away—I couldn't *possibly* tell her about that, and besides, what kind of personality trait was that in the first place? '*I like to collect naughty things?*' Jesus, what the hell was my problem, anyway? Was I too afraid to even look at myself? Is that what Ella meant earlier about an age-old problem?

Thankfully, Ella came to my rescue before I went too far off the deep end.

"Whoa there, Radar. Don't blow a gasket. You don't actually have to answer that."

I tried to play it cool. "I'm fine."

Ella sighed. "Screw it. You wanna know the long answer about my honesty policy?"

"If you really want to share it, sure."

"My dad cheated on my mom."

I made a horrified frown. "Damn. Sorry."

"Oh, you don't have to apologize. The only person who should apologize is my dad. Anyway, I was thirteen when I figured it out—not because I'm some skilled detective, but because my dad was *that bad* at hiding it. I was furious. I went to him and told him he'd better tell Mom first, or I would. He told me not to, that she already knew, and it'd only upset her if I told her that I knew about it, too. I didn't believe him. I thought he was just trying to prevent me from telling her."

"And so what happened?"

"I told her. And he was right. She *knew*—she knew all along. She just chose to pretend like she didn't know and ignore it. When I told her, it was like I'd ripped off a painful scab of hers. All it did was make her upset. She was furious at Dad *and* at me for bringing it up."

"Sorry, Ella." I squeezed her shoulder. "That's gotta be a tough thing for a kid to go through."

"Yeah, it was. And that's when I decided I wouldn't live a life that required me to lie—to anyone else or myself. *Especially* myself."

"Lance never mentioned anything about your parents like that ..."

"I'm not surprised. He needed them to stay together for his career. If they got a divorce, does he still become the hockey player he is today? Can you imagine two divorced parents trying to share custody of two kids, while also managing their day jobs and all the travel and day-to-day sacrifices they had to make for Lance?"

"You've got a point." I knew how much time and energy *my* parents had to invest in me for me to reach this level, after all.

The water taxi's motor slowed to an idle as we neared the pier in Boston.

"So, maybe now you can see why we're always fighting," she said with a smile to lighten the mood. "Sorry to make things all dark by talking about my fucked up family history."

"Not at all, Ella. Thanks for telling me."

We filed off the boat and headed for MacAllister's by foot.

"But this is fun, Ryan," she said to me as we walked. "Thanks again for taking me out. Really."

It was the first time she'd used my real name. Not many people call me that. I don't mind being called Radar, not at all, but I always appreciated the sense of closeness that came when a friend used my real name.

"You're welcome, Ella."

"Just don't tell Lance, right?" She must've sensed me go stiff. She pounded my shoulder. "I'm only kidding! Hey, tell me— what do the guys on the team think of Lance's girlfriend?"

"Well, everyone loves to give him shit about it, because the words *butt model* set him off."

She tittered. "So they've all seen her Instagram, I take it?"

"Oh, more than just *seen* it." I nudged her elbow. "We all follow her on Instagram. We don't wanna miss a single pic."

"Gross!" she squealed. "You hockey players are all such huge sleazes."

"You got that right."

"And you're proud of it, too?" She let out a delightfully high laugh. "Awful. You're just *awful*, Ryan."

We reached MacAllister's. I held the door open for Ella and the hustle and bustle of a rowdy Saturday night dinner crowd hit us like a wall. The two of us were totally over-dressed for a joint like this, of course, but that was half the fun.

11

DINNER
RADAR

The duo of young hostesses lit up when they saw me enter.

"*Radar!*" the first one mewled.

"*Welcome back, Radar!*" her partner gushed.

"Girls, I want you to meet Ella Couture. She's Lance's sister. She's visiting from out of town."

The hostesses looked at Ella. They hadn't noticed her standing right next to me. They gave Ella polite but disinterested smiles, and then immediately stared at me again.

I looked at the crowd that was crammed into the waiting area. "So, what's the wait like tonight?" I asked.

The first girl muttered, "Well, er, let's see what we have ..." She tapped away at her monitor and then, quietly added, "Oh, look at that! I just found a booth." She whisked us past the waiting crowd and delivered us to an over-sized booth that could easily fit ten people. "Enjoy your dinner!"

I smiled at Ella. "Not bad, eh? I love the service here."

But Ella looked appalled. "I can't believe they just did that. We just cut in front of that huge line, and I could *feel* everyone staring at us!"

"The fruits of being a pro athlete," I said with a cocky grin. "They treat us like royalty in Boston."

Ella wasn't impressed.

"You hockey guys really are all the same," she said in a jokey tone of voice. But although she sounded like she was joking, I could swear she sounded a little disappointed for real. "*Anyway.*"

And although I showed her my confident smirk, deep down, I felt a little strange. Naked, almost. Normally, girls absolutely ate up the special treatment I received around town ... but not Ella. I guess that made me feel a little vulnerable.

Huh.

Our server swung by the table. We ordered a couple of drinks. I went with a steak and fries and Ella ordered a grilled chicken salad.

"So, Mr. Royalty, how'd you meet this Kara girl?"

"Through an app."

"A dating app?"

"Yeah." I could've left it at that, but Ella's honesty policy had me in the mood to, well, be honest. "Actually, it's more of a hookup app."

"Wait, that's different than a dating app?"

"Well, sure. Some people use dating apps just to hookup. But a hookup app is like, strictly for hooking up. Less drama, I guess."

She didn't look too impressed at that, either. "I never knew that was a thing ..."

"Really? You've never used Tinder or anything like that?"

"No. I've never been on any of those apps," Ella said.

"Oh. Wow. That's rare these days."

"Is it?" Our drinks arrived, and Ella took a sip from her straw. "Maybe that's what I'm doing wrong, then."

I raised a brow. "You're doing something wrong?"

"I have trouble meeting people, I guess. I'm always working, so I don't go out too much. And all the guys I do meet are just ... *blah.*"

I shook my head. "Dating apps won't help you then."

"Why not?"

"You won't meet any quality guys on there. You'll only meet guys like me."

She smiled coyly. "Professional hockey sleazes, you mean?"

"Something like that." I paused. "You know, that's surprising. I would've thought that dating in New York would be really easy for someone like you. You're obviously a smart, attractive girl, and you run your own business. You've got a lot going for you. And there's *so* many people in that city. There's gotta be some quality guys out there."

"Right? That's what you'd think. But there's only one quality man in my life." She swiped on her cell phone and showed me a picture of a mottled gray and white cat. "His name is Eucalyptus."

"Oh, God." I slapped my forehead. "I did *not* have you pegged as a crazy cat lady."

She giggled. "I'm not. I swear I'm not. But look, this is how dating is in New York ..."

I listened as Ella explained her struggles of meeting a decent man in New York City. As she told it, it was a city full of guys who were only interested in a girl long enough to find out if he could sleep with her. No one was interested in something longer term. She also explained that guys were rather intimidated by her tendency to speak her mind and tell the truth—if not put off by it completely.

Then she told me about the last guy she was dating. A lawyer named Matthew. She told me about their breakup—and what he said to her. That he actually couldn't stand her, and the only reason he stayed with her was so he could brag to his beer league team that he was banging Lance Couture's little sister. And, to add insult to injury, he told Ella that she was a "seven at best." That was so far from the truth, and such an insulting thing to say to a woman, I ground my teeth in anger.

"He actually *said* all that to you?"

"Yup."

I clenched my glass of beer so hard I thought the glass might shatter in my fist. "Where does his beer league play?"

She answered right away. "Chelsea Piers in New York." Then her eyes narrowed suspiciously. "Wait, why? You're not going to go beat him up, are you?"

The fantasy made me smirk. "Would you be mad if I did?"

She took a second to think it over before she wore a smirk of her own. "I suppose I wouldn't stop you."

"Add it to my bucket list, then. One of these days I'll have to swing by Chelsea Piers and body-check some asshole lawyer named Matthew."

She let out a dreamy sigh. "Oh, Radar, you can't talk to a girl like that ... you'll only get her hopes up and everything."

I leaned forward and growled. "Sorry, but I still can't get over that. He was only banging you for bragging rights? Who the hell says something like that?"

She bobbed her head from side to side, as if she were considering telling me something or leaving it be.

"Slight correction," she said at last, "but just to be clear, he *wasn't* 'banging' me."

"Hm?"

"We hadn't slept together. He was bragging to his buddies that we were, but we hadn't yet. I guess that's why he stayed with me for as long as he did, even though he found me so insufferable."

They never slept together?

A wave of righteousness filled my heart. That was the best

damn news I'd ever heard in my life. That scumbag lawyer didn't deserve her, and I was *glad* he'd wasted his time trying.

"How long were you together?" I asked gleefully.

"Four months."

"Four months ..." I repeated, imagining the lawyer's four-month anguish—and savoring every last second of it. "Good."

"Why is that good?"

"You made him work for it, and he didn't get it, and I'm glad," I snarled. "Fuck that guy."

She looked at me like she didn't quite know what to make of my jealous outburst. Part of her was surprised. Another part of her, a part she tried to hide, looked deeply pleased.

"Well then!" she snickered at last, speechless.

Our waitress returned and delivered our dinner. I needed to change the topic, because that lawyer guy got my blood boiling, and I wasn't going to have him ruin my steak.

"So, Ella," I asked as I sawed off a hunk of meat, "tell me about your job."

She gave me a run-down on the interior design business she ran. Apparently, she was growing quite a reputation in the city for quality work and had already had some famous names among her clients—a couple actors, a few NY athletes and local celebrities. She even had a waiting list. She'd really made a name for herself, apparently.

"Makes sense," I said.

"What does?"

"That you'd be in your business for yourself. I can tell you're really ... independent. You know. Strong. Capable. Whatever."

"Thanks," she said quietly. "Unfortunately, a lot of guys are intimidated by that."

"Intimidated? There's that word again. Why are guys so intimidated by you?"

She chuckled, but she didn't give an answer. Her cheeks

turned the faintest shade of pink. Was she embarrassed about something?

"Seriously, I don't get it," I said. "Is it because you run your own business? Or that you expect guys to be honest with you? I get that it'd be hard, but jeez. Self-employed and honest. Those aren't exactly qualities that I'd think were deal breakers."

"No ... it's something else."

"What?" I asked, doubting it could be anything serious. "You've got your life together and you want guys to prove they're worth your time."

"Yes—exactly—I do want guys to prove they're worth my time. The thing is, it gets a *little* more complicated than that. And that's what scares guys away."

I was completely confused. "Well, what is it?"

"Swear you won't be weirded out if I tell you?" she asked.

"Yeah, sure," I said. "I swear."

"Okay." She leaned over the table and lowered her voice. "I'm a virgin."

I smiled at her, waiting for her to burst into laughter so I could laugh along with her. But hell, she wasn't laughing—she still looked completely serious.

"Wait. You're serious?"

She nodded. "Yeah."

"Oh. *Oh*, damn." I rubbed my chin and let that info soak into my brain. "Are you, uh, religious?"

She laughed. "Not really. We moved around so much for Lance's career when I was in school. As soon as I managed to snag a boyfriend, it was time to move somewhere else. And I told you that I shared a bedroom with Lance all those years, right? Can you imagine bringing a boy back home to *that* pig sty? I don't think so. Then I was in college, and you don't exactly meet a whole lot of boys in the interior design program at FIT. And then I graduated and started my business, which exceeded beyond my wildest expectations and ate up all my free time, and voila. Here I am, the twenty-two-year-old virgin."

"I'll be damned," I muttered.

"Look, I don't want make a big deal out of it, okay? And don't tell Lance because he doesn't know and I don't want him to know. That's the thing—I never wanted to make a big deal out of it. It just never *happened*. So what? And it's not like I was *trying* to stay a virgin all this time, either. I just thought, since I waited this long, I might as well wait until I knew the time was right. You know? And I guess the time has never been right."

"Hey, yeah, gotcha," I mumbled, my words running together. I stared off into the distance. "Totally."

Virgin. Whoa.

"See, now *you're* acting weird," she said, disappointment in her voice. "And you're just my brother's friend, and we're not even interested in each other ..."

"No no no. I'm not acting weird. I'm not *trying* to, anyway. Sorry. It's just a rare thing in this day and age. I needed a minute to wrap my brain around it."

"It *is* a rare thing," she sighed, taking another sip from her drink. "Everyone else is using hookup apps and I'm still stuck at third base. Ha ha. Oh well, it's my choice, I suppose."

"Wait, third base? So you *have* done things with a guy?"

"Of course! I'm not completely pure—or anything close to it. I *love* to sixty-nine, for example."

I couldn't help it—my cock stirred against my leg. She'd put the image, the sensation, right there in my head: her bare bottom right over my face; my tongue busily lapping at her pink folds; the sound of her muffled moans as she buried me in her throat.

I shifted in my seat and tried to push those completely forbidden thoughts out of my head.

"So, you're waiting for a quality guy?"

"I was." She took a long sip from her drink. "But I don't know what I'm waiting for anymore. I'm kind of sick of waiting, honestly."

No no no. Not what I need to hear.

"Don't give up," I croaked. "You'll find a good guy eventually."

"Yeah, that's what everyone says, but *where?*"

I felt a heaviness in my heart. "You're asking the wrong guy."

A still quiet came between us. Lost in my thoughts, I sawed off one hunk of steak after another and chewed.

So that was it. She was a virgin.

That was ... unexpected.

But it made sense. Sort of. Like I said, she's tough, capable, driven, successful. I could easily see how most guys would fail to live up to her standards.

Once the shock wore off, I have to say, I felt—*relief.* Because, the more time I spent with this girl, I had to admit—I found her even cuter, even more irresistible. And she was so easy to talk to. And that scared me, honestly, because it felt like I was starting to actually *like* her, and making up excuses to be with her. I'd been lying to myself, thinking that I could be around her and control myself.

Shit, I almost kissed her last night ... and here I was, taking her out to dinner?! What was I thinking?

But now that she told me that she was a virgin, I knew that nothing would happen between us. She was a virgin, and she was looking for a good man and, hell, I certainly wasn't that. She was smart enough not to get mixed up with me. And I was smart enough not to get mixed up with the virgin sister of my teammate.

Or are you one of those easily intimidated cowards she's known all her life?

"So how about you, Ryan? How's *your* love life? Do you ever want to settle down, or are you going to play the field forever?"

"Well, I'm definitely not in love with anyone." I pushed my empty plate aside. "So I guess it's the field."

"Ew! Radar!" she squealed.

"What? You asked a question, I gave you an answer."

"No, it was just the way you said it while you pushed your empty plate aside. Like women are nothing but a *prime rib* for you to consume."

I laughed. "Pure coincidence."

But she was right, in a way, wasn't she? In her eyes, I must've looked like a monster, a sexual deviant. Here I was, bragging to a virgin about going out to meet some random chick I picked up on a hookup app. Awful.

Then again, wasn't that perfectly fine? I didn't *want* her to like me. That'd only cause a whole shit-load of problems. So if she thought I was a terrible sleaze, a man-slut ... hey, great.

We made small talk and joked around until our server came by with the bill. I grabbed the check and paid it and left a generous tip.

"Thanks for dinner, Ryan."

"My pleasure. I'm glad I could get you out of the house."

"Me too." She gave a gracious smile. "Are you off to meet your next cut of meat now?"

"Whatever."

I checked my watch. I still had some time to kill until midnight, when I was going to meet Kara at Regret. I could see if some of the boys were around and if they wanted to meet up until then. Or ...

Hell, why not ask Ella if she wants to come? We're already downtown. She doesn't have anything else to do.

"You wanna come with me to Regret? I'm not supposed to meet Kara for another hour or so."

"As long as you promise I won't *regret* it," she said in that over-the-top manner that said she *knew* her joke was atrocious.

"Ba-dum-tssh. But hey, no promises."

We left the restaurant. Outside, I hailed a cab and opened the door for Ella. I slid in after her, and the two of us sped off for Regret.

12

CLUB REGRET

ELLA

R *egret.*

Ryan Ryder and I were in the back of a cab, zipping through downtown Boston, heading to a club called Regret.

Hilarious.

I'm not superstitious, but it sure seemed like a bad omen. Like something out there was lying in wait for us. Would we run into Lance at the club? Would he flip his shit, automatically assuming Radar and I were up to no good with each other?

Whatever. After what Lance did with Quinn, and the trouble he caused me? He didn't have any right to be upset just because I hung out with his teammate. Lance was the one who bailed on me in the first place, after all.

Besides, I knew *nothing* could possibly happen between Ryan and me. Especially after I told him I was a virgin—the look on his face all but confirmed it. He looked like *all* the other guys did when I told them: like I'd just punched them in the gut with a two-ton weight and their world had ended.

On one hand, I wanted to smack Ryan. Why would it matter to him if I was a virgin? It shouldn't matter at all! We'd told each other we weren't interested in each other, and we'd meant it —right?

But on the other hand, there was a part of myself that was deeply satisfied. Especially when Ryan got all mad and huffy, with his giant chest puffing up when I told him about Matthew. That made me so warm and happy inside ...

That's when I realized it: I wanted Ryan to like me.

I *wanted* Ryan to like me, for some reason, even if he fit the cheesy, sleazy hockey player stereotype to a T.

I didn't get it.

In his favor, he was acting like a perfect gentleman all night, and I enjoyed getting to know the quiet tough-guy a little bit better.

Then again—I guess a perfect gentleman wouldn't be heading out to meet a one-night-stand. But that wasn't surprising, either, given what I knew about hockey players. And he was honest and upfront about it, so it didn't feel right to judge him for it.

And I guess, technically speaking, a 'perfect gentleman' wouldn't be stealing the occasional peek at my chest. *That's right, Radar, I caught you looking—more than once.*

Not that I minded too much. Because hey, he's a guy. A hockey playing guy, at that. And when a guy sees breasts, he's just not in control of himself. Right? When a girl offers even a hint of cleavage, guys just have this overwhelming biological drive to look. It doesn't mean that they're even attracted to her, really. He just has to look every so often to make sure that a girl's breasts haven't jumped off her chest and run off, or something. Because *tits*.

I don't know, I'm just rambling. I have no idea what goes through a guy's caveman brain when he sees a pair of breasts. All I know is that Radar said I'm not his type.

And *I* said that he wasn't my type, too. Actually, I said it first!

Yet he's tall and devilishly handsome, broad-shouldered, sharply-dressed yet rough around the edges in all the right ways—

And I said he's not my type.

Somberly, I stared out my window, mesmerized by the hectic blur of busy traffic; long trails of red and white.

Did I *lie* to him?

Did I lie to myself?

I clenched my fists so tightly my nails began to cut into my palms.

I thought of Ryan's date for the night. Kara. I wondered what she was like. Probably like all the other puck bunnies I'd met over the years—girls that were obsessed with Lance and his buddies. Loud, gaudy, and with a penchant for putting all her assets on display. Credit where it's due, those girls knew precisely how to ensnare a jock's attention: leave absolutely *nothing* to the imagination, because lord knows, they never had much of one to begin with.

"What're you thinking about?" Ryan suddenly asked.

His voice snapped me from my trance. I turned to see him, smiling at me, a small and curious smile on his lips.

"Oh ... lots of things," I said. "You caught me day-dreaming."

His grin grew, and so did his desire to know more. "About what?"

I couldn't hold his gaze. I dropped mine to the floor of the cab. "Oh, fine. I was just wondering what this girl you're meeting up with looks like."

"You wanna see? I'll show ya. Honesty policy and all, right?" He pulled his cell phone from his pocket. The screen lit the back-seat of the cab and he showed me a picture of the girl that matched my mental image of her exactly: blonde, too thin, face heavily painted. Her orange skin tone said she enjoyed baking herself on tanning beds. You could call her *attractive*, because she knew how to package herself and attract attention, but you wouldn't call her pretty.

Or maybe I'm just being a catty bitch ...

He swiped to show me the next picture. Kara had pulled down her jeans, exposing her silly pink panties with a bow.

"Wow," I laughed, a jealous lump lodging itself in my throat. "Straight to the point, isn't she?"

"Right?" Ryan chuckled. He stuffed his phone back into his pocket.

The grin he wore—I'd seen it before with other guys from my past. I'd ended up being the defacto 'cool chick' in a group of guys far too many times to count. Grow up with a popular hockey star for a brother, always surrounded by sweaty, trash-talking boys, and you, too, might easily end up as 'one of the guys.'

To Radar, the novelty of having a *female friend* that he could share anything with was just, *so badass, man.* Even *cooler* that I was a girl who lived by an honesty policy, which meant everything had to be laid bare.

Even if all those honest details kinda hurt for me to know and hear.

The cab pulled over to the curb and slowed to a stop. The club's signage was lit in smoky red letters: *Regret.*

Ryan paid the cabbie and hopped out. He gave me his hand to help me out of the car.

Welp, let's see what this place is like ...

———

I joined the end of the line to get into the club. I was digging through my clutch, in search of my ID, when Ryan stopped me.

"No need," he said simply. He whisked us to the front of the line. The doorman saw Ryan, welcomed *Mr. Ryder* back, and let the two of us in immediately.

The crowded club was dimly lit and thumping beats blasted from the speaker system. Ryan took my hand so we wouldn't get separated and led me through a mass of dancing people. The body heat was thick and sweltering, but we emerged on the other side at the bar and were able to breathe again. A bartender spotted Ryan and rushed over to take our order. He made our drinks in a hurry and when Ryan tried to pay, the bartender reassured him that his money was no good here. Ryan stuffed the cash in the tip jar instead.

Ryan passed me my drink. The dance music was so loud, it forced us closer together to be heard.

"Here," he said, leaning in so close he nearly nuzzled me. His whiskers, like prickly barbs, scraped against my skin and sent a shiver down my spine.

"What do you think?" he asked. "Hoppin', right?"

I steadied myself on his arm and stood on my tip-toes, reaching for his ear. This close to him, the scent of his cologne filled my senses again.

"Sure is," I yelled. "And I can see you're no stranger around these parts, either."

"Yeah," he answered.

I waved my hand like a wand over the club—the environment itself, with the ear-splitting music, the alcohol, the rolling clouds of competing cologne, the skimpily dressed women— and asked, "Do you meet all your girls here?"

"Some," he answered with a shrug.

"So where is she?"

He checked his watch. "She'll be here in a little while."

"You don't sound very excited," I said. "You *should* be. You're about to get laid. And what if you met this Kara girl, and she blows you away in every regard? What if she's your *dream* girl? Would you want to date her? Like a steady girlfriend?"

Ryan chuckled. "I wouldn't count on that happening."

"Why not?"

"I don't wanna think about all that right now!" he shouted. "And it's too loud in here to talk! Hey, c'mon, let's dance."

I didn't even have a choice. His giant hand swallowed mine right up, and then a split second later he was leading me on a charge right to the dance floor instead.

God.

Just like that, he could shrug off any questions he didn't like and skip right to what he really cared about: *having fun.* He was kind of charming in a horrible way—if you could look past the womanizing, anyway ...

13

NOT MY TYPE
RADAR

Kara ended up being late. Not that I minded—Ella and I were having a blast just dancing with each other. And after a second round, and then a third round of drinks, we were really letting loose.

I tried not to think about Lance, or the absolute fit he'd throw if he could see me with his sister on the dance floor. My hands spanned Ella's waist. Her arms hung around my neck. The two of us moved together, eyes locked on each other, the music bringing our bodies closer and closer.

The tops of her glowing breasts jiggled and bounced in her dress, I couldn't help myself. I *had* to look.

She caught me stealing a glance. She gasped and wagged her finger in my face.

"I *see* you staring, you know!" she shouted over the music.

"I can't help it. That dress is such a lovely color on you."

"Oh, please."

"No, really. The green matches your eyes and brings out the red in your hair. It's the perfect color on you, actually."

I meant every word of that.

"I'm not dumb, Radar, you were looking at my *tits*."

"Yeah. Yeah, I was." I smirked, and since the cat was already out of the bag, I stole another peek. "Your tits look great, too."

She slapped my cheek, but only lightly. "Stop it, you perv. My eyes are up here. And Lance would kill you if he heard you say that, by the way."

I gave a serious nod. "I know. But I still meant what I said about the color of your dress."

Her eyes fluttered with doubt, like she wasn't convinced it was a genuine compliment.

"Are you always this cheesy when you're trying to woo some club girl?" she asked.

"Nah. If anything, I'm kind of a dick to them."

"Why?"

I shrugged. "Because it always works."

"I doubt that. Try me. See what happens."

"What? No way."

"Why not?"

"Because you're a cool chick and I like you. And I'm not trying to sleep with you. Remember? Teammate's little sister and all that?"

She let out a piercing laugh. "Is your ego really that big? You truly believe that if you start flirting with me, *poof,* we'll magically end up in bed together?"

I liked hearing her say that. I liked the image she put in my head, too: the two of us trying to quietly bone in my bed—but miserably failing at the whole 'being quiet' part. We're naked and sweaty and our faces are wrought with this twisted, guilty pleasure—like we both knew what we're doing is insanely bad and wrong, but we just can't help ourselves. It was wrong as hell just to imagine it, but that didn't make the thought any less appealing, nor did it stop the stirring in my crotch.

But she wanted me to be a dick to her, so I wasn't going to let her know any of that.

"Who said I wanted to sleep with you?" I asked, and I knew exactly what was coming when I saw her fist clench. "You're not my type, remember?"

Her jaw came unhinged and then suddenly, *bam,* there it was, her fist smashing right into my abdomen. But I was ready and waiting for it, and instead of knocking the wind out of me, her fist futilely deflected off a flexed and armored set of abs.

"Yeah, I *do* remember you saying that," she said with a fire still smoldering in her eyes.

"You said it first," I reminded her.

"So?"

"Don't feel bad." I tried to pull her closer, but she resisted with an indignant squeal and pushed me away. "Just 'cause you're not my type doesn't mean I don't think you're cute anyway."

She raised a still-angry and now skeptical eyebrow. "Oh, so after insulting me, this is the part where you butter me up so you can try to get in my pants, right?"

"I already told you, nothing can happen between us. I'm just telling you the truth: yeah, when I first saw you, I didn't think you were my type. But the more time I spend with you? The more I start to think you're kinda insanely cute. You're growing on me. That's all I'm saying."

She softened, only slightly, but her nostrils remained upturned in disgust. "Well *I* still think you're gross."

"Too bad. We could've had something. Imagine how fun it'd be, running around in secret behind Lance's back for the rest of your trip?"

"That doesn't sound fun at all. But *you* sound drunk right now, and you're acting like a creep."

I raised my hands in defeat. "Damn. Alright, Ella, you win. I gave it my best."

"Wait, that was you being a dick?" she giggled. "And that's it? That's *all?* You're surrendering already?"

"Yeah. I got nothin'. You're player-proof."

She rolled her eyes. "Too easy. I can't believe girls fall for that 'negative asshole' shtick."

"Me neither. But they do." I pulled her closer again, and this time, she didn't resist. "You really think I'm gross, though?"

"I think you're handsome as hell," she said, her hands flat on my chest, "but if you talked to *me* like that? I'd never let you kiss me in a million years, let alone *anything* else."

"Damn!" I had to laugh. I wasn't used to girls talking to me like that.

"Surprised?" she giggled.

She hadn't just resisted me, she'd straight up won this round. I didn't know what to say or do and I wondered if this was how Lance felt growing up with this girl—stunned to find yourself suddenly on the losing end of a verbal or physical battle.

"Yeah, actually," I muttered.

She laid her palm on my cheek and sarcastically cooed, "Aww. The playboy is just so used to getting his way, isn't he?"

With her palm still on my cheek, I put my hands around her waist again. She looked so pleased with herself, smiling from ear to ear. She basked in her victory, and I mean she absolutely *glowed* in that moment, and for once in my life, I didn't mind losing. In fact, it made me feel closer to her, somehow.

With my hands on her waist and my eyes on hers, I felt like everything around us—the shoulder-to-shoulder crowd, the stifling heat, the deafening music—muddled together into a distant background distraction. All those things were still *there,* but in that moment, Ella's bright eyes and sparkling smile drowned it all out.

I had a terrible urge. Same as I did last night. Something I knew was totally out of line, totally inexcusable, totally inappropriate ... but it felt like the only answer, the only thing I knew how to do.

I need to kiss her. This time for real.

I think she knew what I was thinking, and although neither of us moved and neither of us said a word, her eyes seemed to scream at me, *no, don't do it, don't do it you idiot! You'll regret this! We both will!*

But that just encouraged me more.

My eyes darted to her mouth, her lips so pretty and pink, and my breathing began to slow, and she looked at *my* lips and I knew then that we both wanted it, even if we understood perfectly it was a terrible idea.

And then, right then, *right* as I started to lean in, there was a finger tapping on my shoulder.

We both turned, slowly.

Kara.

"*Radar!*" Kara squealed.

Without warning, the girl launched her body into the air and threw her arms around me. She hung from my neck, letting her legs dangle and kick in the air as she pressed her lips into the collar of my shirt again and again. She smelled heavily of fruity perfume and rum, a cloying cloud of nauseating sweetness that burrowed into my throat and overwhelmed my senses.

"I've been looking all over for you! You didn't answer my texts! I'm so glad I found you!" she said, piling her words together.

A choking heat grew around my neck. I felt embarrassed, ashamed—like I'd been caught doing something wrong, although I didn't know what or why. My eyes stayed fixated on

Ella. But Ella retreated from me and Kara, slowly, cautiously, as if she were perfectly content to be forgotten.

No, I thought. *Don't go. Not yet.*

"Um, hey, hey Kara," I stammered. "You mind? You're choking me."

I pried her off my neck and returned Kara to her feet.

Kara demanded my eyes, but still, my eyes flickered over to Ella. I couldn't help it. I felt awful. We both knew that this was what my night was leading up to. But now that the moment had arrived, it felt so wrong to leave her like this.

Kara noticed I was distracted by someone else. She turned a cold, judgmental gaze to Ella. I'd seen it enough times to know: puck bunnies could be cruel and heartless when they thought another woman had wandered onto their territory.

"Sorry, am I interrupting something?" Kara asked, but her tone was anything *but* sorry.

"No," Ella said. "I'm leaving."

"That's what I thought." Kara pressed herself into my side and began to glide her hand down my chest, across my waist, slowly inching towards my crotch. It was more of a show for Ella than it was for me.

Ella turned away and carved a path through the dancing crowd. I watched as she pushed her way through the mass of bodies, hurrying towards the club's exit.

Kara grabbed hold of my jaw and directed my gaze at herself. "*Hi.*"

"Hi," I said.

"You look really hot tonight, Radar. I can't believe how *tall* you are! They said you're even bigger in person than you look on TV and they were right."

"They? Who's they?" I asked, distracted and guilty.

"The other puck bunnies."

"Oh ... oh, right."

"That's how I knew about your *collection*." She winked. "Remember? The picture I sent you earlier?"

I knew what she was doing; trying to shift my attention away from Ella and towards herself. She was trying to win my affection for the night, planting the image of her panties fresh in my mind.

I swallowed tensely. My eyes darted over Kara's head and I glanced at the crowd, trying to find Ella again, curious if she'd made it out.

Kara folded her arms and her tone went short and snappy. "Okay, there you go again—what's the deal with you and her, anyway?"

"She's from out of town. She's visiting from New York."

"So?"

"I don't know if she even knows how to get back to the condo."

"Sounds like *her* problem."

"No, it'd definitely be my problem, since I'm the one who invited her out. She's my best friend's little sister. He'd kill me if something happened to her."

"She's got a cell phone, doesn't she?"

"Well, yeah, of course."

"I don't care what city the bitch is from, no one should be getting lost in 2017. And if someone does get lost, fuck 'em, they deserve whatever happens."

I tilted my head and looked at Kara—really *looked* at her. Who was this girl? How did we meet? Obviously we 'met' on *MeatMarket,* but *why* was I talking to her? I looked so deeply into her, I felt like I was looking into myself. What the hell was all this about?

I didn't know. All I knew was that she looked *very* annoyed that I was concerned about my buddy's little sister.

"Whoa, you're awful," I said, staggering backward.

"Excuse me?" she panted. "*You're* the panty-collecting weirdo. Fucking pervert *creep*."

I shrugged. "Hey, listen, sorry to waste your time. But I gotta run."

"Whatever, dickhead!"

I left Kara and pushed my way through the crowd, hoping it wasn't too late to catch up with Ella.

14

MIXED MESSAGES

ELLA

My heels clicked on the sidewalk as I hurried down the sidewalk. I kept one arm in the air, hoping to hail a cab. But cabs in this city weren't nearly as ubiquitous as they were in New York.

The temperature was perfect when we'd left the condo—but now it was *freezing* cold. I had to keep my other arm snuggled tightly across my torso for warmth. The early morning chill was even more unbearable after being entrenched in the humid body heat of the dance floor at that stupid club.

I checked my phone and discovered yet another problem: my battery was completely dead, and that meant I didn't have Lance's address. I didn't know the way back to his condo. All I could do was describe the area he lived in and hope the cabbie might recognize it.

And that was Club Regret, I thought to myself, snickering cynically as I walked.

The club had lived up to its name. I would've been better off just heading home after dinner. But I guess I fooled myself— thinking I could be *friends* with Radar. Once he started flirting with me? He fucked my mind up. I might not fall for his games, but that doesn't mean I'm completely immune to the emotional bullshit a guy like him will put a girl through as he attempts to get laid.

Stupid jock, I muttered under my breath. *Ugh, why are they always the same?*

They had a way of creeping past your defenses and charming you with their oafish ways. But if you made the mistake of letting your guard down, and if you chose to see them as a gentle giant instead of what they *really* were—sleazy horn-dogs with no sense of loyalty—then the punch to the gut was always lying in wait for you.

I rolled my eyes at myself. The fact that I was even *mildly* upset about any of this just proved how pathetic I was in the first place. How could I even be this upset right now?

You know why.

It was because of the look Radar gave me on the dance floor. After all the shit-talking, the fake-flirting, the promises that we weren't into each other—that look he gave me was *real.* Just like last night. He really wanted to do it, didn't he? He *really* wanted to kiss me and if he'd had a single second longer, he would've done it!

And that's what fucked me up the most. I couldn't believe it at the time. I wanted to *slap* him! How could he? How could he *actually* want to kiss me after all we'd already said to each other? About how we weren't interested in each other? About how it was a bad idea for so many reasons?

How could he be so *dumb* to even think about trying it again? Didn't he know the damage he'd cause? And didn't he know it wouldn't get him laid?

And yet ... I didn't slap him. I didn't slap him when I should've: the very moment I could tell the wheels were turning in his head, and his eyes began to soften with intimacy, and I knew damned well that he'd begun to desire my lips. The *horror* of it all was sort of entrancing. Maybe even alluring. I guess I wanted to see if he could really go through with it. And I was curious if *I* could go through with it, too—if I could let myself give in to a moment of weakness.

And then, right then, right when it seemed like it was about to happen—

His girl showed up.

And oh man, the look of pure horror on his face, as his big fateful moment was snatched away from his grubby paws, as if by divine intervention. Like God was personally telling him, *you don't deserve this girl, Radar.*

What was going through his mind in that moment? Oh, how I'd love to know. I hoped it burned him. I hoped it gave him a serious case of whiplash, as he shifted from working up the nerve to take a chance on something so uncertain, to suddenly having his sure-thing, arranged-lay for the night show up and throw herself all over him. God, that was poetic justice. I hoped he felt dumb and awful. Frankly, it served him right that she showed up at that very moment.

For my part? I appreciated Kara's timely intrusion. It was a perfect reminder of the kind of guy that Radar was: a guy who went for easy lays. He liked girls who squeal his name while they run up to him, girls who jump into his arms and plant their kisses all over his neck, who dress in skin-tight dresses with their tits and ass hanging out, who smell like booze and cheap perfume ...

They were probably all over each other at this very moment, freak-dancing in the club, tongues lodged in each other's throats. I could just picture her jumping into his arms, her legs over his shoulders, shrieking in a fake and obnoxious falsetto as Radar powered her into the air with his obscene dry-humping dance moves. All the blood in Radar's brain would drain straight to his cock and he'd forget I was ever with him tonight.

Gross. He's such a pervert. After tonight, I don't care if I ever see him again. I'll have to go out of my way to avoid him at Lance's ... but it can be done. Oh, it can be done.

Another stream of traffic passed, but still no taxi to be found. I groaned.

And then I thought I heard my name in the distance.

"Ella!"

But I didn't turn and look because I was *sure* I was imagining it. No one in this city knew me.

Then I heard it again, closer, and this time followed by the hurried stride of an athlete in expensive leather shoes.

"Ella! Hey! Ella!"

I stopped and turned. It was him. Radar sprinted after me, his arm waving madly to grab my attention. A gush of relief displaced the bitterness in my heart, but I remained determined to keep him at a skeptical and healthy distance.

This guy is just so full of mixed messages. He's fucking my head up.

———

I don't know if he was expecting me to throw myself in his arms and have some romantic kiss like out of a movie, but once Radar caught up to me, the moment seemed to grow awkward. I stood with my arms folded and he bent over, his hands on his knees as he panted for breath.

"Hey," he said.

"What are you doing here?"

"I couldn't let you leave like that," he said, still puffing for air.

"Why not? That was the plan all along, wasn't it?"

"Yeah, but ..." Radar trailed off. He didn't have the words and that fact made him look briefly annoyed at himself. "Damn.

Look, Ella, you're covered in goosebumps. I told you you'd be cold."

He took his suit jacket off in a hurry and held it out for me to put on. But I regarded the jacket, and the act itself, with suspicion.

"Oh, come on, just wear my jacket," he urged. "You're obviously cold."

It was true, I *was* freezing. Begrudgingly, I stepped forward, and Radar helped me into it. The jacket was still sizzling with his blistering body heat. I pulled the jacket tight over my chest and one final chill ran down my spine.

"There," he said. "How's that?"

"Better. Thank you." The smell of his cologne surrounded me, mingled with my senses, my thoughts. "Why are you here, though? Where's your hot babe?"

"I left her back at the club."

"Why?"

"Really, Ella? Do I have to explain it?"

"Yeah, actually, you do."

"Because you're our guest. And the way you left didn't feel right. Nothing about tonight felt right and I didn't want to leave you all alone in a strange city."

I huffed. "I told you, you don't have to worry. I can take care of myself. I can find my way home. I live in New York, remember?"

"Oh, really, Miss Big City? I guess you know you're walking in the wrong direction then, right?"

I gulped. "Er."

"Yeah. That's why it took me so long to catch up to you. I left almost the same time as you did, but I ran a few blocks in the other direction first." Radar pointed in the opposite direction. "The condo is that-away."

"Oh. Um. My phone died," I whimpered, feeling about two inches tall. "I don't have your guys' address memorized."

"Damn. Thank God I found you then." Radar shook his head. "If I got you lost in the city? Lance would be right to kill me."

"So ... what do we do now?" I asked.

"We're gonna get you home." Radar pulled out his phone and called for a cab. He gave them the address and hung up.

"They said five minutes," he told me.

"Thank you."

The two of us passed the minutes rather quietly. It felt like there was a lot we could *both* say in that moment, but no one had any desire to talk. Instead, we toed at the sidewalk and milled around in place. We watched the traffic fly up and down the street. We stepped aside for the large and boisterous groups of club-goers that roamed the sidewalk.

Radar sidled next to me and let out a gentle breath. "Hey. What's on your mind?" he finally asked.

I gave a short laugh and shook my head. "My mind's fried."

He gave a nod. "Yeah. I hear you. Same."

I thought that was an invitation to ask. "What's on *your* mind?"

He shook his head. "I shouldn't say."

This time, I wasn't tempted to convince him otherwise.

But then Radar blew out a breath. "To hell with it, I'm just going to say it: I had a fun time with you tonight, Ella. Like, an actual good time. Once you left? I just looked at Kara, and like ... I dunno. I didn't even know what happened. It all happened so fast. I just didn't want you to leave. I shouldn't even say it, but—" He grit his teeth. "I like you, Ella. I know I'm not supposed to, but I do."

My mind knew better, but the heart was always a fool. My

heart pumped and churned with waves of warmth, and good vibes flowed outward through my whole body.

He neared confidently, a man on a mission. He pulled me against his warm body and nestled me tightly. I didn't look up. He tried to stroke the hair out of my face but I let out a short burst of laughter and turned away. "No. Don't. Don't even."

"Why not?"

"Because you're drunk and you're acting ridiculous, Radar."

"How am I ridiculous?"

"You know you shouldn't touch me like that." I planted my hands against his hard stomach and shoved, separating us. "You know nothing good can come out of this. Only bad."

He nodded gravely, guiltily. "I know."

With brakes squealing, our cab slowed to a stop at the curb in front of us. Radar held the door open for me.

"And the *only* reason you like me," I told him as I climbed into the cab, "is because you can't have me."

He didn't deny it.

15

ALONE

ELLA

Radar gave the cabbie our address and the car rolled forward. The only sound was the hum of the road below us and the quiet whisper of the radio. Disappointment was in the air. It was Radar's, not mine. While he silently suffered the sting of rejection, I was certain that I'd done the right thing.

We were nearly home when Radar broke the silence.

"Y'know," he began in a low, gritty growl. "It's not because I can't have you."

I buried my face in my hands and laughed. I couldn't believe he was seriously going to try to argue with me over this ...

"I don't *want* to like you, Ella. But you're not like any other girl I've ever met. I can't help it."

I noticed the cabbie's eyes dart into the rearview mirror and watch us with a hint of amusement. *I'm so glad we could be your drunken late night entertainment, sir.*

"Don't you get it?" I asked. "You're used to being able to sleep with any girl you want—any girl but me, that is. What you like is that I'm this forbidden fruit, this best-friend's-little-sister taboo that would wreck your life if you *dared* to touch me. Ryan, you're just after trouble. You don't even know your own self well enough to know that, but I do, so you should listen to me."

One look at him and I knew my pleas had fallen on deaf ears. His irises seared into mine. Telling him *no* had only stoked the embers of his interest, and now he was consumed with burning desire. I knew he wasn't used to hearing a girl mouth the word 'no', in fact, those two letters might be the most powerful aphrodisiac the athlete had ever taken in his entire life.

But the way he looked at me, with such brash and undying interest, made my head woozy and my thighs throb.

"You felt it, Ella. Back at the club *and* last night, too. I could see it in your eyes. We've got something, even if neither of us wants to admit it."

My heart began to race and I didn't say a word. I knew damned well what he meant. And thanks to the heat rushing into my cheeks, I was sure that he could see it in my face, even in the dark backseat of the cab. I knew he still wanted that kiss. And I knew that he was going to come for me soon, and I had better be committed to fending him off.

"I wanted to kiss you," he began, "and you wanted me to kiss you, too."

"No ..." I panted.

But he cupped my face with his titan hand, so huge and so strong, yet so gentle. "I mean, trouble *is* kinda hot, isn't it?"

"Ryan ... don't ... we're almost home—"

But he stroked a lock of hair out of my eyes and my stomach fluttered and hell, maybe he was right, maybe trouble *was* hot, because the next thing I knew? I'd closed my eyes and surrendered to him, waiting for his kiss.

Part of me stubbornly screamed, *um, hello! This is still a terrible idea, Ella!* But the other part of me was far too curious to see where this could go. When Ryan's mouth grazed mine, any thoughts about this being a bad idea were immediately snuffed out of existence. His lips touched mine like sweet and silky rose petals brushing against my lips. I was surprised. Who would have guessed that the hockey tough guy, the awful playboy, could be so soulful with his embrace? I didn't kiss him back so much as I opened for him, as if I never had any choice in the matter, and my lips melted into his mouth.

My insides twisted and knotted as I kissed Ryan in the backseat of that cab. I liked it, I liked it a lot, and I lost any sense of time—but with each kiss going deeper, and with a throbbing between my legs, I remembered again, with conviction, that *yes,* this was indeed a bad idea. I didn't trust myself. I *wanted* to lose my virginity, after all ... and *yes* I found Ryan gorgeous ... but that did *not* make any of this appropriate or smart.

I planted my hands on Ryan's chest and pushed, separating our lips.

He looked at me, his brows raised, "No?"

"No," I said, shaking my head solemnly. "I'm sorry, but we shouldn't."

The cabbie cleared his throat. "Ahem."

I looked out the window. We were already stopped outside Lance and Ryan's building, and come to think of it, the car hadn't moved in some time.

"For God's sake, how long were we here for?" I asked.

"I didn't want to interrupt the first kiss, miss," the driver answered in a heavy Boston accent.

I groaned. "Oh, how kind of you."

Ryan paid the cabbie and we hopped out, and then the two of us waited for the elevator in the lobby.

My mind was swamped with worries about what waited for us at the condo: would Lance be waiting on the sofa, in total darkness, like your parents did back in the high school days when they caught you sneaking out? Was Lance just *waiting* for us to sneak in, so he could surprise us and ask in an ominous tone, 'so, what were you two up to tonight?'

The elevator arrived. We rode it up to the top floor in a sort of stunned silence. I didn't dare look at him. I was too afraid he'd just suck me right back in ... and I was still too damn worked up over that kiss.

"Shit!" I gasped, remembering I was still wearing his jacket. "Thanks for this, but you better take it back." I hurriedly took it off and handed it back.

"Good thinking," he said.

That's when I noticed the red paint of my lipstick on Ryan's lips. I wiped it off with the tip of my finger, swearing under my breath about how stupid and screwed we were.

Ryan broke into a grin.

"You think it's funny?" I asked him.

"Sorta."

"It's not." I held my breath and gave myself a nervous once-over. "How do I look?"

"Beautiful."

I rolled my eyes. "Oh, God. Stop it. You know what I meant."

With a *ding,* the elevator reached our floor. Ryan unlocked the door to the condo and I stepped in, holding my breath. The condo was dark, just like I'd imagined in my dreaded nightmare scenario—but after Ryan flipped on the light, I let out a quiet sigh of relief. Lance wasn't on the couch. I took off my heels and quietly tip-toed down the hallway. Lance's bedroom door was wide open and the room was empty. He wasn't home.

Whew.

"Looks like Lance never made it home," I said.

Which, of course, means that the two of us are alone.

With several feet separating us, I stared at Ryan and he stared at me. A silence and a tension filled the space between us. *Just look at him.* Even after a night of drinking and dancing, he still looked so damn handsome, so sharp and put-together in his suit ...

I sighed.

"What's wrong?" he asked.

"This is the part of the night where, instead of going to bed, you try to make one last move on me, isn't it?"

Ryan chuckled. "It's like you've read my game plan."

"Oh, I've lived it," I said with a sigh. But I wasn't sure I'd have the willpower to stop *him*. "Don't you guys have a game tomorrow?"

He neared with purpose. "We do."

"You're going to get us caught," I whimpered. I backed away from him until I was against the sofa's arm rest. "Shouldn't you go to bed? Won't you be tired for your game tomorrow?"

"I might be."

Trapped between the sofa and Ryan, I hopped on the armrest. He neared, his huge body pressing against my legs, until I had no choice but to open my legs and let him in.

He gently brushed the tip of his thumb over my lips, reigniting the fire in my belly.

"Just one good night kiss?" he asked.

With Ryan's body heat pulsing between my thighs, I was down to my last line of defense.

"If only you would've gone home with that girl," I said. "Forget a good night kiss, you could've been getting *laid* right now, Radar."

"Enough about her," he said. He lifted my chin with his big hand and raised my eyes to his. "She's not what I want."

"What do you want?" I stammered, gently squeezing my legs against his rear.

"You. You're so fine, Ella."

"Ryan," I muttered softly.

He leaned in and kissed me. Just as gently, just as perfectly as he had in the back of that cab. I moaned as he kissed me, knowing the next kiss would only be deeper, hotter—

But there wasn't a next kiss. I opened my eyes to see Ryan pulling back with a devious glint in his eye.

"I *said*, 'just one kiss.' "

"*Ugh*," I grumbled. "That's just cruel."

I grabbed him by the lapels of his suit jacket, whipped him around, and gave him a shove. The big man bowled over the armrest and crashed into the cushions of the couch.

On his back, Ryan looked at me and laughed. "I knew you had a thing for trouble."

I leaped over the armrest and landed on him.

"Yeah, yeah. Save it." I ran my hands over the mountainous pecs that bulged beneath his Oxford. "You're lucky you're so jacked."

He put his hands on my hips and held me in place. "It's not luck at all. It's a lot of hard work and time spent in the gym."

"Shut up and kiss me."

I leaned in, my fingertips grating against the coarse grit of his stubble, and pressed my lips lightly onto his. I kissed him modestly, savoring the humble little *pops* and wet *smacks* of our innocent lip-locking.

Ryan's manly desire quickly grew. He *needed* to kiss me deeper, but I enjoyed only letting him have a taste. Since he'd wanted to torture me with his 'just one kiss' gimmick, it was only fair to return the favor. I was wondering how long I could tease him like this, until—

Ryan grabbed my hair, bunching up a ponytail in his fist, and pulled my head back.

"I *know* what you're doing," he growled, his breath hot on my exposed neck.

He planted his lips on my neck and sucked. I let out a moan, my whole body going limp, a sudden heat radiating between my thighs ...

In one fast and powerful move, Ryan flipped me over. He was on top now, on all fours like a wild animal, his pupils darkened with lust. I clung to his sexy forearms, so thick and muscular and hairy, and writhed beneath him.

His eyes on mine, Ryan lowered himself onto me until I was smooshed between his solid mass and the couch cushions. I'd never felt so perfectly content to be crushed—he was so much *man,* so warm and big and sturdy.

He gripped my hair and pulled me tighter to him. And then he kissed me, the way he *wanted* to kiss me: wild, hungry and dominant.

"Ryan," I panted breathlessly, my tone uncertain. He was a *wonderful* kisser, and if we were going to stop before we got too carried away? *Now* was the time.

But he silenced me with his tongue, and we moved together, tongues circling, pushing, pulling, an intimate dance that grew closer and more passionate with each movement. With each kiss, we sank deeper into the couch, deeper into each other. His large hands cupped and squeezed at my breasts, and my knees began to weaken.

I could feel him quickly growing in his pants as the two of us gently rocked back and forth against each other. He was *huge,* big and long, bigger than any guy I'd ever felt. The presence of his rock-solid arousal against me made my pussy clench and throb.

"I can feel you, Ryan," I moaned in his ear. "You're so big and hard."

But after mentioning his manhood, a seriousness gripped Ryan. He pulled himself back, a sober look in his eye.

"What? What's wrong?" I asked.

"I—I don't want to make you do anything you don't want to do."

Wow. I'd never heard those words from a guy before. Ever.

We stared at each other, wondering what came next.

"It's okay," I said at last. I grabbed his hand and lowered it to my thigh. "We can do other things?"

The pads of his fingers climbed my legs, painting long, torturous lines up my inner-thighs. When he reached my crotch, I was more than ready for him—I *needed* him. Delicately, Ryan stroked the crotch of my panties. He let out a growl, thick and throaty and full of conflicted desire.

"You're dripping wet, Ella."

Driven wild by my wetness, Ryan pressed himself closer against me. He shoved his tongue into my mouth and his thick hand slid under my panties. His skilled fingers caressed my bare flesh and neared my folds.

His voice was dry, coarse, demanding. "I *need* to taste you."

With my pulse thumping in my neck, I nodded.

And I watched as Ryan slithered off the couch and onto the floor.

16

WAITED THIS LONG
RADAR

I was sure I could stop before things got *too* far. She was a virgin and I wasn't going to be the one to steal that from her. All I needed was a goodnight kiss, just one little kiss, to get it out of my system. A taste would hold me over, right? I mean, I wasn't going to *actually* try to sleep with Lance's little sister ... right?

But, *fuck,* Ella's lips felt so right against mine. I loved kissing her, I loved the way she smelled, the way she tasted, the way she writhed and moved against my body. God, this was exactly what I was fantasizing about all night, whether or not I even knew it myself ...

The soft little moans she made sent tingles down my spine. I *knew* I wanted her, of course I did! Those sounds of hers, those gasps and sighs, well, they made my balls heavy and I needed to touch her all over. I loved the weight of her tits in my hand, and wondered what they'd look like if I could get her out of that dress. I wanted to feel the damp warmth of her breath against my neck, as she screamed in orgasm—

No, Radar, don't think like that.

Still. We couldn't stop. I wasn't sure where we were heading, but I knew it wasn't good.

She wrapped her legs around me and pulled me into her. Even through my trousers, I could feel her blistering heat, calling for my cock like a siren's song.

Oh my God. Her pussy's so hot.

I couldn't help myself. I had to stop. *Had* to stop, before it was too late.

I tried. "I—I don't want to make you do anything you don't want to do," I said.

But she took my hand and lowered it to her legs.

Oh, wow, okay.

I couldn't control myself anymore. My hands, with a mind of their own, traveled up her legs. She wanted it, she opened her thighs for me, and I touched her panties. Stunned, my mouth fell open. She'd completely soaked her panties. Sweltering waves of her animal heat radiated against my fingers, daring me to enter her and see just how hot and tight she *really* was.

And any restraint I might've had left just went flying out the window.

I threw myself into her and my fingers quickly found their way under her panties. She was shaved, completely smooth, and so moist my fingers glided across her wetness. Her blazing heat grew hotter as I neared her slit.

"I *need* to taste you," I roared.

She nodded, and I slipped right off the couch and onto the floor.

I pulled her to the edge of the couch. She hiked up her dress and spread her legs. I grabbed hold of her white lace panties, pulled them down her legs, and tossed them thoughtlessly over my shoulder.

"Your pussy's so pretty," I told her. Actually, it was beautiful, a work of art. Her pussy was so pink, with the cutest folds that glistened with her wetness. I didn't feel like I deserved it, like *any* man deserved it.

She didn't say anything, she just blushed. She was so cute. I knew she was a little shy, but then, she wanted this, too.

Gently, carefully, I ran the tip of my tongue up her silk-smooth lips. Her taste could drive a man insane: sweet like strawberries, with an intoxicating touch of salt and spice.

"You taste so fucking good, baby."

She made the cutest sounds, stunned little gasps and feather-delicate moans, as I traced her folds and began to tease her clit.

I took my time. I wanted to savor her. But when her hips began to buck eagerly at my face, I knew what she wanted. I gave her my finger and gently pushed in, one torturous inch at a time.

"Oh my God," she moaned.

When I tried to pull back out, she clamped herself tight on my finger and I couldn't move an inch.

"God, you're tight."

"Deeper," she urged.

I didn't have a choice.

I finger-fucked her slowly at first, but always building pace, always thrusting and licking with purpose.

Soon, she had her hands on the back of my head. She pulled my face against her mound, grinding her pussy wildly all over my mouth, slathering her sticky juices all over my mouth and lips and nose.

Her whole body trembled. "I'm coming!"

I buried myself in her, licking and sucking and finger-fucking, until her gasps grew to a crescendo of screams. "Yes, yes, *yes!*"

Her limbs thrashed and flailed and her pussy quivered against my finger. And then it was over, and she was a gasping, smiling heap of flesh, sinking into the new leather couch.

I pulled my finger out of her. It was covered in her cream. A primal urge possessed me and I sucked her juices right off my finger.

"*Ooh,*" she cooed, "you're so dirty, Ryan."

"I love your taste."

Her eyes rolled back in her head, and she bit her lip, and she looked like she was thinking something over, when she finally blurted it out: "Do you have a condom?"

My manhood throbbed at the sound of those magic words.

Was she really serious?

"In my bedroom," I answered, stunned.

She jumped off the couch. "Let's go."

She grabbed my hand and led me to my room.

My cock ached for her, but—*fuck me* if something about this situation didn't seem right.

I shouldn't have her.

I wasn't supposed to and I knew it.

"Ella ..." I trailed off.

We stepped into my bedroom and she closed the door after me.

"Ella ... wait."

"No." She beamed. "I'm done waiting, Ryan." She spun around and showed me the back of her dress. "Unzip me, please?"

With a conflicted knot in my throat, I pinched the tiny zipper between my thumb and finger and slowly pulled it down. She wiggled out of the dress, and the item fell to her ankles with a soft *swish.*

She climbed into my bed, her hands covering her breasts, and waited for me to join her. "Well?"

I took off my jacket, kicked off my shoes, and methodically took off the rest of my outfit. My boxers were the last item to go—and she licked her lips at the sight of my erect cock, freed from my boxers and swinging up and down.

"*Wow,*" she gasped, her eyes running over me from head to toe. "You are so chiseled ... and hung."

But I laid next to her with a heavy heart.

She rolled onto her side, reached between my legs and found my cock. "*God,* it's so big," she said with a wild look in her eyes. She wrapped her tiny hand around it and tugged. I gasped. My throbbing cock was hard as steel. Yeah, this felt great.

But still, she knew something was wrong. She could see it in my eyes.

"You don't want me, do you?" she asked sadly.

I kissed the top of her head. "I do. So damn bad. More than I've ever wanted any woman."

"But you don't."

I let out a deep, mournful breath. "I'm sorry. It doesn't feel right. I shouldn't be your first, Ella."

"Why not?"

"Because you deserve better. You've waited this long."

"I'm tired of waiting," she said with a whimper.

"You won't be. You'll be glad you did when you meet someone worth your time."

She huffed. "How would you know?"

"You're right. I wouldn't know. I've only had sex with women I don't care about, but ... you're Lance's sister."

"Idiot," she snarled. She struck the bottom side of her fist against my chest. "This is *exactly* why I kept trying to turn you down."

"I know, Ella. I'm so sorry. You were right. I should've listened to you."

"*Idiot.*" She hit me again. "You shouldn't have kissed me. I practically *begged* you not to."

"I'm sorry."

She hit me once more. "*Why* didn't you just leave me alone?"

"I'm sorry, Ella. I really fucked things up."

She pummeled her fist into my chest again and again. "I hate you, Ryan Ryder."

I grabbed her wrist and restrained her. "Don't say that."

She struggled against me. "Why shouldn't I?"

"Because it's not true."

"I feel like such an ass! I'm naked in your bed, and you don't even want me. I've never felt so rejected in my life—"

I silenced her with a kiss. Her lips resisted mine, but I waited until she finally yielded and let me kiss her. We kissed, long and deep, a *real* kiss, not one fueled by raw lust or carnal desire—but a deep current of passion instead.

And then we separated. I stroked the hair from her eyes and cupped her face with my hands.

"Ella, believe me, it's not your fault. I told you, I want you more than I've ever wanted anybody."

She buried her face in my chest. "But I'm Lance's sister. His virgin sister."

I sighed. "Yeah."

"Then I should go," she whispered.

But I squeezed her against me. I couldn't let her go just yet. "Just a minute longer."

"Fine." She rolled onto her side. "I want you to spoon me."

I didn't need to be told twice. I wrapped my arm around her and pulled her into me. She nestled her body against me, until we were a perfect fit, like two puzzle pieces made for each other.

But something was missing. We were too naked, too exposed. I pulled the bed sheets over us, and all felt right with the world.

"Don't get too comfortable," she warned me. "I can't fall asleep in here."

"Yeah. We definitely can't fall asleep like this. That'd be the last thing we need." That's what I *said,* but I still pulled her even tighter against me. "Just a little bit longer."

I pressed my nose against her head. With every breath I took, the smell of her hair filled me.

She smells so nice.

I loved having my arms wrapped around her, the warmth of her body against me. I closed my eyes to enjoy the moment just a little bit more.

17

WAKEY WAKEY

ELLA

I woke to the sound of a door slamming shut.

My eyes shot open. *Please tell me I imagined that. Please tell me that was a dream.*

Because sure enough, I'd fallen asleep in Ryan's bed. I was completely naked and snuggled up with Ryan's hulking arm wrapped tight around me.

But my worst fears were confirmed when I heard Lance call, "Yoooooooo! I'm home!"

Oh my God. Lance is home, and I actually fell asleep in Ryan's room.

I knew this would happen.

I knew it!

Fuck!

"Hello?" Lance called from the living room. "Ella? You here? Huh."

Ryan slept through it. I shook his great big body and spoke as quietly but as urgently as I could.

"*Radar!*" I whispered. "*Wake up! Lance is home!*"

His eyes bolted open with a look of terror.

"*Shit,*" he whispered back. He sat up in a panic. "This is bad. Real bad."

I raised my arms at him as if to say, *well!?! What'd you think was going to happen?*

"I *told you* not to fall asleep!" I said.

"I got too comfortable," he mumbled.

We heard Lance's footsteps. He was coming down the hallway—heading for us. "Radar? You up, buddy?"

"You have to hide," he whispered to me.

"What?" I asked, appalled.

Lance banged on the door. "Yo Radar. Wakey wakey! Don't be late for morning skate, bud!"

Radar's eyes were huge. He spoke without making a sound. "(*Quick!* Hide!)"

"(Where!?)"

"(Under the bed!)"

I hopped off the mattress and crawled underneath the bed. I immediately noticed Radar's snake-skin treasure chest—since the last time I'd seen it, he'd moved it from the top of his dresser to beneath his bed. I wondered why, but I didn't have much time to solve the mystery, as the bedroom door opened.

I watched from beneath the bed as Lance's feet came into view.

And—oh *no*—I spotted the green dress that laid on the floor right by door.

My dress.

Lance started to step into the room before Radar yelled, "I'm naked, bro, don't come in!"

"Whoops, my bad."

I had a view of Radar's feet as he climbed out of bed. He stepped into the boxers he wore last night and pulled them up his legs.

"(My dress, Radar, my dress!)" I tried to quietly warn him, but he didn't hear me.

Radar opened the door and let Lance in. A nausea spoiled my stomach as I watched Lance step right over my dress.

"What's up?" Radar asked him.

Had he seen it? Did he know?

"Just making sure you're up in time. We've gotta be at the morning skate in a few."

"Yeah, yeah. Thanks. I overslept."

"Yeah?" Lance asked, and I could hear his smile. "Must've been a good night, huh? You up pretty late last night?"

"Heh, yeah ... you know ..."

"So how was she?"

Oh my God, I thought. *We are so busted.*

"Who?" Radar asked, suddenly sounding guilty as hell.

"The *puck bunny,* duh," Lance said. "Who else?"

I hoped that neither of them could hear the deep sigh of relief that came from beneath the bed.

"*Oh,* ha, right. Yeah man. She was uh ... incredible."

"Did you go to her place or bring her back here?"

"Her place," Radar said huskily.

"Ha! You liar," Lance said with a great glee in his voice. "Did you forget something last night? A little piece of evidence, maybe?"

"Wha'?" Radar stammered.

"There's a pair of white panties lying in the living room. Yeahhhh! That's right. Thought you'd get away with it, didn't you?"

A flashback from last night played in my head: Radar pulling my panties down my legs and tossing them over his shoulder. Neither of us had remembered to pick it up afterward.

Oh my God. Great.

Lance continued. "You're fuckin' *sick,* by the way. And the boys on the team are gonna *love* hearing about this one: I buy a new couch, and you fuck some puck-slut on it less than twenty-four hours later?"

"Ha ... sorry man."

"You're lucky I love you, Radar. But you know you owe me for that couch now, right? You christened it before I did, you fucker. I can't believe you."

"Heh ... yeah. Sure. Sorry about that." Radar gulped.

"Did Honey Badger hear you guys?"

"No ... she was fast asleep ..." Radar was desperate to change the subject. "But hey, how was your night?"

"Great, great. Spent the night at Lindsay's. I *finally* tapped it, bro. Finally."

"You did?!"

"Oh yeah. That fuckin' *ass*, man. It's unreal." I heard the slap of Lance's back-hand on Radar's bare chest. "Let's just say, Sir Lancelot *came-a-lot.*"

"*Ew,*" I whispered.

Radar laughed, and Lance laughed, and they were slapping at each other, *hoo boy,* over how funny that terrible joke was.

God, are hockey players even worse when they don't know a woman is around? That's great news.

"Anyway," Lance began, "I'm gonna run across the street and grab us some coffee and doughnuts, but I wanted to make sure you were awake."

"Thanks bud. Appreciate it."

"Yup. Don't mention it." My guts twisted with anxiety as Lance's shoe stepped *right* on my dress. He stopped walking and slowly turned around. "Don't forget to pick those panties up, by the way. Because I ain't gonna touch them. And I don't want Honey Badger to see them, or you know she'll flip her shit and rant about what sleazy horn-dogs men are, blah, blah, blah."

"Right. I will. Sorry again."

"No prob." Lance turned around, and his foot lifted off my dress. Radar must've noticed it now, because he put his foot on it and quickly scooted his leg backward. My dress swooshed across the floor, scooping up a bunch of under-the-bed dust-bunnies, before the dusty mess smacked me right in the face.

Gee. Thanks.

Lance turned around again. "Hey, speaking of Honey Badger —you wouldn't happen to know where she is, would you?"

"Oh, yeah, um—she told me she was going to the gym."

"This morning?"

"Yeah."

"She woke you up to tell you that? Huh. Weird. Anyway, I'm gonna go grab those doughnuts. I'll be right back."

Radar shut the door after him. When we heard the sound of the front door open and shut, he crouched by the bed. "I'm sorry, Ella," he said, extending his hand to me.

"I think I meant it last night when I said I hate you," I grumbled. I gave him my hand and he pulled me out.

He nodded, wearing a frown. "Yeah, that's fine. I deserve that."

I clutched my dress over my body to hide my shame. "What do you keep in that box, anyway? I noticed you moved it."

"What box?" he asked.

"Don't play dumb. The one that was on top of the dresser but is now beneath your bed."

"Did you look inside it?" he asked as if he was accusing me of something.

"Wow. No, I didn't, but it must be something sensitive."

"It's private. Don't look in there."

"Forget it. I don't care about the box. We've got bigger problems, like what do we tell Lance *now*?"

"What do you mean? He doesn't suspect a thing. We stick to our story and we're fine."

"Yeah. He doesn't suspect a thing." I rolled my eyes sarcastically. "Until he wonders where *I* was sleeping while you were banging this 'puck-slut' on his new leather couch last night. The way you guys talk about women is really gross, by the way."

"Don't overthink it, Ella. You'll just say you were sleeping in Lance's bed. You went to bed early and you didn't hear or see anything."

"You want me to *lie,* is what you're saying." I tutted. "Did you *not* listen to what I told you last night? Don't you get it?"

He buried his face in his hands. "I know how important it is to you to be honest. Believe me, I get it."

"No, you don't. Or you wouldn't be putting me in this position."

"Do you know how important my career is to *me*? If Lance finds out, he could have me shipped off to some other team. Hell, I could end up in the AHL again! Ella, all I'm asking is that you make an exception. Just this once. Don't you believe that sometimes, a lie can be for a good cause? Like, if it helps somebody out?"

"No, I don't believe that at all."

"Please, Ella. Hockey is all I've got."

"Then last night was a huge mistake for us both," I said, seething. "You want me to lie for you? Fine. I will. But don't ever talk to me or ask me for anything again, because I swear you won't get a damned thing from me, Radar."

"Ella—" He reached out to give me a hug, but I batted his stupid arms away.

"I said *don't.*"

I marched off to the shower, to wash away the grimy layer of regret that clung to my flesh.

———

When I emerged from the shower, Lance and Radar were huddled at the kitchen table.

"Hey sis," Lance said.

"Hi Lance," I muttered.

"How was your workout?"

"Honestly?" I let the question hang just to see Radar squirm in his seat. "Not so good. I didn't really have it in me today. In fact, it's almost like I didn't work out at all."

"Uh. Okay." Lance laughed uncomfortably and wolfed down a doughnut in a single bite. I saw him catch Radar's eye, as if to silently communicate some thought like, '*women, what crazy bitches, am I right?*'

"Did you sleep alright last night, Honey Badger?" Lance shot Radar another sly look. "Any strange sounds keep you up at night?"

"You mean *besides* the grunting and groaning at three in the morning?" I countered. "Radar was banging some slut in the living room, as I'm sure he told you."

Lance burst into laughter, but Radar slumped in his seat.

"Okay, wait. You mean you actually heard them fucking?! Because Radar seems to think that you slept through it ..."

"How could I sleep through *that*? Her screams were just awful. Like a thousand wolves being burned alive."

Lance practically fell out of his chair. "Ohhh my God! A thousand wolves—aaah! I would've loved to have heard that!"

"You laugh, but I was worried. I actually came out to check on them and make sure everyone was alright."

Lance's eyes grew as big as plates. "You *what*???"

"I mean, what if someone was having a medical emergency? I had to make sure."

"Well, what'd you see?" Lance asked.

"Um." I covered my mouth and snickered. "Well, I saw Radar, butt-naked and covered with sweat, jack-hammering away at this blonde chick on the brand new red leather couch."

Radar turned as red as a tomato, but Lance beamed with delight.

"So you actually caught them in the act?! I am laughing my fucking ass off right now! Dude! Figures some shit like this would go down the one night I'm not here! Can you believe he fucked that girl on the new couch? I told him he owes me five grand. Look at how red Radar is—you can tell he's ashamed of himself, haa!"

"How do you think *she* feels? She's probably really regretting her life choices today," I said. "Especially once she realizes she left her panties here and everything. How embarrassing for her."

"So you saw the panties in the living room, too?! Dude, Radar, you really fucked up, bud!" Lance howled, clapping his hand against Radar's shoulders. "But don't you worry, Ella, I doubt she'll be missing those panties too much. I mean, all the puck bunnies know about—"

"That's enough," Radar roared, and the room fell suddenly quiet and tense.

"Jeez." Lance leaned back in his chair. "Hey, sorry bud. Just playin' around, that's all."

Radar checked his watch. "Look. We need to get going or we're going to be late."

"Right, right." Lance rose from his chair. "Lemme grab my shit."

Lance went off to his room. I started to walk away too, but Radar spun me around with his hand on my shoulder.

"What the hell was all that?" he growled quietly.

"I'm just doing what you asked. You wanted me to lie for you, right?"

"Not like *that!* The more ridiculous details you add, the less believable it is!"

I rolled my eyes. "So now you're dictating *how* I should lie."

"Ella, please! Be reasonable!"

Lance stepped back into the room, ready to go. He raised a suspicious eyebrow at the two of us. "What's up, you guys?"

"Radar was just apologizing for his behavior last night." I strutted away. "You two have fun at your morning skate."

18

MORNING SKATE

RADAR

The water taxi chugged towards Boston, but I kept my eye trained on our building. Somewhere in there, Ella was busy hating my guts.

And even if I wasn't happy with her little stunt at breakfast, I knew why she'd done it. I'd made her lie. The one thing she built her personal code around ... and I'd made her trash it. Just for me.

I wished I didn't have to go to morning skate. I wished I could call in sick, but that never goes over well with your teammates or your coaches. All I wanted more than anything right now was to be back in that building. *Alone* with Ella, so I could really try to ... I dunno. Talk about last night? Explain myself?

But what else is there to explain? You tried to do the right thing—you didn't even fuck her! Besides, she's covering for you and now you guys won't get caught. Nothing to worry about. The end.

But if all that was true, then why did I still feel so rotten?

Lance elbowed my side. "You alright, man?" he asked.

"Huh? Yeah, why?"

"You're all quiet and moody today. Never seen you like this."

He elbowed my side. "You didn't go *falling* for that girl last night, did you?"

If he had any idea the girl he was talking about was his little sister—

"What? No way," I panted.

"Good. Because the Brawlers can't have you going all soft on us." He leered at me. "You sure you didn't fall for her? Sounds like she was a real wild one. Maybe that's what you've been looking for all this time."

"I don't wanna talk about it, Lance," I groaned.

"Okay. Whatever, man."

Lance was right. I *was* quiet and moody. The rest of the way to the arena, I didn't say a word. I felt so damn conflicted about everything.

Ella's taste still lingered on my tongue. Every so often, I'd get a whiff of her musk and memories from last night flooded my mind: I saw myself between her thighs, spreading her legs apart. Her dress hastily bunched up around her waist. The way her eyes fluttered, how she bit her lip, the expressions on her face, God, her *screams!* ...

Everything about her drove me wild. Just thinking about last night made me hard. She took off her dress, climbed into my bed, and—somehow, *somehow,* I managed to do the right thing and turn that beautiful girl down.

And now she hated my guts.

———

I was a disaster in our morning skate. I flubbed pucks left and right. I whiffed on passes. I turned one-timers that *should've* been goals into duds that sailed ten feet wide. I lost an edge and took a spill to the ice more than once.

I might as well have been Ryan Ryder from four years ago—

the player who couldn't hold a steady roster spot in the NHL. A scrub who didn't have the confidence to be on NHL ice.

"The hell's wrong with you today?" Shea barked at me.

I shook my head. "Dunno."

Lance glided by and announced with a shit-eating grin, "Radar had a lady friend last night."

Shea wasn't amused. "Oh, another pair of panties for the collection, huh." He blasted a heavy slap-shot at the goalie and turned to me. "If your social life is starting to become a problem on the ice, it's time to grow the hell up and knock that shit off, Radar."

Bitterly, I swallowed the captain's sage advice with a reluctant nod.

This can't be over soon enough.

———

After practice, I sat at my stall like a zombie while Lance recounted Ella's version of last night to all the boys in the dressing room.

"... yep, she literally said, the girl screamed like a thousand wolves being burned alive. ... I know! I know! ... Hell, she'll hang out with us after the game tonight, I'm sure. You can ask her yourself ..."

"It's not true," I grumbled at last. "None of it is true."

"What?" Lance chuckled. "You're going to just deny it?"

"Yes. It's not true."

"What about it isn't true, then?"

I stared at Lance. I couldn't possibly tell him Ella made the whole thing up, or he'd ask why. And then that'd only make him more suspicious. I was trapped.

" ... Nevermind."

The boys all laughed uproariously. Yep, surely, I was just all bent out of shape because Lance's sister caught me in the act. Ha ha ha. Oh, boy. What a riot. I even left her panties in the living room—talk about a smoking gun.

Our coach came in and interrupted the chuckle-head session. He said *some* of us didn't look like we came ready to play, so we'd better pull our heads out of our asses before the game tonight and come ready to play. He didn't call anybody out by name, but we all knew exactly who he meant.

I couldn't wait to head home. We'd have a few hours to eat lunch, take a pre-game nap, and then it was time to head back to the rink for game time.

And, somewhere in there, I hoped I could talk with Ella to make myself feel better.

19

SOMETHING IN THE AIR

ELLA

While Lance and Radar were away at their pre-game skate, the door-bell started ringing. The first item to arrive was the gorgeous salvaged wood coffee table we snagged at the antique shop. All morning long, delivery guys were arriving with our other purchases. I was glad to have the distraction, and I hopped right into action and started decorating the condo.

I hoped that work might be able to take my mind off other things—but while I unpacked boxes and rearranged furniture, my thoughts were elsewhere.

Like the nauseating guilt I felt over lying. Yeah, yeah. It wasn't the end of the world. But to me, it mattered a lot. It went against my principles. Frankly, I had to wonder *why* I even bothered to lie for Radar in the first place. Why should I care if he nuked his relationship with Lance? I warned him not to kiss me. What did it matter to me if he damaged his own career? He *knew* that those were the consequences of getting with me in the first place.

But as soon as I started covering up for him, I enabled his crimes. And so *I* had to live with the guilt while *he* got away with his misdeeds. He probably didn't even learn anything from this whole experience. I'd bet he'll be all over the next forbidden piece of ass that he stumbles across. What would he do next? Try to sleep with Lindsay the butt model when Lance wasn't around?

Worst of all, I couldn't even say last night was a total disaster. *Yes,* he got me all excited to lose my virginity only to leave me stranded at the altar like a jilted bride. And somehow, disturbingly, that fact only made me want him *more.* But all morning long, filthy little memories from last night flashed through my head. And I couldn't help but be turned on, as pathetic and horrifying as that sounds. But I couldn't help it. He was *so good.* His perfect kisses, his electric touch, the panty-melting bulge that towered in the crotch of his pants ...

Or, *ugh,* how good he was at oral—teasing my folds with his tongue, licking me until I thrust at his face uncontrollably. Or how he kissed and sucked my clit and finger-fucked me until I screamed so embarrassingly loud in orgasm.

And, after I came, Radar sucked my juices right off his finger. God, that was so dirty, but *so* hot at the same time. I felt like he wanted me *so* bad, that, well, he deserved me. And besides, I wanted to lose my virginity. And who better than Radar—a guy who wouldn't get attached to me or make a big deal out of it. A guy who'd just *take me* and then it'd finally be over.

At least, that's what I thought.

But then, Radar got me into his bedroom, got me naked, ... and then he turned me down.

My thoughts turned inward at the moment. *Is something wrong with my body? Why doesn't he want me?*

But no. It wasn't me, or at least that's what he swore. Apparently, he'd just decided to grow a conscience. He didn't have a problem with kissing me or groping me or eating me out on the brand new couch. But *fucking* his best friend's little sister? Well, that was a bridge too far, and something only a *bad friend* would do.

What I did with Radar wasn't some new milestone for me. I'd given, and received, oral with my past boyfriends. But it was always my boyfriends who pushed for more, only to get gently turned down and end up complaining about their severe case of 'blue balls.'

Last night, for once, *I* was the one to get turned down. And now I had my *own* case of the 'blue balls.' My insides ached with frustration ... abandonment ... misery.

I guess this is how my boyfriends always felt. There might have been a hilarious irony in that, but I certainly wasn't in the frame of mind to appreciate it.

And yet, nearly lost in all my suffering, were two curious and bothersome questions: if Radar turned me down ... wasn't he *actually* the kind of guy that I'd basically given up on trying to find? And why would I lie for a guy if I truly thought he was worthless?

You're just getting your hopes up, I thought to myself with a sigh. *He only cares about himself.*

———

When the duo of hockey bozos returned, I was standing on the top rung of a step-ladder, struggling with the new curtains we bought for the giant living room windows.

"*Suh-weet!* This place looks so fucking legit already, Ella!" Lance cheered as he stepped in and saw the chaos. Radar lurked behind him. "I love it, Honey Badger!"

"I'm glad," I said, focused on my task.

Radar neared and steadied the base of the ladder. "Can I help you with that? I'm tall, I'll be able to reach up there easily."

"No thanks," I said in a perfectly polite and cheerful tone

that I hoped was another dagger to his heart. "How was practice, Lance?"

"Ah, you know, it was just a morning skate, not a big deal. Except for *this* guy!" Lance ran up and put Radar in a head lock. "Radar was a total scrub out there!"

"Oh, was he?" I grinned—maybe enjoying that bit of information a little *too* much.

"Oh, yeah. You should've seen him, Ella. The guy must have some seriously weak knees after last night. That's why Coach always tells us, don't blow too big of a load the day before a game—you gotta save a little cum in your balls, or you won't have any legs left to skate!"

"That is so freakin' gross," I wailed.

Radar fought to get out of Lance's hold, and the two began to rough-house right in my work area.

"Would you mind?" I asked, annoyed. "Last thing I need on this vacation is for you two jerks to knock me off this ladder and put me in the hospital."

They separated.

Lance gestured down the hallway. "Well. It's about nap time. Shall we, Radar?"

"Sure," Radar grumbled.

"Aw, that's cute," I mewled. "But aren't you supposed to store up your cum for the game?"

"Shut up," Lance whinnied. "You know I didn't mean it like that. We *all* take naps before a game, in our own beds, thank you very much."

"I'm just giving you shit, like you would me."

Lance walked off and made for his bedroom. But Radar stood in place, staring and watching as I hung the curtains. I could feel his gaze on me but I didn't dare return it.

Lance called for him from down the hallway. "C'mon, Radar,

leave Honey Badger alone and get some shut-eye, will ya? You obviously need it ..."

Quietly, Radar exhaled and walked off.

———

An hour later, the boys were napping in their bedrooms and I took my lunch break. Quietly, I ate my lunch at the coffee table, flipping through a magazine.

I heard a bedroom door crack open. Quiet footsteps followed as someone deliberately sneaked down the hallway. I waited, with an eyebrow raised, for what I knew what was coming.

It was him, alright.

"Hey," Radar whispered as he lowered himself onto the cushion next to mine.

"What do you want?"

"I want you to know that I'm sorry."

"For what?"

"Last night. Making you lie to your brother today." He sighed. "Everything, really."

"Mm."

"I went too far last night. I should've listened to you. You were the voice of reason, and you knew things would only get fucked up, and you were right. But ... I couldn't help myself."

A silence grew between us.

"Seriously, what can I do?" he asked.

"About what?"

"About *this*. I want to make things right. I hate that you're mad."

"What do you care? I'll be gone tomorrow and that'll be that. Besides, we'll probably never see each other again. And you got what you wanted, didn't you?"

He chuckled quietly. "No," he said. "I wouldn't feel this empty if I did."

"Well." I paused to thumb through a flurry of magazine pages. "I know how *that* feels."

"Ella, I only tried to do what I thought was righ—"

Radar stopped talking when we heard Lance's bedroom door open and his footsteps came down the hall.

Uh oh.

Lance stepped into the living room. For the second time today, Lance walked in on us having a private chat, and I could see the wheels turning in his head—even if he wanted those wheels to stop. "I thought I heard voices out here ... what are you two up to?"

"I couldn't sleep," Radar said, rising from the couch. "So I came out here to see how Ella's decorating was going."

I tutted with a quiet *tsk tsk* under my breath. *Still lying.*

But Lance bought it, probably because he wanted to buy it. "Oh, okay. Well, you really ought to try to nap, man. Even twenty minutes would help you a lot."

Radar slapped Lance's shoulder as he walked past. "Yeah, you're right, Lance."

After Radar's door shut, Lance neared. "Everything alright with you, Ella?"

"Yeah, Lance. Why?"

"I dunno. I can't quite put my finger on it, but, God, it seems like there's a weird feeling in the air today." He shrugged. "Who knows. I'm probably imagining it."

I smiled at him. "I'm fine. Thanks for asking."

Lance scratched his head. "Well, okay. Hey, after the game tonight, you wanna come out with the boys? I told 'em you were visiting and they're all pumped to meet you and go out afterward."

"Hmm." I pretended to think it over. "No, I don't think I'm in the mood, really."

"Aw c'mon, Ella. It's your last night here, and I haven't even gotten to take you out anywhere but our shopping spree. I know how bad you wanted to do something last night." He grabbed my arm and began to tug. "At least come to dinner with us after the game."

"Fine. I'll do team dinner."

"And maybe the club after?" he asked, wiggling his eyebrows.

"I'll think about it, but no promises."

"Alright, alright." Lance dropped my arm and backed away. "Back to bed for me."

"Sleep tight."

20

EMPTY

RADAR

The pre-game nap was a waste of time. I tossed and turned in bed for two hours, but I couldn't sleep at all. I knew I was going to pay for it later on the ice, too ...

All I could think about was the new look in Ella's eye. The way she looked at me had changed. Sounds crazy, right? But it really wasn't the same. There used to be something else in her eye when she looked at me. A bright, glittering spark. But now, when she looked at me, it was just ... cold. Cold and unhappy and like I was a nobody.

And I knew it was my fault, but I couldn't grasp *why*. Where the hell did I go wrong? I *liked* Ella. That was the only reason I tried to kiss her. Was that a mistake? Yeah, okay, I guess. But wouldn't it be an even worse mistake if I'd slept with her?

For once, I actually liked a girl, and I tried to do the right thing—and that ended up making her even more mad at me.

I couldn't wrap my brain around it.

I knew the worst thing I'd done was making her lie. But what else was I supposed to do when Lance was standing in my bedroom and Ella was naked, hiding underneath my bed? Tell him the truth? God, no! If I did that, I can basically guarantee a fist fight between me and Lance would've immediately erupted, followed by an unholy war between siblings.

I didn't get it. I didn't get why she was so mad at me. Yeah, she was leaving town tomorrow, and yeah, I'd probably never see her again. But that didn't make it any easier to stomach. And hell, that fact also *sucked* to think about, too.

When 'nap time' was finally over, Lance knocked on my door. I hadn't slept a wink.

"You ready to head out to the rink, bud?"

"Sure," I grumbled.

"Get any sleep?"

"Nope."

"You normally sleep like a rock," Lance said, rubbing his chin.

"Yeah. Not today."

"Huh. Weird."

Our tradition before every home game was the same: we cleaned up, put on our suits, grabbed our bags and took the water taxi downtown then walked the rest of the way to the rink. The only difference in that routine today was that Ella would be joining us. When she emerged from the bathroom, in a breathtaking little black dress, I felt my heart drop into my stomach. She'd pinned her long hair on top of her head like a crown, opening her bright and round face to the world.

She's so gorgeous.

My heart thumped in my chest as she neared. I wondered if I could tell her how nice she looked without Lance getting suspicious—

But she walked right past me and went to her brother instead. "I'm ready! Are you?"

"Yep. Let's go."

The boat ride across the harbor was tough. Lance and Ella were trading memories from their youth, joking, laughing, playfully reviving decades-old disagreements. It was good to see them getting along, but it was obvious that I was the outsider. If I tried to joke with them? Lance might chuckle, but Ella would just stare over the water, off into the distance, and wait for me to butt-out out of the conversation before she went back to talking to Lance.

It was only a matter of time before I withdrew myself totally from their conversation and watched them from afar.

I knew what she was doing: erasing me from her life. I was nothing but a bad mistake now, and this was how she was moving on—by forgetting about me entirely. She'd meant what she said earlier, when she swore I wouldn't get another thing from her. Ella was a woman of her word, after all.

When we made it to the rink, Lance and I split paths with Ella. She headed off to the press box where she'd watch the game, and we took the VIP elevator down to the rink-level.

"Does she seem strange to you?" Lance asked me as we stepped off the elevator and made our way to the dressing room.

I swallowed tensely. "Huh? I wouldn't know. I thought you guys were getting along just fine on the way over here, though."

Lance punched my shoulder. "Thank you! That's exactly what I mean."

The two of us stepped into the dressing room and our teammates greeted us with hoots and hollers.

"Dinner's on me tonight, boys," Lance offered with a wink. "My little sister's in attendance tonight. Let's treat her to a win."

21

VIP SEATS

ELLA

Just one last night of this, I thought to myself as I had a glass of wine and watched the game from the press box. I shared the box with a few of the Brawlers team officials, some suit-and-tie business executive types, and the casually-dressed hockey media people.

But the game wasn't the worst thing in the world. It was fun seeing Lance play again. And I'll admit, it was pretty awe-inspiring seeing all the people in the crowd who wore our surname, *COUTURE*, emblazoned on the back of their jerseys.

Of course, I couldn't watch Lance play without seeing Radar, either. They played on the same line. The hockey media people around me started openly questioning what was wrong with Radar. According to them, Radar looked sluggish and disinterested—like he were 'wearing cement blocks for skates.' He lost all his board battles, gave up on plays, looked winded, was the first skater back to the bench for a line change ...

At first, I enjoyed listening to them trying to figure out what was wrong with him. It was a small thrill knowing that *I* was a large part of what was bothering him. Little ol' me, sitting right there in the press box with those media people, innocently sipping on a red wine in a plastic cup. Who would ever suspect it? Certainly not the hockey journalists.

But before long, the media people's observations about Radar's game turned nasty. Once they noticed the problem, they seemingly enjoyed seeing him struggle on the ice. And then they were free to let their imaginations run wild, gossiping like children:

Has Radar quit on the team?

Does he want to be traded?

Does he hate playing for this coach?

Is he unhappy with his contract?

Eventually, the wine kicked in and I jumped into one of their conversations.

"Or maybe he's just human," I proffered loud enough for them all to hear. "Do you guys ever stop to consider that?"

Ten sets of eyeballs stared at me as if I were a strange monstrosity.

"Excuse me?" one of them countered.

"He's human, right? So he has the same stuff we have to worry about, on top of being a professional athlete. Right? You don't know what's going on in his personal life. Maybe give him the benefit of the doubt for once." I downed the rest of my wine. "And that's coming from *me*. I don't even like the guy."

Someone cleared their throat. An anxious quiet set over the press box, but at least they stopped talking about Radar as if he were some kind of criminal mastermind who was purposely sabotaging the team.

Can't believe I'm defending him now. Lying for him, and defending him from the media.

I stared at him as he chased the play on the ice. I'll admit, I watched some of his highlight videos on YouTube after I first met him and thought he was cute. And, it was true, watching him now, he looked like a totally different player—like one with half as much heart.

I knew it was because of me, but ... the only part I didn't understand was *why*. Why did he feel so bad about what happened last night? He was supposed to be this heartless, womanizing sleaze.

Something didn't fit the picture, and I couldn't understand what or why.

———

Even though Radar didn't have the best game, the Brawlers still won, thanks to Lance's two goals. Someone from the team escorted me down to the room after the game.

I stepped into the locker room where the players were peeling off their sweat-drenched jerseys and protective equipment. The athletes were in good spirits, laughing and shouting about their victory.

No one even seemed to notice me, until—

"Well *hello*, sweetheart," someone called. "Who are you and why are you so beautif—"

In a huff, Lance threw a roll of tape at his teammate. "That's my *sister*, you idiot!"

The cat-caller ducked the roll of tape, but turned bright red. "Shit! Sorry Lance! You're Ella, right? Please forgive me, I'm an idiot!"

Lance, still wearing his ice skates, clomped over and gave me a hug. "Thanks for coming, Ella."

"Ew, Lance, you're dripping with sweat!" I griped, wiggling away from him.

He grinned. "How'd you like the game? Did you like your seats?"

"Minus the media jerks, yeah, it was fun. Good job scoring those goals."

"Thanks." Lance turned to his teammates and grabbed their attention. "Everyone, this is my sister, Ella. She'll be joining us for dinner."

"Hi Ella," twenty-some deep voices boomed back at me.

"Hi," I answered meekly.

"This is your sister?" another voice asked. "The one you left alone? With *Radar*?" another voice joked, and the whole room suddenly exploded with laughter.

Gulp. Maybe it was my turn to turn bright red? I hoped no one would notice.

"Shut up," Radar growled at the perpetrator from his stall in the locker room. "Don't joke about that. It's not funny."

While everyone else looked joyous and triumphant after their win, Radar looked like ... well ... like he'd just suffered through another game entirely; a bad defeat. His brow was heavy, his features dark. He tore off his shoulder pads and angrily stuffed them into his locker. I watched as he struggled to get his sweaty undershirt off his body. My eyes swept up and down his muscles for the last time.

I *almost* wanted to tell him what had happened in the press box with those reporter jerks ... but I was giving him the silent treatment, after all.

Lance turned to me. "Anyway. We have to shower up and do some media interviews, but we'll be ready to go in an hour or so. You can kill time in the club room if you want. There's a bar, internet, TV, whatever you want."

"Sounds good, Lance. See you later, boys."

"Bye, Ella!" all twenty voices boomed at me as I left the room.

22

____

TAKE IT TO THE GRAVE

RADAR

"Huh, Lance, your sister's kinda cute," Ilya joked. "Lucky for her, she doesn't look a thing like you."

Everyone busted up into a great big belly laugh. *Ha ha ha ha.*

Everyone but me. I'd played a lousy game and I didn't feel like I deserved to bask in the good vibes of our victory.

Lance rolled his eyes. "Oh, *ha* ha. By the way. If any of you guys think you're hot shit and try to flirt with my sister tonight? I'll personally ask the GM to trade your ass to the coldest fucking city in the league. What city would be that anyway—Winnipeg? Winnipeg, boys. That's where you're heading if you even look at my sister the wrong way."

I didn't laugh at *that* joke, either, for obvious reasons.

Lance strutted by and patted my shoulder. "Tough game, Radar, but you'll bounce back."

"Yeah."

It killed me to think that Ella had been somewhere in that crowd, watching me suck all over the ice. She probably enjoyed it, too, after what I put her through.

We did our media interviews, hit the showers, and then dressed for team dinner.

"I don't feel like going," I muttered. "I'm feeling all fucked up. You guys go without me."

Everyone booed and hissed.

"It's a team dinner, Radar," Shea began. "If you go home, then someone else has a reason to cut out early, too. And then suddenly everyone else on this team has some other place they'd rather be. Then it's not much of a team dinner anymore, is it?"

I sighed. "Yeah ... I'm just really not feeling well."

"Order a pepper vodka, then," Ilya yelled. "That's what we do in Russia when we're not feeling well. Oh, and go to the sauna!"

"Pepper vod—" I made a horrified face. "You know what, I'll be fine. Where are we going, anyway?"

"I was thinking MacAllister's," Lance shouted from across the room.

"Shouldn't we take Ella some place she hasn't—..." I caught myself and swallowed down the rest of the incriminating sentence.

"Some place she hasn't what?" Lance asked.

"I meant, shouldn't we take her some place fancier?" I muttered.

"Nice try, Radar." Lance wagged his finger at me. "Nice try. But I know exactly what you're doing."

Gulp. "You do?"

"Yeah. You heard me say I'm buying dinner for the team, so now MacAllister's isn't nice enough. Lemme guess, you want to go to the most expensive steak house in Boston, right? You're just trying to drive the bill up as high as possible, you fucker!"

I let out a breath of relief. *Whew.* "Ha, yeah, you caught me ..."

"I knew it, bud. I should make *you* pay for dinner, since you owe me that five grand!"

Once everyone was dressed and ready to go, the entire team

headed over to the club room where we picked up Ella. I stayed away from her, since I knew that was what she probably wanted. But it kinda hurt to see her joking around so carefree with all the others.

We went outside where a fleet of cabs was waiting for us. Lance grabbed the first car, opened the door for Ella, and shouted, "who wants to ride with me and Ella? Radar? Ilya?"

I jumped into an empty cab before he could spot me. Shea climbed in after me and shut the door.

———

"So what's up with you?" Shea grumbled at me.

"Huh?"

"You. You're acting fucking weird. So what's up?"

"Nothin'."

"Bullshit. I've seen you play with the flu. I've seen you play a game after a night you didn't get any sleep. I've seen you play so hungover, I could smell the alcohol pouring out of your sweat. But tonight? That's the worst game I've ever seen you play. By *far*." He paused. "You might manage to fool Lance and the others, but you're not fooling me. So what is it? What happened that's got you all fucked up?"

"I, uh." My throat grew chalky. I couldn't speak if I wanted to.

"You know, I saw the way you and Lance's little sister looked at each other back there in the dressing room."

I played dumb. "Huh?"

"I also heard you almost slip-up. You almost said something like, 'Ella's already been to MacAllister's.'"

Shit. He'd caught me.

Shea stared me down. "I'm going to ask you something serious, Radar, and I want you to answer truthfully. Don't bother trying to lie because I'll see it in your eyes."

I nervously swallowed as I waited for his question.

"Did you do something with Lance's little sister?"

I couldn't lie to Shea. I broke eye contact and turned to stare out the window instead, swearing under my breath.

"Holy shit," Shea muttered. "Holy *shit*, Radar. What the fuck is wrong with you?"

"You can't tell him," I said, or pleaded, desperately.

"No shit! But I got a funny feeling he's going to find out anyway—because you fucked *his sister!* And once she tells him what you did, this team is *done.* Either Lance will ask to be traded or he'll make sure *you're* traded. Either way, the core of this team is gutted. All because you couldn't keep your dick in your pants. Damn, man. I've been telling you to stop sleeping around and get your shit together for two years now—"

I shook my head. "Shea, it's not like that—"

"Oh, I know. You just *had* to fuck her. Had to add those sweet, sweet, teammate's-little-sister panties to your collection. They're so hot and rare, and you gotta collect 'em all, right? Couldn't stop and think for a second what a bad idea it is to fuck your teammate's little sister, could you?" Shea's nostrils flared. "You didn't just fuck her, Radar. This time, you fucked *all* of us this."

"Dude, Shea, I'm telling you, I didn't fuck her."

"Oh, no? You just held her hand, then?"

"I mean, we fooled around, but ..."

"Fooled around, meaning what?"

"Look, yeah, we did stuff, but we didn't fuck. She wanted to but I told her it'd be a bad idea."

"Lance will be very relieved to hear that you were thinking of him when his sister had your dick in her mouth," Shea huffed sarcastically.

"That didn't happen, either," I mumbled.

"Honestly, Radar? I don't care what precise sexual acts you

two did together. Look, do you think she's going to tell him or not?"

"I have no idea. I really don't know."

"So is that why you played like garbage? Because you're afraid Lance is going to find out?"

I had to think it over. "No ... I honestly don't think it's that."

"Then what is it?"

I paused. "It's because she's mad at me. Yeah, we shouldn't have done anything last night, but I tried to do the right thing. And now she hates my guts because of it. I just feel awful. Plus I made her lie about it."

Shea's jaw dropped. "Wait—are you telling me you actually *like* this girl?"

I had to stop and mull it over. *Jesus, I do like her, don't I?*

"Is it worse if I do?" I asked.

Shea smacked his forehead. "I don't even know. I guess it's less worse than if you just fucked her for the hell of it ... but not by much. It's still a train wreck of a situation. And don't think for a second that anything could happen between you two, alright? It's hopeless. Get that through your thick-ass skull."

I groaned.

"Sorry, Radar, but you should've known better than to get involved with a teammate's sister."

"I know. But what do I do now? How do I make things right?"

Shea shrugged. "You don't. You don't tell another soul, and you hope you can take this with you to the grave."

I nodded somberly. "If I'm taking this to the grave, I have to get one last thing off my chest. It's the worst part."

"Oh, God. Do I even want to know?" Shea asked.

"She's a virgin, Shea. That's why I didn't sleep with her. Not because of Lance."

The captain didn't reply. He just turned away, stared out the window and shook his head every so often.

"God damn it, Radar."

"How fucked am I?"

"Pretty well fucked."

The cab pulled to a stop outside MacAllister's. I paid and we hopped out, joining the rest of our teammates outside the restaurant.

23

MACALLISTER'S REDUX

ELLA

In the back of the cab, I was squished between Lance and Ilya, the Brawlers' great big Russian goaltender. I threw my elbows into the two huge human masses, hoping to clear a little extra breathing room.

"Ow! Hey!" Ilya complained. "Her elbows! Man, she hits hard! Should give this girl a contract and put her on the blue line!"

"Tell me about it. She's the Honey Badger, man. She don't give a fuck."

"Honey Badger?" Ilya asked. "What is a honey badger?"

"Ignore my idiot brother," I snapped.

"She is feisty," Ilya said.

"Moreso than usual, too," Lance said.

"Whatever," I huffed. "Is there some other place we can go *besides* MacAllister's?"

"What's everyone's problem with MacAllister's all of a sudden?" Lance asked. "Besides, you're from New York, what would you know about it?"

"It's a sports bar and grill, right? I think we have them in New York, so they must be a chain," I lied.

Great. One lie begets another. Where does it end? Will I have to lie to Lance for the rest of my life, just because of one mistake I made with Radar? I ought to tell Lance the truth. Just to end all this.

"No shit? You've got a MacAllister's in New York?" Lance asked. "That's weird. The restaurant was opened in the 70's by an old-time Brawlers legend, Vern 'Mack' MacAllister, so I always assumed it was a Boston-only joint. I can't see why they'd open one in New York, since Mack was universally hated in NYC ..."

Oh, great. It just figures that Lance's encyclopedic hockey knowledge would be my undoing.

"I can Google it," Ilya said, reaching for his cell phone. But his phone was in the pocket closest to me, and I leaned against the Russian, hard, so he couldn't fish the phone out of his pocket without a serious struggle first.

"Who knows, maybe I'm thinking of something else," I said. "No need to Google it."

"Anyway, we're here," Lance said as the cab rolled to a stop.

We climbed out. A line of cabs had arrived ahead of us, and a dozen athletes in suits and ties waited for us. I spotted Radar, huddled closely with another one of his older teammates, having what appeared to be a serious chat.

There's no way he'd tell any of his teammates about what happened, right?

Radar looked my way every so often, hoping to catch my eye, but still I didn't acknowledge him.

We entered the restaurant as a group. Bright and smiling at the hostess desk were two blonde girls—the same girls, I realized, that were working last night.

They greeted all the players that went past by name.

"Hi Brooks! ... Hi Josh! ... Hi Radar! ... Hi Shea! ... Hi Ilya! ... "

Then we walked past.

"Hi Lance!" one of the hostesses said. "And oh, you brought your little sister tonight! Ella, right?"

"That's right!" Lance said, giving her a wink. But then he turned to me with a suspicious look. "Now how the hell did she know you're my sister?"

"It's certainly not the family resemblance, thank God! Lance is a farm animal, but *Ella*?" Ilya joked.

"Remember what I said about Winnipeg," Lance said.

Winnipeg must mean something to them ... who knows.

Lance turned to me again. "No, but seriously, she knew your name was Ella. How'd she know that?"

"She's probably a huge fan of yours," I muttered. "Don't superfans like to know every little detail about your life?"

When in doubt, always appeal to an athlete's ego.

Lance smirked. "Heh. Yeah, you're probably right."

I'd gotten away with another lie. With each lie, it felt like I slowly transformed into someone else, something dark and monstrous, something I wasn't ...

The hostesses led us to a private event room with a giant table. Lance sat at one head of the table, and I sat at his right. Their older teammate sat at the other head—I'd pieced together that his name was Shea.

Radar tried to sit next to Shea, but Lance wouldn't have it. "The hell are you doing down there? Sit by us, Radar. We've got the guest of honor over here."

Radar neared. He sat on Lance's left, across from me. I couldn't avoid him now.

If eyes could speak, his said, *I'm sorry I got us into this mess.*

If my eyes could reply, they'd say, *yeah, well, being sorry doesn't change a thing, does it?*

"The reason I want you sitting by us," Lance began, "is because I'm sure everyone wants to hear Ella's re-telling of Radar's night last night."

"What? No!" I protested.

But my voice was drowned out by the approving grunts and

jeers of twenty-some grown men. Once they quieted down, all eyes were on me in anticipation.

"I don't really want to tell it again," I said. "I don't really remember what happened now. My memory's fuzzy."

I was met with boos.

"Sorry ..."

Lance frowned at me. "Seriously, sis? You're not going to tell them?"

"I don't want to, Lance."

"Ugh, fine. Okay, for those who didn't hear the story this morning ..."

While Lance launched into a re-telling of the events I'd made up this morning, I caught Radar's gaze from across the table.

If his eyes could speak, they were saying, *remember when I told you making all that shit up was a bad idea? Welp, here you go— hope you're enjoying this!*

And if my eyes could answer, they'd say, *I don't want to hear it! You made me lie in the first place, remember? How the hell am I supposed to be good at lying? I never even do it! At least, I never lied before I met you, anyway—now I'm suddenly getting a lot of practice at it ...*

Okay, maybe he didn't get all that just from my eyes, but that was certainly what was going through my mind.

Eventually, Lance's story came to an end, and everyone joked around about Radar's bad game and openly wondered what could've been the cause of it.

"Obviously, she was too great of a lay. Drained his nuts completely dry, and today he's got nothing left in the tank."

"Look, he isn't even talking!"

"Is that why Radar's so moody today? He just had his mind blown all night, and today he's thinking about the one that got away?"

"The one that got away is the one that screams like a million wolves in hell?"

"Bwahahah!"

"Radar, you're never gonna live this one down!"

I frowned at Radar while he suffered his teammate's jokes in silence.

My eyes said to him, *Okay, maybe I did take it a little too far.*

You think? His eyes said to me.

"Do you think Radar might've fallen in love with this girl?" someone asked. "Like maybe he fell, legit, head-over-heels in love with this chick."

Lance pointed at his teammate. "Yes! Thank you. That's what *I* said."

I spoke up at last. "Oh, I certainly doubt that."

"What makes you so sure?" Radar spoke, his eyes locked on mine with a burning intensity. "Who knows. Maybe I did."

While his teammates exploded into delirious shouts and elated screams of *ahhhh!* and *I fucking knew it!*, I was left breathless, my heart and mind racing.

You don't mean it.

You can't just say that.

Don't fuck with my head any more than you already have.

Beneath the table, he touched his shoe against mine. I wasn't sure what it meant, but I knew it meant *something.*

When the excitement died down, Radar was inundated with questions about whether or not he got this girl's number, what her panties were like (*what a strange question to be asking! God, hockey players are weird!*), and how he intended to pursue her now that she'd escaped him.

"I don't know," he said. His eyes never strayed from mine. "I haven't quite worked that part out yet. But I know I don't want to let her go."

Stop it, Radar! You're going to get us caught!

"Maybe let's talk about something else, yeah?" Shea called from the far end of the table in a serious tone. "How's the butt model doing, Lance?"

"Lindsay's great! She's meeting us at the club tonight and I'll be spending the *second* night in a row at her place."

Radar turned to Lance.

"Hey, Lance. You mind if we chat outside for a few, bud?"

"Uh, why can't we chat right here?"

"I just gotta talk to you about something in private."

Lance shrugged. "Alright, sure. Let's go."

If eyes could talk?

Mine screamed, *WHAT ARE YOU DOING?! DON'T DO WHAT I THINK YOU'RE ABOUT TO DO!*

And his said, *you wanted me to tell the truth, right?*

I was left at the table with their rowdy teammates. They barely noticed Radar and Lance had left.

With my pulse banging in my throat, I looked at Lance and Radar's suit jackets, draped around the backs of their chairs, and wondered.

How's this going to end?

24

COMING CLEAN

RADAR

Outside the restaurant, the air was chilly and each breath turned into a puff of steam. Two cooks were huddled outside the rear loading entrance with cigarettes. Their faces looked long and tired, and their white shirts were spattered with red sauce. They watched us with a distant curiosity, blowing out clouds of smoke.

"So what's up? What's the deal?" Lance asked, sensing something wasn't right.

"Look, man, I've gotta tell you something."

"So what is it? Spit it out already. You're making me nervous as fuck here, man."

I rubbed my mouth, wondering how to say it.

God damn, am I about to make another mistake? Shea said to take it to the grave …

"It's about Ella."

"What *about* Ella?" Lance asked, his fists balling with rage.

"Last night, after you left for Lindsay's, I saw Ella on my way out the door."

"*And?*" Lance asked, wanting me to get right to the point.

"I felt bad for her, Lance. She hadn't eaten dinner. I told her I was going to meet a girl from MeatMarket, so she might be third wheel or whatever, but she didn't mind. She wanted to get out of the house. We came here to MacAllister's."

"So that's why the hostess knew her," he mumbled under his breath. "But what the fuck? Why would Ella lie about that? She *never* lies. And why am I only finding out about this right now? What'd you guys *do*, Radar?"

I took a deep breath. "She went with me to Regret after we ate."

"And?"

"And when I met the puck bunny, Ella went home. But I felt bad, and I was worried she wouldn't know the way home, so I went after her."

"Tell me what the fuck *happened* already, Radar," he growled.

I sighed. "Lance, I don't know what happened. From the moment she showed up, I felt like there was something about her, about us—"

Pop.

A sudden force impacted my face, right below my eye, and a bright flash forked like lightning across my vision.

I staggered backwards from Lance's punch.

"Yep," I mumbled, pressing a hand to the sudden throbbing pain in my face. "I deserve that."

"I don't want to hear your whole fucking love story, asshole, I want you tell me *what the fuck you did with my sister*," Lance snarled.

"I kissed her," I said. "I kissed her, and one thing led to another, and we fooled around, but that's *it,* that's all—"

Lance interrupted me with two more punches—the first to the gut, which made me double over, and the second to the jaw. The latter knocked me off my feet, and I landed on my ass in a sludgy puddle of MacAllister's fry grease.

He grabbed me by the collar.

"*Did you fuck my sister?!*" he yelled, his other fist clenched.

"No, Lance. I swear I didn't."

He let go of my collar and gave me a shove, throwing me right back into the puddle of fry grease. Now it covered the back of my shirt, and the sickly smell of greasy, salty, burnt fry oil made me queasy.

One of the cooks shouted at us. "Hey, uh, everything alright with you guys?"

We both waved and smiled at them. "Yep!"

They shrugged and went back inside, their smoke break over.

Lance squatted over me and stared me down, face-to-face. "Look me in the eye and tell me you didn't add her panties to your fucking collection."

"I didn't add her panties to my collection, Lance."

"Were those her panties in the living room?"

"Yes," I swallowed, "but I wasn't going to take them anyway. They just, uh, ended up there."

"Oh, they just ended up there, did they?" he snickered. "Why should I believe you weren't going to swoop in and take those panties?"

"Because I'm not into stealing a girl's panties. And if I *explained* it to her, first of all, and she'd look at me like a freak. Don't you get it? That was something I only did with puck bunnies or girls I didn't care about."

He gave a snort. "Oh, so now you're saying you care about my sister?"

I paused. I wasn't sure if admitting this part made it better or worse.

"I actually like her, Lance. I like her a lot."

"What the fuck, Radar? You think you like her? You've known her what, two days? And that's enough to know that you like her?"

"I can't explain it. I've never felt this way about a girl before."
I gave a defeated chuckle. "Doesn't matter, though. She hates my
guts."

"Why?"

"Because. That whole story she told you this morning?
About me and the puck bunny I brought home? She made it
all up."

Lance shook his head. "But why would Ella lie?"

"Because I made her. She would've told you the truth about
us, but ... I was afraid you'd kill me if you found out."

"Oh." Lance suddenly looked lighter, and he stepped away
from me. "You fucked up, Radar."

"I know."

"First, you fucked up when you touched my sister. I meant
what I said about getting traded to Winnipeg, bud. Hell, maybe
Winnipeg's not even far enough."

I accepted my fate with a nod of my head.

"But second, man, if you truly had a thing for my sister?
Lying to her is bad, but making *her* lie? You *really* fucked it all
up. That's the last thing you should've done. She'll never forgive
you for that." He snickered at me. I must've been a pathetic sight,
laying in a puddle of trash and grease. "Fuckin' idiot."

Lance wrung his hands.

"Don't bother coming back inside. You look and stink like
shit now. You should head home, clean yourself up, and get a
head start on packing your bags. You'll be getting a call from the
team GM first thing in the morning."

"What will you tell the boys?"

"Don't worry about it—they're not your boys anymore. I can
guarantee you that."

He walked off.

Slowly, I staggered to my feet, and started walking for the

water taxi. I knew there was no point in calling a cab—they'd kick me out as soon as they smelled my fry oil stinkin' ass.

I felt disgusting, covered in that slimy grease. My jaw hurt like a bitch, and my eye was swelling shut. Without my suit jacket, I was cold as hell—especially once I got on the water taxi and had the harbor breeze blowing over me.

But as cold and dirty and miserable as I was? I actually felt better than I had before, now that I'd come come clean. Ella might hate me even *more* for telling Lance the truth, but ...

At least she wouldn't have to lie about it anymore.

25

NAUSEATING

ELLA

The rowdy athletes never stopped talking, sharing dirty jokes, or making fun of each other in that non-stop, rapid-fire way that hockey players do. Eventually, their raucous banter faded into a distant background noise that I was able to tune out. My mind was elsewhere and I nervously fidgeted with my hands while Lance and Radar had their chat outside.

Radar wouldn't *really* tell Lance, would he? But what if he did? How would I feel? Would it change things?

I didn't know.

But when Lance returned ten minutes later, Radar wasn't with him. Lance was smiling, but I could tell he was straining to put that smile on for all of us.

"Hey, where'd Radar go?" one of his teammates shouted.

"Turns out, Radar really *wasn't* feeling well, guys. He headed home."

The room groaned.

Maybe Lance was telling the truth? I didn't know. But then I spotted Radar's jacket.

He would've taken it with him if he was planning on leaving, wouldn't he?

"I bet we got too close to the truth," Ilya joked. "I bet he really did fall for that girl he hooked up with last night."

"I seriously doubt that," Lance said with a scoff. "Anyway, who cares? We can still have fun without him."

Lance grabbed his glass of ice water and took a sip. But then did something strange, something that gave me pause: he lowered the glass to his lap, out of sight, and held the cold glass against his knuckles.

My eyes widened. *Oh my God, did they have a fight?*

I slunk in my seat.

Now what?

The servers entered with our food. While all the starving athletes around me inhaled their meals, I stared at mine. I felt sick.

"What's wrong, Ella?" Lance asked. " Lose your appetite?"

After suffering through dinner, Lance suggested that the team go to Club Regret—then caught my eye to see my reaction.

Okay. He definitely knows. I'm screwed.

Outside, an armada of cabs was once again waiting for us. Lance and I grabbed a cab, but this time, he told Ilya to ride with someone else.

We climbed in.

"I think you'll like this Regret place," Lance said. "Unless, of course, you're going to inform me that Regret is *also* a chain, and you conveniently have one of those in New York, too."

I gulped loudly.

"Is there something you want to tell me, dear sister?"

"Seems like Radar already told you," I muttered.

"He sure did. So, how'd it happen? Did he take advantage of you?"

"Of *course* not. It 'happened' because you bailed on me to go hang out with Lindsay, and then Radar felt bad for me because I hadn't even eaten dinner."

"Oh, so it's my fault."

"It's no one's *fault*. It's just something that happened."

"So Radar treated you to dinner. Wow, he's *such* a nice guy, isn't he?"

I rolled my eyes. "Yeah, he was, actually."

"And that's why you were willing to lie for him, when you made up that ridiculous story about catching him with the puck bunny?"

I sighed. "I guess so."

"It's funny, because I thought you never told a lie, and you lorded that over everyone's head as proof that you were better than everyone else. But I guess, in the end, *that* turned out to just another lie, too."

I tutted. "Stop being so dramatic. It's not like I wanted to lie about it. It's very simple, Lance: Radar and I got caught up in the moment last night, and we did something that maybe we shouldn't have done. And then he begged me not to tell you, because he thought you'd freak out and get him kicked off the team. I went along with it because I didn't want to see his career get wrecked."

"Which it will, by the way." Lance smirked. "I have to say, Honey Badger, sleeping with my roommate is pretty damn low. I wouldn't expect that from you."

I gave him a dirty stare. "First of all, I didn't sleep with him."

He rolled his eyes. "Whatever. You two clearly did *something*."

"*Second* of all," I continued, "you've got some nerve to talk about how low it is to sleep with a roommate."

"What?" He looked genuinely stumped. "What does that mean?"

"Hello—does the name Quinn ring a bell?"

"Oh, here we go with Crazy Quinn again. So that *is* what this is about, isn't it? I asked you if you planned to fuck Radar to get back at me—and you said no. Remember when you said you *weren't* the kind of sister who'd fuck her brother's best friend? What was that—lie number forty-seven you've told so far this trip, Ms. One Hundred Percent Honest?"

"I didn't *plan* on fucking him—and once again, I *didn't* sleep with him, either! This wasn't some plot of revenge. It just—"

"It just sort of happened?"

"Yes ...!" I let out a heavy breath. "He was sweet to me, Lance. Not just last night, but the night before, too. He didn't have to take me out to dinner, but he did, and we started talking to each other and getting to know each other more, and yes, I liked him enough to kiss him."

Lance rolled his eyes. "Oh, great, you like him, too. The more I hear, the more nauseating it gets."

He thought it was nauseating, but my heart fluttered at hearing that.

"... Ryan said he likes me?"

"*Ugh.*" Lance sneered with disgust. "You call him 'Ryan'? Seriously?"

"Forget it. Where did he go, anyway?"

Lance shrugged. "He went home, like I said."

"Did you guys have a fight?"

Lance didn't give an answer, so I grabbed his hand and inspected it. "I knew it! Your knuckles are puffy and bleeding. You punched him, didn't you? Is he hurt?"

He snatched his hand away from me and pressed it between his thighs.

"He'll be fine," he said.

"I can't believe you, Lance. You think you can solve everything with violence? You think you can hit a guy just because he likes me?"

"Radar doesn't *like* you, Ella. The guy always has some new slut he's banging, practically every weekend. Did you know he never brings a girl around a second time after he fucks her? Wanna take a guess who his new slut was last night?"

My jaw dropped and my eyes narrowed with rage, and that was when I caught Lance with a back-hand to the mouth.

He recoiled and dabbed at the blood trickling down his lip. "Funny. I thought violence wasn't the answer."

"You're *such* an ass, Lance."

"Yep. Sure I am. And I guess this is the thanks I get for inviting you out to my place for the weekend. You try to bang my roommate, you hit me—"

I interrupted him. "You are *so* selfish. You lied to me about why you wanted me to visit. You weren't even home the first night I arrived in town. You bailed on me last night to hang out with your girlfriend, *all of which* created the perfect storm of me and Radar hanging out together. You also aren't even sorry about the fact that you fucked Quinn, my best friend, and sabotaged our friendship in the process. But when the same thing happens with me and *your* best friend, suddenly it's some egregious crime?"

"Uh, yeah. Exactly. I'm a guy, so I'm *supposed* to try to sleep with your friends. But if your sister tries to sleep with your guy friends, it's like, wrong and stuff—"

"That is so stupid. *You* are so stupid."

I commanded the cab driver to pull over.

"Wait, where are you going, Ella?"

"I'm going home, I'm packing my things, and I'm staying at a hotel for the night. I've had enough of you and Radar both."

I slammed the car door shut before he could say anything else.

Asshole, I muttered as his car drove off to the club.

26

WHAT'S IN THE BOX
RADAR

Back home, I needed a long, hot shower before I managed to get the greasy film of fry oil off of me. My shirt and pants were ruined, so I threw those away.

I threw on my favorite pair of sweatpants and laid in bed. I had a pounding headache thanks to the punches I'd taken. Wondering what was going to happen next wasn't helping relieve the throbbing pain, either.

Should I call my agent and let him know?

Sometimes it helped to get ahead of the media blitz. If word of this was going to hit the media, it might be best to get started on damage control ...

I really fucked things up.

I had such a good thing going in Boston. Realistically, I know I'm not a top-line player—but Lance and I just had chemistry on the ice. I never clicked with a top-six guy before. My only hope was to compete for a bottom-six roster spot on another team. And I might make that work for a season or two. But once my new team figured out I wasn't the same player I had been in Boston, their patience would start running thin. I'd find myself demoted to the third line, then the fourth line, then struggling to stay with the big club at all ...

You really shouldn't have fooled around with her, moron, I thought.

But then another part of me thought, surprisingly: *it was worth it. You did the right thing, and took a chance because you liked her in the first place.*

An hour or so later, I heard the condo door open and someone came in.

Great, I mumbled under my breath. *If it's Lance, he's probably still furious.*

But it wasn't Lance's body that entered the condo. The foot steps were lighter, softer, more elegant.

It was Ella. She was alone.

I didn't go to see her. I knew well enough to leave her alone, after the train wreck I'd created.

Ten minutes later, there was a soft rapping at my door.

"Knock knock," Ella said.

"Come in."

She stepped in, saw me, and covered her mouth. "Oh my God. Your face."

"Handsome, right?"

"You look awful, Ryan."

She spun around and left the room immediately. I thought, *huh, I guess she really can't stand the sight of me.*

But she returned a minute later holding a bag. "Here. I brought you some ice." She neared, sat at the edge of my bed, and pressed the ice bag to my eye. "How's that?"

"Helps. Thanks." I couldn't look her in the eye. "How was dinner?"

"It was MacAllister's. For the second night in a row. Hardly the place you bring a girl you want to impress, right?"

"Where's Lance?"

"With the rest of your teammates at Club Regret." She paused. "Lance and I had a fight on the way over."

"Funny. We had a fight too."

"Yeah. Our fight was about your fight."

"I figured."

She leaned closer and lowered her voice. "Why would you tell him about last night, Radar?"

"So you wouldn't have to lie to him anymore."

"But why?"

"I told you, I wanted to make things right. Did it work?" I gave my best shot at giving her a cocky grin, but it must've looked pitiful, given my black-eye-and-ice-bag condition.

She smiled coyly. "Well, you certainly pissed him off."

I chuckled. "Tell me about it."

"He says he's going to make sure you get traded, you know."

"Yup. I know."

"Why would you *tell* him all that, Radar? I wouldn't have told him about last night. You could've continued on like nothing ever happened."

"But you told me you vowed to live your life without telling a lie. And here I was, forcing you into a life where you had to lie to your brother. I guess I didn't realize how important it was to you until I made you do it, and I saw how angry it made you."

She didn't answer. She pursed her lips and looked at me with a half-smile, half-frown.

"So, Ella, even if I got away with the lie, you would've had it buried inside you for the rest of your life. Who knows—maybe in the grand scheme of things, that lie wouldn't be a big deal. Maybe, eventually, you'd only think about it once every other year. But it'd still be there, a little piece of proof that you weren't living your life the way you wanted, and worse, it'd be my fault."

She put her hand against my cheek, the non-swollen one. "Ryan ..."

"I like you, Ella." I covered her hand with mine—and then I gently removed it from my cheek. "But I don't deserve you. And that's why I was only trying to do the right thing last night."

"What are you talking about, you don't deserve me?"

"I sleep around. You don't. You're the complete opposite of me."

"I already know that about you."

"And how does it make you feel?"

"I mean ... I'm not *wild* about it. But it's not like you're unique in that regard. *I'm* the odd one, sitting around and waiting—and for what, exactly? I'm not even sure anymore."

I shook my head. "No. See, you don't know how bad it is for me." I climbed off the bed and pulled the trunk out from underneath the bed. "Here. You were asking me what's in the box. You really want to know?"

She looked at me and gave an uncertain dip of her shoulder. "Er ... I don't know ... I don't know what you're trying to tell me."

"What's in this box is proof of how fucked up I am in the head, Ella."

"Um." Frozen with fear, she swallowed loudly. "It's not dead body parts, is it?"

"Of course not. I sleep around but I'm not a serial killer."

"Whew." She let out a breath of relief. "Then show me."

I unlatched the locks and lifted the lid, and Ella peeked in at my shame.

"Um. Okay, it's—a jumbled pile of women's panties? Are you a cross-dresser?"

"What? No! It's a panty collection."

"And what is a panty collection, exactly?"

I sighed and explained it to her. Every last mortifying detail. Each pair represented a girl I'd slept with. They were almost all puck bunnies from MeatMarket, the hookup app I used.

Her brow furrowed with uncertainty. "How did you start something like this?" she asked.

"Once I went pro, one of the first girls I hooked up with accidentally left her panties in my room. I texted her the next day and told her, in case she wanted to pick them up. But she said, 'add them to your collection.' I told her I didn't have one. She said, 'start one then, duh.' And so ... I did. And I guess it kinda grew out of control from there."

She had more questions, and I had answers:

No, I didn't steal any damn panties; the puck bunnies always willingly gave them to me because they knew about my collection and were more than willing to help me add to it.

Yes, of course they were clean; every pair went through the wash before I placed it in the box.

No, I never did anything weird with them ... besides collecting them, anyway.

After I answered all her questions, Ella didn't look at me like I was a monster. In fact, she started to look—*amused.* Like she were biting the insides of her cheeks to keep from breaking out into a grin.

"I guess I'm just confused why you ... *ah* ..." she stifled a giggle, "*ahem,* why you would want all these panties in the first place?"

"Wait, are you laughing?" I asked, appalled.

"Yes! I am! It's sort of funny, okay! Some people collect stamps, or bottle caps, or baseball cards—but you collect panties." More giggles.

"I collect them because ... I don't know." I looked into the stupid box and gave it a shake. "It's kind of dark."

"Tell me."

"I've always had this idea that, as long as I was an athlete, I should never settle down and date anybody. Because, first of all, there's all these girls who just want to fuck me because of my name and profession, right? But that's a double-edged sword. How can I ever trust that someone I meet is actually interested in *me,* the person, and not just 'Radar' the hockey player? All these panties are *proof* that women only like me because I'm a pro athlete."

She nodded while my words sunk in. "I get it, Ryan."

To say I was shocked doesn't even begin to explain my surprise. "You do?"

"Yeah, I think so. I'll be honest, it's a little weird, but I still get it. I've got sort of the same problem going on, don't I? I mean, I don't collect the boxers of men I've rejected or anything"—another stifled giggle—"but I have the same fears about finding a guy who actually likes me and isn't just trying to get laid. It's the same problem, it just manifests itself differently, right?"

Damn. She's so smart.

"I never thought of it like that," I admitted quietly.

She shut the panty box. I took her cue and tucked the box back under the bed.

"Why'd you want to show me that, Ryan?" she asked, scooting next to me on the mattress until our thighs touched.

"Because that's what I meant when I said I don't deserve you. A guy who does something like that shouldn't be your first."

She covered her mouth.

"You're still laughing," I said.

"Only because I think you're a sweet guy who doesn't even *know* that he's sweet."

"How can you possibly think I'm sweet after what I showed you?"

"Ryan, the kind of guy who compulsively collects panties because he's a perverted monster *isn't* the kind of guy to turn a virgin down because he thinks she deserves better for her first time."

"I don't get it. So if I'm not a perverted monster, what the hell am I?"

"A guy who actually cares." She grabbed my arm and made me drape it around her shoulders. "Trust me, I've dealt with enough creeps that I'm *normally* pretty good at spotting them by now." With my arm around her, she snuggled against my side. "I'll tell you this much: you are officially the first guy to turn me down. Which means a lot, if you ask me."

She was so close, her warmth crept over me, and that dangerous scent of hers clouded my mind. I squeezed her against me.

"Hardest thing I've ever done," I said with a smile. "I like you, Ella."

"I know. I like you too, Ryan." She took the ice bag away from my face and smiled at me.

"How do I look now?" I asked.

Carefully, she touched the skin around my eye. "Better. The swelling's already gone down a bit. You kinda look sexy with a black eye, honestly."

I leaned in and softly kissed her. It wasn't the naughty, forbidden kisses that yesterday's make-out session on the couch was. Instead, the embrace of our lips was something deeper, something more meaningful. Our lips locked and we explored each other deeper. Like we were truly *seeing* each other for who we really were for the very first time.

Her head hit the pillow and she invited me between her legs. I climbed on top of her, and she squeezed her legs around my back and pulled me into her.

Ella snuck her hand down to my crotch and fondled my growing penis.

"Ella," I panted. "We don't—"

She put her finger to my lips. "I'm tired of waiting, Ryan," she said with a twinkle in her eye. "I'm ready."

"But … what about Lance?"

"I don't care what he thinks. Besides, he's staying at Lindsay's tonight."

I stared at her. *Should I?*

But as she tugged me through my sweatpants, and my firming cock began to throb in her dainty hand, my troubles grew.

I gulped.

I couldn't … Lance would kill me if I slept with his sister after everything that had already happened … but …

"I want it, Ryan. I want *you*."

27

FIRST TIME

ELLA

I could see it all over Ryan's purple-and-blue eye: he *still* wasn't sure he should do this.

Give the man some credit: even after his best friend punched him in the face and he'd basically lost his job, Ryan still wanted to do the 'right thing.'

But with my legs wrapped around his muscle-bound trunk, and with my hand pulling at his cock, he could fight me off for only so long. With each tug, his cock grew bigger and harder in his sweatpants, and I felt his resistance melt away, like a heap of snow quickly melting under a warm day's sun.

"I haven't been able to stop thinking about how bad I wanted you," I told him.

"I thought you hated me," he said, his voice a gravelly hiss.

"Oh, I did." I nodded profusely. "But that only made my feelings worse."

His pupils darkened with sin. He kissed me deeply, crazily, an undeniable heat in our lips and growing between our bodies.

"You're *so* big and thick and long," I teased him with a warm whisper in his ear. "I bet you'd feel so good inside me, Ryan."

Showing vulnerability in the face of temptation, he grunted.

I knew I was winning this battle. I pressed on. "How do you think your big, hard cock would feel, thrusting insid—"

I was stunned when Ryan cut me off with a roar, a primal noise of pure, pent-up animal need. And with that, he let himself go. He grabbed my dress and quickly whipped it over my head, tossing it aside. He tore off my bra just as hastily and flung it across the room.

Wide-eyed and giggling with surprise, I tried to cover my chest in the name of modesty. But Ryan wouldn't have it. He grabbed my wrists with one hand and pinned my arms above my head. I gasped for air and his eyes feasted on my rising-and-falling breasts with a fiendish craving ...

"Ryan," I moaned, writhing beneath him.

With my arms restrained, Ryan lowered himself to my breasts. Greedily, he groped and pawed at my breasts, tweaking and pinching my nipples—and ignoring my initial too-sensitive yelps and mewls.

"Your tits are *perfect,*" he snarled.

My sensitive cries became deep moans of pleasure as Ryan licked and kissed and sucked at my growing nipples. They elongated, the sight of which—pink and erect and wet with his saliva —only drove him even more wild and crazy.

Ryan dragged his tongue down my torso, licking and kissing and nipping at every inch of skin. His carnal desire for me was so thick, so urgent and real. In the past, plenty of boyfriends had wanted me, but never like this, never like they worshiped every *inch* of me ...

Soon, his mouth was at my waist. He laid a trail of feather-soft kisses above the hem of my panties. I squirmed. He'd already gotten me so wet. I wanted him to touch my panties, I wanted him to notice my wetness for him, just like he had last night—I wanted to see how the sight and smell of my need for his body possessed him once more.

Ryan began to kiss and gently nibble his way up my inner thigh, slowly, tortuously, to my crotch—and then, cruelly, he skipped over my mound entirely, only to start the ritual over again at my other thigh.

"Please," I gasped, clenching at the bed sheets. "Please, *please*, Ryan. I want you so bad."

He glanced up at me with his sparkling eyes. "You waited this long. I want to take my time with you."

"Oh my God ..." I panted as a sudden rush of warmth soaked my panties.

At last, Ryan dug two fingers under the waistband of my panties and pulled. He dragged the intimates until they tumbled down my legs.

Ryan spread me apart with his powerful arms. "Damn, babe. Your pussy's so pink and wet." Tenderly, he began to lick at my heat. I placed my hands on his head—secretly adoring the sharp sensation of his short, prickly hair against my hands—and guided him as he French-kissed my pussy.

Just like last night, Ryan reduced me to a whimpering, moaning puddle in a matter of minutes. And just like last night, I could only withstand a few strokes from his incredibly thick finger before my hips began to quake.

"Oh God!" I announced, pulling a pillow over my face so I wouldn't wake their whole building with my screams. "I'm coming!"

Ryan knew just what to do. He kept a steady pace, lapping at my folds and boring his finger in and out of me, until he broke me.

Wave after wave of euphoric bliss crashed over me, making my limbs thrash against the mattress.

I was a breathless mess when it was over.

"Oh. My. God," I panted, peeking out at the sexy athlete from beneath the pillow.

He grinned so cutely and confidently at me. "I love your taste, Ella."

"Dirty boy," I said. "What do I taste like?"

"You tell me."

He mashed his mouth into mine and a wildfire blazed between us as we kissed. Sure enough, my taste lingered on his lips and tongue; a sharp, yet at the same time, pleasantly mellow musk. My stomach twisted into knots with the taboo: I *loved* my taste on his mouth, with *his* scent and *his* taste. It was naughty, but *so* right, like no two things were ever made more perfect for each other.

Reaching blindly at Ryan's muscled waist, I swiped at his sweatpants. They slid over his round butt and his hefty manhood sprang out, bobbing intimidatingly and bulging with veins. The tip was wet with a glossy trail of excitement that dribbled down his shaft.

"Oh," I moaned, "I want to taste you, Ryan."

He sat back on his haunches, head towards the sky. I knelt between his chiseled thighs and stroked him, my eager eyes on his massive cock. With each tug, he spilled more mouth-watering pre-cum. I *had* to have him in my mouth.

I leaned forward and delicately dabbed my tongue to his wetness. It was *sweet* and I wanted more. I swirled my tongue all around his head, licking and sucking at him as if his solid mass were a melting ice cream cone, and I didn't want to spill a drop.

Needing to taste more of him, I locked my lips around him.

"Oh, Ella," he groaned as I pushed down his length.

With every pass into my mouth, his sweet-and-salty taste trickled against my tongue. I sucked him faster, harder, desperate for more of his pre-cum, when he began to pant in warning,

"Careful, Ella ...! You're gonna make me come—you better slow down!"

But I didn't slow down at all. The idea of him losing control so quickly was an incredible turn-on. I sucked him harder, faster, thrashing my tongue against his member. His whole body trembled and his dick turned as hard as steel in my mouth.

"*Fuck,* I'm coming!" he roared, grabbing a fistful of my hair.

Powerful threads of his cum jetted against the roof of my mouth, but I didn't stop sucking. I swallowed his juice down and kept sucking for more, until he grew too sensitive and had to pry me off his cock.

The two of us collapsed on his bed. He put his arms around me and pulled me near.

"Holy shit," he panted. "That was amazing, Ella."

I buried my face against his hefty pecs. Each breath carried his salty, masculine scent.

"I liked it, too," I said, shyly biting my lip. "But ..."

"But what?"

"I just made you come, and I was hoping that ... y'know ..."

He pulled me near. "I'm not done with you yet."

I grinned uncontrollably. My hand found his cock and I stroked him and, sure enough, he grew rigid in a hurry.

"I love how big you are," I told him.

I watched as Ryan rolled off me and opened his nightstand drawer. He fetched a condom, tore the package open, and slowly rolled the ring of rubber down his throbbing thickness. My nervous heart beat with excitement.

My very first time.

After having waited for so long, I always wondered how this very moment would go. I'd always tried to picture what the 'perfect guy' might look like, or what we'd done in the day leading up to it.

But having reached my wits' end with hopeless men, I was ready to give up on all that. At age twenty-two, my virginity had become such a burden, such an obstacle, such a needless distraction that I couldn't stand it anymore. After Matthew, I was sure I just wanted to be *rid* of it and fuck the first guy who met the most basic requirement, that is, *not a total dick-bag.*

Last night, when I was ready to fuck Ryan, I thought he was the perfect guy for a meaningless first. I didn't care that he wasn't the guy I'd been waiting for. He was *a* guy who had experience and would gladly fuck me and that would be that.

But no. Instead, he'd turned me down and sent us both on this whirlwind journey. And here we were again, less than twenty-four hours later—naked, in his bed, and all over each other once more. Only this time, I felt a lot closer to him. And maybe it was just the fact that his poor eye was bruised and swollen, but I could've sworn he was a lot more vulnerable to me than he was last night.

And I realized, as crazy as it was, this *was* the moment I'd been waiting for. Ryan was a guy who was willing to risk it all— his best friend, his team, his comfortable lifestyle, maybe even his career—because that's how badly he wanted me.

Maybe, in an ideal world, we'd wait a little longer before we jumped into the sheets. Maybe we'd get to know each other a little more, meet each other's friends, go out for coffee—something 'normal' like that. But tomorrow, I'd be gone. And who knows where he'd be tomorrow? All that mattered now was that I liked him, and he liked me, and we both wanted this.

He mounted me in missionary, his soft eyes holding me with reverence and respect, making sure I still wanted this. No words needed to be spoken. I encouraged him with a nod.

Ryan slid the tip of his sheathed manhood against my opening. He glided his bigness up and down my folds—a tease. Each time his cock glanced over my slit but didn't enter me, my whole body quivered with disappointment.

"Please, Ryan," I begged him, "I want it. Please don't make me wait any longer."

My words were like a spell to the athlete. With an obedient glaze in his eyes, he stuck his tip at my opening. Slowly, he sunk his weight forward, and his thick cock parted my folds, one inch at a time.

"*Yes*," I whispered when his hips touched mine and he ground to a halt.

Yes. Finally.

Ryan didn't move. His presence was warm, long and thick and solid inside me. He was the first man to have me, and he was more than happy just to stay buried in my pussy. I never imagined I could feel so satisfied, so filled and stretched, so *complete*, as I did with Ryan's cock pulsing inside me.

And then Ryan did something a little crazy.

"I love you," he whispered.

I gasped with surprise—but surprise for what? Because Ryan had said those words so quickly, or because I felt the same exact way?

I opened my mouth and said something a little crazy myself.

"*I love you, too.*"

Those magical words had been said and Ryan gave me his lips. We kissed madly, two people in love, until I could feel his huge cock begin to swivel and turn inside me.

He backed out and heavy breaths escaped us both. After feeling so whole, the absence of him was excruciating. I *needed* him back inside me.

"Fuck me, Ryan," I pleaded him.

I dug my nails into Ryan's round, firm ass, and moaned for him as he thrust his length into me again.

28

I MEAN IT

RADAR

"I love you."

Holy shit, did I just say that?

I've never been in love. I wasn't sure I ever *could* fall in love. I wasn't sure I'd know what it felt like ... or if it was even real.

But I've also never told a girl I loved her before. And I wasn't planning on saying it to Ella, either.

The words just ... had a way of coming out, all on their own.

And then I'd done it. I'd said those words, alright.

Ella reacted the only way she could: her mouth cracked open just the tiniest bit, and her eyes went wide with surprise. I was sure I'd blown it.

But then she surprised me.

"I love you, too."

Were we serious? Had we lost our minds? We barely knew each other! How could we say those words when we'd just met two days ago?

I couldn't possibly answer those questions rationally. But I guess love wasn't the most rational thing, either. All I knew was that I'd never felt this way about a girl before, and I wasn't one to throw those words around to impress somebody. Hell, those words had always scared me.

But with Ella, they felt ... *right*. So right, I'd spoken them without planning on it. And once she'd said it too, something magical happened. It was like we'd sealed a sacred bond, something we'd share forever, something bigger and more important than space and time itself.

We locked lips and kissed like we never had before, so hot, so raw, so deep. I pulled out and we both trembled and gasped in agony, both of us waiting to be put back together again.

"Fuck me, Ryan," she moaned, clutching two handfuls of my ass.

I pumped myself back into her tight, steaming-hot pussy. She truly opened for me now and I slid in even deeper than before, until every last inch of my cock disappeared inside her. With a devious smile, Ella squeezed me so tight, I couldn't even pull out.

"Fuck me?" she sang. A taunt. She knew what was she doing. I tried again to withdraw, but her grip was too strong.

"You're so tight, Ella," I grumbled vulnerably.

"C'mon, Ryan! I *said*, fuck me," she teased in a tone that told me she knew it was an impossible task.

With a roar, I pulled against her with all my might, fighting against the sweet, blissful friction of her muscles. The intensity of our struggle ratcheted higher, until at last, her hold gave way and we were torn apart, separated in a crescendo of grunts, groans and moans.

"I'm not gonna last long if you keep squeezing me like that," I gasped.

"Try again. I promise I'll let you out this time." She gave an ornery smile and I knew she hadn't meant it. Not that I minded. I gave her my tongue, eased forward, and slid my dick right back into her sopping-wet tightness. She let me right in. But when I tried to pull out, sure enough, she clamped down on me.

"You are *such* a liar."

"Fuck me, Ryan?" she sang again.

I didn't hold back. I pulled and pulled against her until at last she lost her grip, and then we shoved ourselves back together again.

She teased me with her strength, her tightness, and I began to realize why: she'd kept herself pure all this time, and she wanted me not just to appreciate it, but to claim it, to *own* it.

We fucked, harder and faster, each thrust a tussle, until her resolve finally gave away and she couldn't hold me anymore; she could only grip her muscles *against* me as I plowed in and out of her, and then things *really* got loud and out of control.

With her tightness, her wavering screams of pleasure, her tits bouncing and jiggling as I fucked her, I didn't last long. My cock pulsed and throbbed inside her, shooting my load into the condom.

After I'd spilled my seed, I held her tiny body against mine, and the two of us didn't speak a word. We just grinned like fools, basking in each other's warmth and the bliss we'd just created together.

"I love you," she said again, once we finally caught our breath and settled down.

I gave her a kiss on the top of her head. "I love you, too."

We made sweet love. We fucked like animals. We screwed with dirty, pent-up frustration. We were up for hours, and we did it all.

We fucked on the bed, on the floor, up against the wall, and all over the bed. We did her favorite sixty-nine, too, which was just as hot with Ella as I'd imagined.

I was the first man she'd ever had, after all, and she wanted to try it all. She had a penchant for hard, athletic sex—sex that took us both to the physical limit. Sweat dripping, flesh clapping, bed creaking, headboard banging, *hard* sex.

Once, Ella sweetly asked if she could be on top and be the one in control. I'd just grin and tell her if she wanted to be in control, then she should just *be in control.* Without another word, she hopped on top of me, dug her nails into my chest, and rode me in cowgirl. She rode me rough, just like she wanted it: pelvis gyrating, hips bucking, clit grinding against my shaft with every pump. When she came, she let her hair cascade over my bare chest. She kept going, her hips slowly swiveling on my hard cock, until she milked me for my orgasm and I came inside her.

Every time I exploded inside Ella, I was left feeling totally drained. Like I had nothing more to give. The only I desire I had was to shut my eyes and let sleep take me. But then she'd sneak a hand down and massage my balls, or put my soft cock in her mouth and swirl it around until it was hard, and, well, the whole process started over again.

And then we'd collapse into each other again, clutching each other near, our sweltering bodies even sweatier and stickier than before. On and on and on for hours, until the first crack of daylight started to appear out the window and the bed sheets beneath us were damp with our sweat and mess. We knew we needed to get our hands off each other and at least try to get *some* sleep.

I watched as she climbed out of bed and started pulling her panties up her legs.

"Where are you going?" I asked.

"I shouldn't sleep in here, should I? It's already so late, and if

Lance comes home in the morning, and I'm still in here, he'll kill us both ..."

I blew out a gust. "I want you with me. Lance is *not* going to get between us."

"You actually mean that, don't you?" Smiling, she rushed and jumped back into bed and wiggled out of her panties. She pinched the item between her fingers and held it out to me.

"I guess you want these?" she asked. "For the box? Your collection?"

I didn't take them. "God, no."

She pouted. "Why not?"

"They don't belong in there." I shook my head. "I'm throwing that damn thing away. I can't stand the thought of it anymore."

"Nooo!" Ella squealed sarcastically. "But how will you ever remember all the babes you've boned!"

I jealously put my arm around her and squeezed her into my body. "They don't matter to me. All I want is you."

She giggled with her lovely laugh, but she pushed herself away from me. "You know you shouldn't talk like that, right?"

"Why not?"

"Because I've gotta go back to New York tomorrow."

"So?"

"You *really* think you'll still want to be with me once I'm gone and all this craziness is over?"

"I said I love you and I meant it. I'm not letting you get away from me that easily, Ella."

"But what if you get traded to ... what did Lance say? Winnipeg?"

I wrapped my arm around her even tighter. "I'll figure it out. I'm not letting you get away. I've been waiting for a girl like you my whole life. I just never knew it until I found you."

"God." She quietly sighed and melted in my arms. "I love it when you talk to me like that."

"Good. Because I mean it."

29

LAST DAY IN BOSTON

ELLA

Ryan's alarm woke us up at 8:00 AM.

"What time is your flight?" he asked, his voice gritty with sleep.

"2:00 PM ..." I trailed off, disappointed by the thought.

"We should get up, then. I don't want to spend our last few hours together in bed."

"But then again?" I teased, running a finger through the carved-out valleys of his stone-hard abs. "We absolutely *could* spend our last few hours together in bed."

"You don't know how tempting that is." He growled hungrily. "... *But,* I'd feel bad if I didn't take you out to breakfast and have a proper morning with you first."

I perked up immediately. "Ooh, breakfast! Where?"

"MacAllister's," he said.

I searched his face for a clue that he was joking, but I didn't find one.

"Wha'? Really, again?" I muttered.

"I figured we'd go for the MacAllister's hat trick: three times in three days. What do you think?"

"God, no! Ryan Ryder, if you even *try* to take me there again—"

He laughed and hugged me. "I'm kidding, I'm kidding! There's a fancy French place that does an over-the-top prix fixe brunch special. It's delicious, it's crazy hard to get a table, and it's expensive. You'll love it."

I clapped my hands with excitement. "*Now* you're talking."

"Then we'd better get up."

We staggered out of bed, both of us bleary-eyed and exhausted. My skin was covered in a salty, sticky glaze—a reminder of last night's marathon love-making session. We'd truly done it *all* until the sun came up. I liked to think that I was making up for lost time, and making sure my 'first time' was plenty memorable.

But it was a new day, and that meant a new start. I took a shower and when I emerged fresh and clean and soft, Ryan was waiting for me in his bedroom with a steaming mug of coffee.

"Here you go," he said, passing the mug to me. "My turn to shower."

Ryan showered and dressed in a hurry, magically trans-forming into a crisp, clean-shaven, and devastatingly hand-some man who, in another fantastically fitting suit, could've graced GQ's cover. Minus the slightly swollen black eye, anyway.

"You ready?" he asked me.

"Yep." I took his arm. "You look dashing, by the way."

"And you look lovely."

The plan was to eat brunch and spend the rest of afternoon in downtown Boston. We'd go to the airport from there, so I had to pack my bags to bring with us. I felt a sadness in the air that we were going to leave each other so soon.

Ryan carried my bags, and we took the elevator down to the lobby. We waited at the curb outside for the valet to return with

Ryan's car. It almost slipped my mind that he would have a car, but, *duh,* of course he'd have a car.

While we waited for the valet to deliver his car from the parking garage, I tapped my chin and wondered what sort of car Ryan drove. I imagined a brightly-colored exotic sports car that would come roaring up the garage ramp, tires screeching to a halt in front of us, the engine's idle a menacing, organ-rattling hum. He was a professional athlete, after all, and that was the kind of exuberantly tacky stuff they filled their lives with to signal their status.

But when the valet emerged with Ryan's car, I was pleasantly surprised to see a perfectly modest cobalt-blue BMW coupe. A fancy car, no doubt, but not one that screamed *rich millionaire athlete.*

"What a nice car!" I told him.

"Thanks."

Ryan got his keys from the valet, slyly slipped the young man a tip, and opened my door for me. The cabin was infused with that new car smell, and the comfortable black leather seats were taut and pristine.

"Is this car new?" I asked.

"I got it three years ago. When I signed my contract with the Brawlers."

"Wow, it still looks and smells new." I ran my fingers over the smooth and flawless dashboard. He'd obviously taken good care of it. It was a comfort to know that he cared for his things.

Ryan put the car in gear and off we went. He mused, maybe a little self-consciously, "I don't drive a bright red Lamborghini like Lance does."

"No, but Lance is loud and obnoxious, and he needs a car that projects those qualities out into the world. This? This suits you. It's classy and luxurious and elegant on the surface, but it packs a lot of *rawr* under the hood."

Ryan laughed. "Nice. I like that."

"Not to mention … it's got sex appeal." I reached over to his lap and walked my hand across his built thighs, teasing the long bulge that thickened down one leg of his pants.

"Damn, Ella. Don't get me too worked up."

"Why not? You don't want to walk into your posh brunch spot with a raging boner?" I giggled.

Ryan shook his head and stifled a laugh. "Man. See. You *know* you're bad, don't you?"

"Maybe." I snuck my hand into his lap and started rubbing his length.

"Oh, God," he sighed. "That's so good …"

But then there was a buzzing in his pocket, against my hand. It was his cell phone. I fished into his pocket for it and handed it to him.

Ryan looked at the screen and frowned. "Shit."

"What?"

"It's Shea. I better answer."

I listened to his half of the conversation.

"Hey, what's up, Shea? … Uh huh … yeah … Right. Yep. I know. … Okay. … I'm taking Ella out to brunch. … In two hours? Yeah, I guess I could make it … Alright, bye."

He hung up and, without a word, stuffed the phone back into his pocket.

"Well? What was that?"

"Shea is trying to set up a team meeting. I'll have to stop by the rink after brunch." Ryan tried to reassure me with a smile that this was normal, but I could see behind his eyes that something was wrong.

"A team meeting? On your day off? With such short notice?"

"Yeah, well—"

"Is it because of us?"

"Who knows?" Ryan shrugged. He looked at me and knew I

wasn't buying it. "Okay, yeah, it is. But look, I don't want to let it ruin our morning. I can't control what happens, Ella, what's done is done. I just want to enjoy my time with you."

"I'm so mad at Lance. He's such an idiot."

"He can be hard-headed, but he's a good guy."

"How can you say that after he punched you and everything?"

But Ryan shook his head. "He only did what any good brother should do. I'd do the same thing if I had a sister."

"Oh, really? You'd beat some poor guy up just because he liked your sister? That's *so* stupid."

"If you say it like that, sure, it sounds stupid."

"That's because it *is* stupid."

"Maybe you're right. But us hockey players have a code we live by, and maybe it's stupid, but I still broke it."

"I guess it's just one of those guy things," I reflected with a sigh.

He grabbed my hand. "Let's just enjoy our time together, Ella. Whatever happens, I'm gonna find a way through this. I'm not letting you go that easily."

I fought back a smile. Secretly, I loved it when he talked about us like that—like we were destined to be together, to love each other for all time. Part of me thought it was absurd, that I should know better, because we'd only known each other for so short a time: how could he possibly mean what he was saying?

"You seem so sure," I said.

"Sure about what?"

"That we'll end up together," I said.

"All I know is that I'm crazy about you, Ella. If you tell me that you don't feel the same way about me, and you want me to leave you alone, then I will. But until that happens, you're mine, and I'm not letting anyone get in our way."

Every time I doubted him, he answered in such a way that

told me he *meant* those words. And why shouldn't I believe him, after everything he'd done already?

I laid my head on his round shoulder. Comforted by his warmth, his scent, I was sure everything would work out.

30

BRUNCH

ELLA

Ryan couldn't have picked a better brunch spot. The atmosphere was warm and relaxing even though the place was crowded. We got our table right away, and Ryan looked at me across the table and smiled. I noticed the gap in his teeth that wasn't there last night.

"Hey! You're not wearing your implant!" I said excitedly.

"I left it out for you. You said the missing tooth was kinda cute, didn't you?"

"I sure did."

"Still think it's cute?" He simpered, showing off his smile in all its imperfect glory. "Or should I pop the implant back in?"

"Leave it just the way it is."

He chuckled. "You're strange. I think I look like a hobo without it."

"No, you look like a hockey player."

"I thought you didn't like hockey players?"

"But I like you, and you're a hockey player, so leave the tooth out just for me, okay?"

He looked pleased with my answer. "Sure thing."

Our food came—Ryan was right, the food here was delicious. We had a perfect date. We made each other laugh and shared all the intimate stories and secrets that are reserved for the people you truly care about and trust.

Brunch was so lovely, in fact, I *nearly* forgot the fact that I was leaving soon, or that Ryan had to cut into our last day together to attend some mysterious team meeting at the rink.

Soon, our food was gone and Ryan paid the bill, and then we were back in his car riding towards the rink again. The cabin was eerily silent and I knew that Ryan was nervous about the meeting.

"Will Lance be there?" I asked him.

"I don't know. Maybe."

"For real, Ryan, what did Shea tell you over the phone?"

"The GM has a trade lined up. Looks like I'm going to Vancouver."

I gasped—I'd started to buy into the fairy tale that Ryan and I could maybe make something work. Boston to New York wasn't a terrible trip by any means, but—

"*Vancouver?*" I repeated, aghast.

That was even further away than Winnipeg. And that fairy tale story, that unlikely picture of 'us' as destined lovers, started fading in my mind. Ryan might have meant it when he said he liked me, but how could we ever expect to survive a distance like that, when we barely knew each other?

"Yep. Vancouver." Ryan took his eyes off the road long enough to give me an ironic smile. "Last night he was saying Winnipeg, because it's the coldest city in the league. But Vancouver ... that's the furthest hockey city from New York."

"Lance ... I *hate* you ... I'll never forgive you for this ..."

"Well, just for the record, I'm not traded *just* yet. Who knows, if they wait long enough, the deal might go sour and I could end up somewhere else. Hopefully some place closer to the east coast."

"What's the hold up?"

"Shea's trying to get everyone together before the trade goes down. Me, Lance, the GM, and him. He says he wants to talk the problem over first and see if cooler heads could prevail."

"Yeah?" I asked, with a sudden injection of pure hope in my voice.

But Ryan shook his head. "It's a nice thought, but I wouldn't count on it. I like you and I'm not backing down, no matter what."

"Ryan ..."

It seemed so romantic, but so tragic at the same time. Wasn't there some way we could continue on, without this being such a big deal? But no ... he'd tried to do it that way, and *I* helped turn it into the disaster that it was now.

I sank lower into the passenger seat. "I'm sorry I didn't just go along with this in secret like you wanted. Everything would've been so much easier if we just did things your way from the very beginning—"

"No way. Don't say that. It wouldn't have worked out between us if we tried keeping it a secret. Your way—telling the truth—is the only shot we've got."

I stared at my handsome athlete.

This was really him.

The guy I'd been waiting for all along.

———

We arrived at the rink just in time for their meeting.

Ryan parked the car and switched off the engine. With a deep breath, he turned to me. "Might be better if you stay in the car. If they see you with me, we might unleash hell all over again."

I shook my head. "No. I want Lance to see me so he knows

I'm serious. If he thinks he can throw a tantrum and get you traded to Vancouver, then I want him to know he's saying goodbye to *me*, too."

He took my hand in his. "Thanks, Ella. That means a lot to me."

So we walked, hand-in-hand, and made our way into the arena through the staff-only entrance. We took an elevator to the top floor. A long hallway led to a set of mahogany double-doors. Ryan knocked and a gray-haired middle-aged man in a business suit answered.

"Hello, Radar," he said.

"Morning, Mr. Tremblay. This is Ella Couture. Ella, this is our GM, Mr. Tremblay."

I smiled at the older man and shook his hand. "Nice to meet you."

"Likewise," he said politely, although he wore a pained smile, as if he were saying, *but boy I wish the circumstances were different!*

We entered the GM's office. Lance and Shea were already seated inside. When Lance saw me, he shot up from his chair. "You guys can get started. I need to have a word with my sister."

Lance whisked me out of the office and into a press box overlooking the arena's empty, blinding white sheet of ice.

"So I take it you didn't go to a hotel last night like you said you would," he mused. "You probably ran home to Radar, didn't you? I heard you guys had brunch this morning, too?"

"It's none of your business what we did."

"Well, I hope all that quality time together was worth it, because he's about to be traded to Vancouver." He stared at me, shaking his head with disbelief. "I can't believe you're actually standing here right now."

"I'm here because Ryan took me to brunch this morning, *and* he was going to take me to the airport for my flight. Because he *cares.* Unlike you, the so-called brother who lured me to Boston because you had some selfish ulterior motive. Would you have taken me to the airport? Or would you have put me in a cab to get rid of me? Considering you spent the whole weekend with your girlfriend rather than with me, I think I already know the answer."

"Whatever. You shouldn't have come here with Radar, end of story. If you thought you could show up and change my mind, you're wrong. You're only adding to my embarrassment—that's the *only* thing you're doing."

I folded my arms angrily. "Is that what this is about? You don't care about me or my feelings at all. You just think it's *embarrassing* that your little sister might like your teammate."

"Damn right, I think it's embarrassing. He *used* you, Ella. And you think you *like* him? Don't make me laugh."

"I *do* like him. And he likes me."

Lance rolled his eyes. "So I've heard."

"Actually, he said he loves me."

"He said he lov—" Lance couldn't finish the sentence. A rage boiled in his eyes, his fists balled and his forearms trembled, and he began to pace the floor outside Mr. Tremblay's office. "I oughtta barge in there and kill that bastard."

I grabbed him by the shirt, dug my heels into the ground to keep him from going into that office.

"I love him, too, Lance."

"Bullshit. You've known each other for *three days.* You don't love him, you're just high on emotions. And he only told you he loves you so he could get in your pants. It's just like what happened with me and Qui—" Lance stopped just before he damned himself.

"Excuse me?" I laughed, but it wasn't a funny *ha-ha* laugh. "You were about to say 'me and Quinn.' Weren't you?"

He swallowed. "Well, er—look, I don't remember if I said it or not."

"You're *such* a liar, Lance. For once in your life, just be honest with me."

"Ugh. Okay, yeah, I told her I loved her. Happy now? That's what guys like us *do*, Ella. We lie to get what we want. Sometimes, we don't even know we're doing it—but we need to get laid so bad, we'll say whatever it takes. We might even trick ourselves into feeling like we *do* love the girl! It's only *afterward* when we realize we don't actually love her. So, technically speaking, it wasn't a lie, y'know?" Lance crossed his arms. "Anyway, that's why I'm trying to protect you from Radar. He's *just* like me."

"Thanks, but I don't need your protection. And no, actually, he's *not* like you at all."

"You don't even know him, though. And you definitely don't know him like I do. I told you he's a player, but I didn't tell you the sort of thing he's into. Ella, I could tell you something about him that would make you sick to your stomach."

"Like what?"

"He's into some *weird* shit. He takes something from every girl he sleeps with. I mean every single girl. If you knew, it'd turn your stomach—"

"Oh, you're talking about his panty collection, right?"

Lance's jaw dropped. "He—he told you about that?"

"Yeah."

"How? Why?"

"He showed it to me, Lance, because he wanted me to know why I didn't deserve to be with a guy like him."

Lance was speechless. He hemmed and hawed and scratched at his head. "That's ... surprising, actually ... I only found out about it because I snooped in his room and found it ...

he got so pissed at me ... he was even more pissed when I told our teammates about it ..."

"Well, that doesn't surprise me, Lance. He seems pretty ashamed about it."

"If he's ashamed about it, then why the hell did he do it in the first place?"

"I don't know why he did it, Lance. People are messy, people are flawed and complicated. Life is hard and people do strange things to cope with it. The point is, he told me about his panty box, thinking it'd scare me off forever."

"And?"

"It didn't, obviously. It just made me like him more. He's honest with me, Lance. More honest than any guy I've ever known."

"But just last night, you were saying he made you lie ..."

"Yep. But then he felt horrible about it and came clean to you to set things right with me. He didn't have to do that, you know. He could've gone on with his life and you never would've found out that we'd done anything. And before you even start to think it: he didn't set things right *just* to try to get with me, because he kept saying he didn't deserve me."

Lance clutched his head between his hands. "I'm so confused. This isn't like Radar at all."

"Maybe you've never seen this side of him before. Maybe he means it when he says he loves me, Lance."

His brow furrowed. "But it's only been three days?"

"I know. And when I think about it, believe me, I think it's a little crazy, too. But sometimes, Lance, you meet someone, and the heart just *knows*. From the second I met Ryan, I felt a pull to him—even if I didn't want to be pulled in." I paused. "It's like how you feel with Lindsay, right?"

That love-struck, dopey grin that he reserved for any

mention of Lindsay returned. "I mean ... the first time I saw that round, *thick* fuckin' ass? Yeah. I knew."

I slapped my forehead. "Nevermind."

"But it's the same thing!" Lance protested.

"Listen, Lance," I said seriously, "let's put everything else aside for the moment. I don't know what's going on with this trade stuff, but if you have any part in it, I'm asking you to try, just *try* to work this through with Ryan before you do something crazy. Please? Just talk to him? Remember, he's your best friend. I know you're angry now but if you cut him off forever, you're not going to realize how much you miss him until it's too late."

He looked at me, sighed, and finally relented. "Fine. I'll talk to him."

"Thanks, Lance."

"But no promises, alright? First, I have to see what his intentions *really* are."

"Just talk to him," I said. "That's all I ask."

We hugged.

"I love you," he said.

I gasped. "Lance! How can you say that?! It's only been twenty-two years!"

"Damn it, Honey Badger! That was really *hard* for me to say just then, okay?"

"Aw. I'm just kidding. I love you too, Lance."

We headed back to the GM's office.

31

THE BIG DEAL
RADAR

While Lance and Ella were outside, I sat with Shea across from Mr. Tremblay. The mood was dark and somber, like we were attending a funeral—we all hated that we had to be here.

And maybe we were attending a funeral, in ways: mine, as a Boston Brawler.

"So you've got a deal in place with Vancouver?" I asked to get the ball rolling.

Mr. Tremblay nodded dourly.

"That's nice. Is it good for you?"

Mr. Tremblay shook his head. "Not quite. Vancouver straight up said they don't have a spot for you. The most they're willing to offer up in return is a couple of B-rate prospects and draft futures. They're confused why you're even being offered up to them and suggested we look for a deal elsewhere."

"Then why make the deal? Why not another team?"

"Lance is the face of this franchise for the next ten years. We have to keep him happy."

I gave a shrug. "You'll do what you have to do."

"This sucks like hell," Shea said in a burst of rage. "Everyone knows this makes no sense. The team's going to be emotionally gutted when we lose Radar. He is a *huge* part of this team. Hell, Lance didn't even turn into the player he is today until Radar joined the team and started doing the heavy lifting on his line! And here we are, trying to trade him for a bag of pucks? Fuck this."

"We've been trying to talk Lance out of it all morning," Mr. Tremblay said to me with a frown. "But he's drawn a line in the sand: it's either you or him. And he wants you as far away from his sister as possible."

I blew out a heavy breath. "Well, if it's between me and him, the choice is obvious."

"Is it?" Shea asked rhetorically. "Because sometimes I wonder. I get it, Lance puts a lot of butts in those seats and he sells a lot of jerseys for this franchise. But it sure seems like we give these young kids *everything* they want, not because of what they've accomplished, but based on their 'potential.' Doesn't seem smart to me. Seems more like we're creating an entitled monster that we'll have to deal with later on down the road. You know, back when I broke into this league, no one gave you *shit* until you accomplished something. You had to earn your keep and prove you could play the game before you inherited the kingdom."

I clapped my captain on the back and tried to bring some levity to the situation. "I'm so glad you gave me one last 'back in my day' rant. I'm gonna miss you, old man."

"I'm gonna miss you too, bud." He stood and we hugged. "I *told* you not to tell him, Radar. I told you to take it to the grave, didn't I?"

"You sure did."

"Knucklehead. See what happens when you don't listen to the captain?" He gestured at my eye. "Now you've got a real nice shiner."

"I took my licks last night. Thought I owed it to him."

"You know, for the sake of the team, I *wish* you would've taken my advice. But ... I'm kind of impressed that you didn't."

"Yeah?" I asked. "Why's that?"

"You must really like that girl."

"I do."

"Does she like you?"

I couldn't help but smile. "Yeah, I think so."

"Then there's nothing Lance can do about you guys, is there."

"I'm not letting her go. No matter where I get traded."

"Hell." Shea chuckled.

Mr. Tremblay's office door opened, and Ella and Lance stepped in.

"Hey, um, Radar. You mind if we talk in private for a moment?" Lance asked meagerly.

"Sure."

"Really?" Shea asked. He wasn't so sure that was a good idea, and he started to rise from his chair.

I stopped him. "Don't. We're fine, Shea."

"Okay, but no more fighting, guys."

Lance and I stepped outside into the quiet hall and looked over the empty ice.

"So ..." Lance began. "I'll just come out and say it. Ella told me that you said you love her."

"I did tell her that, Lance. And I do love her."

"We both know that's impossible, Radar. Sounds to me like you're just trying to get laid."

"I don't blame you for thinking that. I know it feels like it happened way too fast. And yeah, we haven't had a lot of time to get to know each other. But I love being around her. She's so cute and fun and off-the-wall. She's like no other girl I've known. And most importantly ... I can already tell. There's just a certain something about her, dude. She doesn't care that I'm some famous athlete. She makes me want to be a better person."

Lance sighed. "She told me you showed her your collection."

"I did."

"Why?"

"I thought she should know who I was before we went any further. I wanted her to see it, and see who I was, even if I knew it might be a deal breaker for her."

"No ... it wasn't a deal breaker. I think, somehow, you actually scored *more* points by showing her that." Lance made a *harumph*. "Women. I swear, some things I'll never understand."

I chuckled. "That's what I'm talking about. She makes me feel like I can be myself around her. But I'm sorry it started behind your back, Lance."

He laughed. "Trust me, that's the *only* way it would've started, because I wouldn't have let it happen in front of me. That's for *damn* sure."

"Right. But I'm just trying to say ... I get why you're mad. And I'm sorry for how it went down. But I'm not sorry about the way I feel about her. And if you want me off the team, I understand, but I'm not going to let her slip through my fingers. I like this one, Lance. I really like Ella and I *will* see her again."

His face twisted as if those words were utterly incomprehensible. To be fair, to a brother, I guess they would be.

"Well, as confusing as it is to hear all that, you're saying the right things, Radar. To her and now to me. So, um, I'm sorry I did the crazy over-protective older brother thing. I could've sworn you were just trying to fuck my little sister for the hell of it and add her panties to the collection."

"I threw the collection away this morning. I'm done with it."

"Jesus. So you really are serious about my sister, then?" he asked, probing my eyes one last time.

"I am, Lance."

He took a deep breath. "Okay, man. Then fuck the trade."

A thousand tons dropped from my shoulders. "You're serious?"

"I'm serious, as long as you agree to a couple things," Lance said. "Don't forget we still live together—and that's not going to change, either. In other words, if you cheat on her, I *will* find out about it. And not only will I rat you out, I will then proceed to cut your fucking nuts off in your sleep. Understand?"

I laughed. "Understood."

"Second, I never, ever, *ever* want to hear you two having sex when she visits. So take her to a hotel, or invest in some quality soundproofing, or better yet, just don't ever bang when I'm home. Got it?"

"Got it."

"Good." He wrapped his arms around me and we hugged. "Then welcome to the family, bud."

"Thanks, Lance. That means a lot to me."

The two of us went back into Mr. Tremblay's office. Everyone's eyes were glued to us as we entered, nervous expressions all around.

"Well?" Shea asked.

"Ah, what the hell," Lance bellowed. "So Radar wants to date my sister. What's the big deal? Vancouver's offer *sucks*, anyway."

"Lance!" Ella cheered. She jumped up and hugged him. He quietly gave her some brotherly words of wisdom, how he would always be there for her, and if I ever treat her wrong, she needed to let him know.

Smiling from ear to ear, Shea shook my hand, and Mr. Tremblay did, too, and both men let me know how happy they were that this whole thing could be peacefully worked out.

And then the room hushed as Ella and I gravitated towards each other. She leaped into my arms and I scooped her off her feet, squeezing her tight in my arms.

I won't lie, part of me was afraid that, even though Lance had just given us his blessing, the sight of me embracing his sister might trigger some suppressed rage and send him rushing at me. Thankfully, that didn't happen. Ella stayed right by my side and we clasped each other's hands.

And then we all watched as Mr. Tremblay picked up the phone and made a call. "Hey Jim. Jean-Paul here. Deal fell through on my end. Thanks, catch you later."

Click.

And a collective sigh of relief went around the room.

"So now what?" Lance asked.

"I gotta get this girl to the airport," I said with a frown. "You wanna come with us, Lance?"

He looked at his watch. "Can't."

Ella rolled her eyes. "Lemme guess: you're meeting Lindsay?"

"Yeah, actually."

"Next time I visit, you're introducing me to her, okay?"

"Sure."

Lance and Ella hugged one last time, we hurried through our goodbyes, and then I rushed Ella out to my car to make her flight.

32

GOODBYE
ELLA

"What a whirlwind," I said with a sigh as we sped down the highway. "These past few days went by so fast." I gave a long, tired yawn. "And *jeez*, I'm drained from all the drama."

"I'll say. Feels like I aged five years this weekend."

"In a good way or bad way?"

He looked at me like I was nuts. "There's a *good* way to age?"

"Yes," I said, as if it were the most obvious thing in the world. I looked at Ryan and tried to imagine this rugged, handsome man, five years older and entering his thirties. I started to run my hands through his hair, methodically looking for gray hairs.

Ryan caught on to what I was doing. "Hey, what the hell? Are you looking for gray hairs?"

I giggled. "Yeah, I am."

"You find any?" he asked nervously.

"Unfortunately, not yet ..."

"*Unfortunately?!*"

"You'd look *so* hot with some salt-and-pepper, Ryan. You'd look all distinguished but macho, too. And you score double points if you're still super jacked."

He tutted. "Huh. Well ... if you say so."

"Oh! Hey! Found one!" I cheered and pinched my fingers shut on the lone gray hair.

"No you didn't," he said gravely.

"I'm not a liar." I plucked it and showed it to him.

Ryan took his eyes off the road to inspect it. "I'll be damned. You really think that hair turned gray because of this weekend?"

"No, that's silly. But I do think we both grew up a lot this weekend."

He nodded. "I definitely did."

We drove on for miles, my hand in his. My head was spinning—from today, and last night, and hell the whole weekend, really, and also the things I was going back home to ...

Eventually, Ryan noticed I was in my own world.

"What's on your mind?" he asked.

"God, what *isn't* on my mind?"

"Tell me everything."

"I was just thinking about us ... this weekend ... work ... how I'm not at all excited to go back to New York ... and how nervous I am."

"Nervous about what?" he asked.

I sighed. "Don't get me wrong. I'm so happy that things worked out, Ryan. But ... now it feels like there's all this *pressure* for things to work out between us. You know?"

He shook his head. "I don't feel any pressure."

"What if you end up not liking me?"

He chuckled. "Not happening."

But I began to spiral. "Really? What makes you so sure? What if, the second you put me on that plane, the reality of everything we did suddenly hits you? Everything we said, everything you went through with Lance and the team and *everything else,* dawns on you in the darkest of ways. And you start saying to yourself"—I puffed my chest up and did my best gruff Radar voice—" *'what the hell was I thinking? I almost nuked my career over a girl I only see once a month? Plus, why should I settle down? Wherever I go, girls wanna bang me, because I'm hot and my name's Radar, and—'*"

He cut me off before I went too far off the deep end.

"First of all, you do a terrible impression of me. Second, I don't want to 'bang' anybody else. Third, *once a month?* We'll be seeing each other more than that. New York isn't that far from Boston at all. Besides, we'll find ways to sneak in visits. We'll make it work."

"You really think so?" I asked, my voice tinged with doubt. I needed to be reassured.

"I do." Ryan snapped his finger as if a great idea just came to him. "Oh! Hey, what are you doing next weekend?"

"Pft ... probably working." I rolled my eyes. "Why, what are you doing?"

"The team's got a road trip to New York. If you can take time off, I'd love to see you."

I squealed with delight. "Of *course* I can make time for you."

But then reality, and a small bit of dread, started to soak in. "For this to be a thing, though, I'll have to start taking more time off work in general. I work through the weekends, you know. I've gone *months* without taking a day off."

Ryan gave me a side-eyed glare, like I ought to know better. "And from what you've told me about yourself, your 24/7 work schedule has become a problem for you."

"True." I pursed my lips. He had a point. "You're right. God, it's a hard habit to break, isn't it? I feel so guilty when I take time off."

"Don't, Ella. Everyone needs to take time off. And I'm going to make sure you take it, by the way. You work too hard. If you keep that pace up, you're going to burn yourself out eventually."

I rest my head against his shoulder. "Thank you."

It felt so nice that I'd found a man who was already watching out for me; a man who would firmly tell me the things that, in my heart, I *knew* were true, but was too weak to tell myself.

"I don't want to go home," I said forlornly. "I wish I could stay with you."

He gave me a sweet smile. "I wish you could, too."

"I'm tired of New York."

"Move to Boston, then," he said.

I couldn't tell if he was serious, but I perked up like he was anyway. "You really think I should?"

"If you think you'd be happy here, sure. I could introduce you to the Brawler WAGs so you could make some connections for your work—"

"WAGs?" I asked.

"Wives and girlfriends. They're like a social and support club. Plus, they're all really good friends. They keep each other company when the team's out on the road."

"Ooh."

"Point is, those ladies are great, and more than a few of them are also hard-working professionals. I'm sure they'd help you out any way they can. I can start asking around, if you'd like."

"Mm. Let's not rush into things *too* quickly now," I said, biting my lip. But I'd be lying if I said the idea of starting new somewhere else didn't excite me.

An airliner overhead hung low in the blue afternoon sky. We were nearing Logan Airport. As we drove closer and closer to my destination, an awful sense of loneliness began the inevitable slide down to my stomach.

Soon, I'd have to say goodbye to Ryan—and although we'd weathered our first storm together, now we'd have to weather a whole other storm separately: being apart from each other constantly. And at such an early stage of our relationship, too. I'd be lying if I said I wasn't a little scared.

The closer we came to the airport, the harder I squeezed his hand.

And just like that, Ryan was parking the car and slinging my bags over his shoulder and walking me to the airport.

This is it ...

———

Ryan stayed by my side through the baggage check-in process. Thanks to the impromptu meeting at the hockey rink, we didn't have much time to spare—my flight was leaving soon. But there was one last thing I wanted to do before we said goodbye.

"I better run to the bathroom before I get on that plane," I told Ryan, thankful I'd worn a skirt today.

When I emerged from the bathroom, I told him to give me his hand. I made him open his fingers, then stuffed something into his palm, and made him squeeze his fingers tightly shut around it.

"Now don't peek at that until you're in your car," I said, my heart racing with excitement.

"I *know* what this is, Ella," he said, sounding dark and accusatory, but undeniably turned on.

I bit my lip. "I was just wearing them."

"I know. I can feel your warmth."

"And what do you think?"

"That's so hot," he growled. "But I told you, I threw my collection away."

"Start a new one. This time, they'll be just mine."

He swallowed, loudly, and a thrill swept over me when I noticed the way his Adam's apple moved thirstily in his neck.

"Do you like that idea?" I asked him quietly.

"Yes," he whispered. He pulled me near and kissed me, deep

and passionately. My body pressed against his, and I could feel his hardness growing in his pants ...

"Uh oh," I whispered, sneaking a hand between his legs. "You're awfully excited."

"I want you so bad," he whispered, and he *meant* it, because his words sent a shiver down my spine, and terrible ideas began to fill my head: did we have enough time for a quickie? What if the two of us turned right around and rushed out to the parking garage for one last moment together? Thinking about riding Ryan in the passenger seat of his BMW, I could *feel* the stifling, window-fogging heat building between us ... hell, who even *cares* if I missed my flight? I could just get another one.

But I shook my head, and sanity returned. I couldn't just throw everything aside. I had a schedule. I had to return to work.

"I need to catch that plane," I told him sadly.

"I know." He clutched me tighter. "I'm so glad I met you, Ella."

"Me too."

"Thanks for making our condo look like nice, by the way. It looks like actual humans live there now."

"You're so welcome!" I patted his cheek. "So ... I guess this is it?"

"Until next week," he said.

"Next week," I agreed.

We shared one last goodbye kiss, our tender lips so juicy, sweet and yet mournful.

And then I had to tear myself out of his strong arms.

Ryan stood and watched through the glass partition as I made my way through security. Before I disappeared from view, we gave each other one last bittersweet smile and reluctant wave.

I mouthed the words: *next week.*
He mouthed back: *can't wait.*

33

A LITTLE MORE HOCKEY

ELLA

One week later.

The crowd at Madison Square Garden gnashed their teeth and groaned, but I cheered as Ryan and Lance and the rest of the Brawlers on the ice celebrated another goal with a group hug. The Brawlers were dismantling the hometown New York Scouts, and it was *all* because of Ryan and Lance's spectacular play together.

Ryan spotted me in the front row, skated by, and gave me a wink. With butterflies in my stomach, I blew him a kiss.

An older couple sitting next to me, dressed in Scouts jerseys, put two and two together. The wife asked me, pointing Ryan out, "is he your boyfriend?"

I could barely contain my smile when I responded with an emphatic "yes!"

"Well," the kind lady began, "he's the enemy, so we're obligated to hate him. But ... looks like you picked a good one."

"Thank you!"

I couldn't *wait* for this game to be over so we could be together again at last—seven days had never felt so long in my life. I was a huge Boston Brawlers fan now, having watched all three games they'd played since my visit to Boston.

It was so much fun watching Ryan's heroics on the TV. And Lance's too, for that matter. Ever since last week, Ryan and Lance had somehow grown even closer, and their play on the ice showed it. Not only were they skating circles around their opponents, but if anyone looked at Lance the wrong way—or God forbid, hit him—Ryan turned into an angry bull-dog, jealously and rabidly defending his teammate.

As soon as Ryan made it back home or to his hotel room after the game, he would call me up on the phone and ask sweetly—"Hi Ella, how was your day?"—as if he *wasn't* just scoring goals and crushing grown men in a nationally-televised hockey game only an hour or two ago.

I loved our conversations on the phone—there was nothing so uplifting as being able to hear his voice and feel like there *was* a light at the end of the tunnel. But then again, talking with him was a special kind of torture, too—because after we hung up, I felt sad and empty and wished more than anything I could have him near.

When we couldn't talk during the day, there was always a text here or there to keep each other in mind. I may have sent him a few dirty pictures ... and I may have even gotten a few in return! Not a day went by without him letting me know how badly he wanted me, how he couldn't stop thinking about the way I left him at the airport.

It's pretty safe to say that, once the horn at Madison Square Garden sounded and the game was over, I was expecting Ryan to change out of his hockey gear in a hurry. Surely he'd come find me, throw me over his shoulder like a possessive caveman, and rush me back home where he could have his way with me, right? We'd been teasing each other all week, building up to this moment ...

But that wasn't what happened at all.

Who came for me instead? Lance, with Shea and Ilya in tow. The three of them were in suits and fresh out of the shower, with their hair wet and neatly styled.

"Hey, Honey Badger!" Lance said, greeting me with a hug. "You remember Shea and Ilya?"

"Of course. Hi, guys," I answered. Skipping right to the point, I frowned at Lance. "Where's Ryan?"

"He snuck out the back entrance a little while ago, actually," Lance said as if it were *totally normal* for a guy to evade his brand new girlfriend.

"*What?*" I asked, my worried heart pounding.

Was this it? Was Ryan just another coward, the kind of guy who couldn't even look a girl in the face when he broke up with her? Had I been played that badly? Lance said he never went for the same girl twice, after all ...

"What do you mean, he *snuck* out?" I asked. "Why would he do that?"

Lance shook his head. "Come with us. I'll explain in the car."

I followed them out, down to the staff entrance, where a car was waiting. The four of us climbed in and the car took off and exited the arena.

"Would you tell me what this is about already, Lance?" I asked, growing shrill and testy with my brother.

"Settle down, Honey Badger. It's not my fault. Look, Radar said he, uh, felt like playing a little more hockey tonight."

"He wanted to play a little more hockey tonight." I repeated the sentence slowly, punctuating the absurdity of it all, hoping Lance could hear how ridiculous the words sounded.

My stare must've been burning through his skin, because Lance shielded himself from my gaze. "Hey, don't shoot the messenger, man. I'm just repeating what he told me."

The guys all chuckled—and I figured, if *they* were laughing, then this must not be a bad thing ... maybe some sort of practical joke of Ryan's ... I didn't figure him to be the joker type, and this stunt didn't make me happy, but whatever ... there wasn't anything I could do about it now.

I loosened up a bit, resigning myself to the fact that whatever was happening was apparently Ryan's idea. I quietly watched the city roll by my window, hoping that his idea was a good one.

We headed west. The driver turned on the West Side Highway, and then we headed south. Chelsea Piers came into view on our right, and the driver turned into the parking lot.

"Here we are," Lance said.

"Chelsea Piers," I mumbled, remembering my conversation with Ryan during our first dinner date at MacAllister's. "Is this what I think it is?"

Lance wouldn't say. "They're about to drop the puck. We better hurry!"

We rushed into the building, made our way to the rink, and stood in the front row right behind the glass. Two teams were warming up—a beer league game. After watching a professional hockey game, watching this rag-tag group of guys lumber around the ice reminded me of drunken snails on ice.

"These guys are awful," Ilya remarked.

"Scrubs," Lance laughed. "Absolute scrubs."

"This won't be pretty," Shea said, shaking his head.

Of course, one player among them didn't look nearly so bad. Ryan circled around the ice humbly. I could tell he was trying not to showcase his skill and was trying to blend in instead—but even in the way he glided, you could see he knew what he was doing. He was too big, too smooth, too elegant, to be some random beer league player.

At the other end of the rink, skating for the opponent, was my ex-boyfriend: Matthew, the asshole lawyer.

I turned to Lance. "Ryan's not *seriously* going to do what I think he's about to do, is he?"

He smirked knowingly. "Radar doesn't let anybody harass *me* without making them pay for it. You think he's going to let this sleaze get away with insulting *you*? Not a chance, sis."

The ref dropped the puck, and the game began.

It was only a matter of time—Matthew, the puck-hog 'star' of his team, took the puck from his own defensive end and started skating at top speed in a straight line. Ryan, playing defense and skating backwards, matched Matthew's top speed with a single stride. He pinched off Matthew's lane and began to steer the lawyer towards the boards. We all knew what was coming—it was like watching a car accident unfold in slow motion.

Ilya turned his eyes away. "This is too brutal, I can't even watch!"

"Here we go, boys!" Shea shouted.

Right in front of us, Ryan lowered his shoulder and powered his mass right through Matthew, sweeping him off his skates as if he weighed nothing, and pasted the dirt-bag face-first into the glass.

BOOOOOM. The thud of Matthew's body smashing into the glass echoed around the empty rink. Only inches away from my ex's smashed face, I waved at him, though I doubted that he could see anything but stars at the moment.

Matthew tumbled to the ice.

"Gotta keep your head up, kid!" Ryan yelled as he skated off.

Slowly, Matthew staggered to his skates. "That was a cheap shot!" he screamed. He skated towards Ryan, throwing his gloves to the ice in the process. "You're fucking *dead!*"

"Oh, no." Ilya winced. "He's not *seriously* challenging Radar to a fight, is he?"

"Uh oh." Shea shook his head. "He definitely shouldn't have done that."

Lance laughed. "Yuuup. This is about to get ugly."

Ryan threw off his gloves, and when Matthew neared, he easily blocked Matthew's first strike like someone swatting away an annoying fly. My boyfriend then grabbed the collar of Matthew's jersey and fed him one solid right after another: one, two, three, and then Matthew's legs turned into jelly and he spilled to the ice.

The referee skated over and told Ryan he was ejected from the game.

"There's no fighting in this beer league," Shea said. "They're both banned now."

Ilya looked at his watch. "Radar's beer league career lasted what, fifteen seconds? Damn, too bad. Guess we'll have to keep him on the Brawlers."

We watched as Matthew needed help climbing to his legs. The refs escorted him off the ice, too. Blood ran freely from his brow. He looked over his shoulder to see me and the boys. The four of us happily waved back at him. He looked so mad and embarrassed.

"It's nice having him stand up for you, isn't it?" Lance asked.

"I could *definitely* get used to this," I giggled.

"Well, boys, you ready to go?" Lance asked. His two teammates nodded. "You stay here, Ella, and wait for Radar."

"Where are you guys going?"

Lance and his teammates smiled like a trio of troublemakers. "I heard this Matthew guy is a big fan of mine, right? I just wanna pay a fan a little visit."

"Don't do anything stupid, guys. He *is* a lawyer, don't forget."

"We won't do anything illegal," Shea said.

34
———

THE TOUR
RADAR

I threw my gear in my bag as fast as I could and nearly ran out of that rink. I couldn't *wait* to see Ella.

I found her smiling at the entrance, waiting for me. The space between us was so *small* now but *ugh* I couldn't wait until we were together ...

She jumped in my arms, and I kissed her like I hadn't seen her in *years*. Because even though it was only seven days, it felt a whole heck of a lot longer.

"That was so *awesome*," she squealed. "He got what he deserved!"

"C'mon, let's go," I said, putting a possessive arm around her waist.

We hurried out of the arena, where I had a car already waiting.

"I thought you were joking when you said you were going to clobber that moron," she said.

"No way. That guy was a total dick to you. Besides, I told you it was on my bucket list, didn't I? I'm a man of my word."

"Apparently, you are!"

I opened the car door for her and slid in after her. She gave the driver her address, and off we went to her place.

"I've been thinking about you all week, Ella," I told her. "I haven't been able to get you out of my mind."

She smiled, so sweet and innocent. It was that same lovely smile that wrenched at my heart; the same one I fell in love with when we first met back at the condo.

"I've been waiting all week for this, too," she admitted quietly.

With the driver's eyes on the road, Ella climbed into my lap. Our lips met, and we showed each other just how bad we missed each other.

After a car ride across Manhattan, we arrived at her building. We took the elevator up to the fiftieth floor. She unlocked the door and we stepped in.

"Nice place," I said.

"Thanks, but it's small. Here's the tour: living room, kitchen, and that's Eucalyptus." She pointed at the cat who perched proudly, almost arrogantly, on top of the coffee table. Hell, he almost looked like he was sizing me up—and he wasn't impressed by what he saw.

"So this is my competition, eh? I think he hates me already," I laughed.

"He'll come around to you."

"Think so?"

"I know so."

"What makes you so sure?"

"Because you won *me* over, and if you can win me over, you can win my cat over. Now, on to the rest of the tour." She grabbed my hand and led me down the hallway to her bedroom, a sultry pout on her lips. "Or the only important part of it, anyway."

She shoved the door open and crawled into bed, beckoning for me to go and get her. I prowled right after her. Our lips met and my fingers popped the waist-button of her jeans open. She sighed as I tugged her jeans off her long legs, and then her panties followed. I spread her legs and lowered my mouth to her heat.

"You're mine," I growled before I gave my tongue to her pink and glistening pussy.

"God, I missed you," she sighed, before surrendering to a rising chorus of moans.

EPILOGUE
ELLA

One year later.

I never thought I could have such a hard time telling the truth, but I was a nervous mess the whole flight to Boston. I'd only just found out yesterday. It was still very early on, but I'd already developed the habit of cradling my stomach and pondering my life with Ryan, and the life inside me ...

I wasn't sure how Ryan would react when I told him. He'd been nothing but wonderful to me ever since we'd started dating a year ago, but we'd never had the discussion about what we'd do if *this* happened.

Jeez, it's been over a year already? Time flies ...

I guess part of the reason was that *I* wasn't sure how to feel about it, either. Would I have to give up my career? I couldn't do that ...! Business was booming, thanks to the lovely ladies that were the Brawlers wives and girlfriends. Just like Ryan thought, they helped put me in touch with the right people. I did a few projects, word spread, and more projects started rolling in. And that's how it happened, that's how the city of Boston sucked me in—just like Ryan himself had. The Brawlers ladies weren't just business contacts, either—they became the missing piece of the puzzle for me: the close-knit group of friends I'd always wanted. When our boys were out of town, we always got together for ladies nights, which made getting through those week-long road trips so much easier.

Ryan's career was going great, too. At the end of last season, he ended up scoring a career high in goals and points—something he's always thanking *me* for, because he said I helped him settle down and focus more on hockey. Even better? This year, he's on pace to break last year's career high, too. He was realizing his potential as a hockey player—and realizing that he belonged in the NHL just as much as any other player.

But ... a *baby*? How did that fit into the picture? Having a baby was such a serious thing, such a huge commitment—it was like a magnifying lens that forced you to examine *everything* in your life under the closest scrutiny. What if a baby changed things? What if Ryan wasn't sure about me? What if he liked me but he just didn't want to raise a family with me?

Argh. I almost wished the plane could stay in the sky forever, just circling and circling, and I'd never have to come down and break the news.

But it was a short flight, after all, and before I knew it the plane's tires chirped as they touched down on the runway. While the plane taxied to the departure gate, I convinced myself that I'd just blurt the news out to Ryan as soon as we were in the privacy of his BMW.

But when that moment came, I grew gun-shy. He rest his giant hand on my thigh and smiled at me, as devilishly handsome and well-dressed in a sharp suit, like always.

"Missed you, Ella," he said.

"Missed you too, Ryan."

God, the hormones were already making my brain chemistry all out of whack—I couldn't look at Ryan now without seeing him as the sexiest, most *adorable* Dad ever, wearing a puffy knit sweater on a chilly wintry weekend, the three of us cuddled around the warm and crackling fireplace. Our child would think his hockey-playing Dad was a real-life superhero ...

Sure enough, I felt myself breaking out into the gushiest, most over-the-top smile. I couldn't help it.

"What's up, babe?" he asked. "You look like you have something on your mind."

I gulped. "I do."

"I do, too," he said, trying to hide a gooey smile of his own.

"You go first," I said.

He stared at the road ahead. "Hey, I asked you first."

I shook my head. I couldn't. I didn't have the courage yet. "But ... you should really go ..."

"Stalemate, then." Ryan laughed. "So, how were things in ol' New York?"

"Good," I said, giving Ryan a run-down of my work week. "How were things for you?"

Ryan filled me in on his past week with the team and at home with Lance. Yep, they still live together. They love to joke around about the time Lance flipped his shit when he found out Ryan and I were fooling around—because ever since, our relationship has only brought those two closer than ever. They're basically like brothers. I'd like to think that Ryan is even rubbing off on Lance a bit, and Lance is starting to mature ... but the jury's still out on that one.

Then Ryan said something that surprised me a little. "But, you know, I'm starting to think it might be a good idea to move out and get a place of my own soon."

"Really?"

"Yeah ... you know ... with you spending more and more

time in Boston and all. I dunno, it's kinda weird at the condo, always having to be quiet around Lance ..."

Shit, I thought. *Ryan wants to ask me to move in with him.*

I didn't say a word. I was too freaked out to possibly speak. Ryan wants to ask me to move in, and *I* need to tell him I'm pregnant. He'll be in for a big surprise when I ask if the baby I'm carrying can move in with us, too ...

Sigh.

"You sure you're alright?" he asked.

"Uh huh."

———

When we made it back to the condo, Ryan was having a harder time trying to hide that smile.

"What's gotten into you?" I asked.

"Nothing. I told you, I missed you." He pulled me near and smothered me with kisses. "Man, you *really* look beautiful today. You look like you're glowing."

"Thanks," I said shyly, while my insides silently screamed, *that glow you're seeing? That's your body noticing that I'm carrying your child!*

It was time to tell him.

"Where's Lance?" I asked—because the last thing I wanted was Lance to rush into the room and yell, *wait, did I just hear you say you're pregnant?!*

"I dunno," Ryan said. "Hey, why don't we go up to the rooftop? Have a drink? Maybe it'll help you relax."

"I'm, um—not drinking," I said.

"Since *when?*" he laughed.

"Since ..." I took a breath, mustering up the courage to say it —*since I missed my period and took four pregnancy tests before I managed to haul my sorry ass to the doctor to confirm what I was seeing!*

But Ryan stopped me before I could. "We can just drink a sparkling water, then. I just want to be with you up there and look over the harbor. It's a beautiful day."

I nodded, suddenly thinking that breaking the news to him up there, overlooking the harbor might not be such a bad idea after all. It was one of the first places we started to get to know each other, after all.

"Yeah, okay, that sounds nice."

We took the elevator to the roof, hand-in-hand. The doors opened and we stepped out—and I gasped with surprise.

Everyone was there, all the WAGs and the friends I'd made in Boston and all Ryan's, too. The entire Brawlers team was there, Lance and Shea and Ilya and all the other teammates I'd gotten to know. Everyone was dressed so nice and elegantly and my mind flipped through all the dates in my head—was it my birthday? No, of course it wasn't ...

"What ... what is this?" I stammered.

I turned around, and Ryan dropped to one knee. "I wanted everyone to be here when I asked you if you'd make me the happiest man alive."

"Ryan ...!"

He pulled a box from his pocket and showed me the gold ring. A diamond, big and white as snow, glittered under the bright blue sky.

"Will you marry me, Ella?"

"*Yes! Of course, yes!*" I screamed, and he put the ring on my finger and I pulled him to his feet and we hugged and kissed in front of all our friends who went *yay!* and *aww!*

Lance aimed a champagne bottle into the sky and *pop*, sent the cork sailing. "Let's get this party started!" My brother began pouring champagne, and gave us the first two flutes. "Here you go! Congratulations, Ella!"

"Thanks, Lance!" I took the champagne from him, but I didn't sip from it.

Lance went passing out his flutes to everyone, and they all milled about, engaged in lively conversation and passing by to give Ryan and I their best wishes and ambush us with questions:

So when I was moving to Boston? (*The sooner the better! I'm ready!*)

Would we let Lance move in with us? (*Ha ha ha—NO!*)

During a lull, I found myself in Ryan's arms, just the two of us, away from the boisterous chaos and overlooking the serenity over the harbor.

"So, I have to ask—why'd you pop the question here?" I asked him.

"Remember when we first met, and I showed you around the building?"

"Of course."

"When we were on the rooftop—that's when we first started to really talk. That's when I realized there was something about you, something that just drew me towards you. I thought you were so cute, Ella, and I was so dumb, thinking I wouldn't fall for you. God, I really thought I could ignore my feelings for you and they'd go away ..."

I put my hand on his cheek. "Aw, Ryan. That's so sweet."

"Yeah, so I figured I had to propose either right here on the rooftop ... or at MacAllister's," he said with a smirk.

"Oh my *God*. Don't even joke about that!"

Ryan finished off his champagne. He glanced at my glass and frowned. "You haven't had a drop."

"I told you, I'm not drinking."

"Not even tonight?" He narrowed his eyes at me. "What's up, Ella?"

I held my breath. *Should I tell him now? What if it goes badly and I screw this whole celebration up?*

Oh, whatever.

I didn't want to make a big scene out of it. Gently, I took Ryan's hand and simply placed it over my tummy and held it there.

His eyes grew wide. "Are you saying what I think you're saying?"

I nodded. "Yes, Ryan."

Ryan smothered any doubts or fears I might've had with a soulful kiss.

"Ella ... that's amazing!" he said at last.

"Yeah?" I asked, nervously laughing.

"Oh my *God,* yes! We're gonna have a *baby,* Ella!" Then he hushed his voice and looked around, hoping no one had heard. "Shit, I shouldn't say that so loud, eh?"

"Yeah ... we shouldn't announce it just yet ..."

"How far along are you?"

"Six weeks. I found out yesterday."

"Oh, man, that's gonna kill me. We gotta start getting *ready!* So what do we do now?"

I grinned. "First, let's enjoy our night. We'll start planning later. We've still got plenty of time."

He nodded and offered me his arm. "Let's go visit with every-one, then."

A couple hours later, the party had dwindled, and the rest of the stragglers went home or out to the club. News of the baby had put a wild spark in Ryan—and he barely managed to keep his eyes or hands off me all night. Now that we were home alone, Ryan rushed me into his bedroom, his mouth on mine, his hands hungrily groping at my breasts, his erection pressed against my rear.

He tore off my clothes in a hurry, then his own. He mounted

me and set the tip of his manhood at my opening.

"Ella, I love you so much," he said as he widened me open with his thick, throbbing cock.

"I love you too, Ryan," I moaned as he filled me.

THE END.

ABOUT THE AUTHOR

June Winters believes every romance is hotter on the ice. Born in Minnesota, June grew up knee-deep in hockey and quickly learned to love the sport—but especially its strong and sexy heroes, who will do anything for their teammates ... and the women they fall for.

Keep your eye out for more hockey romance from June!

If you'd like to be the first to hear about June's latest releases, sign up for her private mailing list!

Ice Daddy

(Boston Brawlers Book 2)

Once upon a time, Boston's best player **scored** *-- and never even knew it.*

Love him or hate him, hockey superstar Lance Couture makes *no* apologies for being the best -- or for living life to its fullest. He's hot, rich, and girls can't get enough of him. Why would a player like him *ever* settle down?

Nashville nursing student Paige McMillan only wanted to get over a cheating ex. But a few sinful hours with a tall, muscular bad boy left the good girl with a **lifetime of responsibility** -- and no idea who her adorable daughter's father really is.

When a pro hockey team comes to town, Paige learns that the father of her daughter is Lance Couture, star of the Boston Brawlers. But the pro athlete isn't interested in talking about lost time. He'd rather replay

their steamy one-night affair -- and his lips and tongue are *oh* so
seductive ...

Can Paige resist the hockey hunk's advances and tell him the truth?
Can Lance's career survive another off-ice controversy? *Is there hope for
a happy little hockey family?*

EXCERPT FROM ICE DADDY

I.

Paige McMillan

Paige's best friend, Emily, jabbed her with an elbow and quietly whispered, "*Pst.* Paige. There's a really cute guy in a suit across the bar. And he's *totally* checking you out."

Paige didn't look. She didn't care how cute the guy might be; her wounds were too fresh, too raw.

"If I'd known you were going to point out every hot guy that walks by, I think I would've stayed home instead," the Vanderbilt University junior muttered.

Emily groaned. "You've been cooped up in your apartment for a *month*, Paige. I know you're hurting, but that's why it's good to remember that there's plenty of other fish in the sea." She made a subtle gesture across the bar. "He's seriously *hot*, Paige."

"If he's so hot, why don't you talk to him?"

"Because I have a boyfriend. And he's not looking at me, he's looking at *you*."

Paige frowned. "So? Sleeping with some random guy really won't help me feel any better. It'll only make things worse."

"How would you know?" Emily asked with a defiant shrug of her shoulder. "You've never even *had* a one-night stand."

The idea made Paige snicker. "Some things you don't have to try. You just know."

"I'm not asking you to *marry* the damned guy and have his babies," Emily griped. "I'm just asking you to *look* at him."

A tinge of guilt settled in Paige's belly. Emily was only trying to help, yet Paige was being needlessly stubborn. She let out a small breath of surrender. "Fine. I'll look."

Slowly, and with an air of disinterest, Paige turned her head. Across the bar, she saw there wasn't just one guy in a suit—there was an entire raucous group of them. But instantly, she knew exactly which one Emily had meant. He had clean-cut hair and a day's worth of blond stubble that perfected his wholesome, All-American-Man look. And, most tellingly, he didn't shy away from her gaze. Instead, he seemed to be waiting for her with a glint in his eye and a smile on his lips. He gave a slight nod of his head, as if to say, *I'm your man.*

Careful not to send any unwanted signals, Paige broke eye contact with the guy in the suit before he could get any ideas.

"So? What do you think?" Emily asked.

"I see what you mean. He's handsome." She was almost surprised to hear herself admit it.

Emily beamed. "Told you. Man, all that trouble just to get you to look at a hot guy ..."

"But you have to understand, Em, it's just *so* soon. I still can't get over what Adam did—"

Emily was quick to cut her off. "We're not talking about that idiot tonight, remember?"

"My point is, objectively speaking, yes, the guy in the suit over there is super hot. But I'm really not in the frame of mind to meet anyone right now."

Emily gestured in the guy's direction. "Him and his friends—

they're all in suits. Think they came from a wedding? God, I'd happily marry any one of them ... they're all so hunky and *big*."

Paige peeked over again. Emily was right; the guy and all his friends were tall and statuesque and healthy looking. Enormous men, really.

"Maybe," she said. "Who knows?"

The All-American said something to his friends. They laughed, shoved him, and clapped him on the back. He downed the rest of his glass and pushed his way past his friends.

Startled, Paige quickly looked away and shielded her face. "Oh God, is he coming over here?"

Emily's eyes grew wider as he neared. "Yes. Yes, he absolutely is."

Paige didn't dare look to confirm it for herself. She couldn't believe this was happening. She didn't want this—and if this guy had *any* idea what a hot mess she was right now, he'd probably go running for the hills. Poor guy had no idea what he was getting himself into.

Sure enough, she felt his presence at her side a second later. He nudged her elbow with his rather large hand. His voice was deep, smooth, confident. "Hi, I'm Lance."

Can't believe I have to do this right now, she thought to herself as she met the stranger's pine green eyes with a look of skepticism. *This is the last thing I want right now.*

"Hi, Lance," she mumbled.

"What's your name?" he asked. He'd looked tall from across the bar, but up close, he was even taller. And handsomer. He had to stand at least 6'0 tall. He was blessed with broad shoulders and a wide, sturdy frame.

"Paige," she muttered.

His smile was bright and his presence warm—all of which slightly annoyed Paige. Couldn't he feel the cold waves of *brokenness* emanating off of her? She almost felt sorry for him for even trying to talk to her ... until she heard what came out of his mouth next, anyway.

"Paige," Lance repeated. "That's funny. Pages have numbers, but I don't have yours."

A hand darted to cover her mouth, and Paige stifled a mortified laugh. She glanced at Emily to make sure she'd just heard it, too—possibly the worst pickup line of all time.

"*Wow*, Lance," Paige said at last. "That was *bad*. Truly bad."

He set his rather large hand on her shoulder and gently squeezed. "Yeah, but it made you laugh, didn't it?"

Her back arched at his touch, whether she wanted it to or not. "If you're planning on using any more bad pickup lines on me, you better get them out of your system now."

"Hm. Okay." Apparently, Lance saw this as a challenge, because his eyes looked skyward for inspiration. "If your name is Paige, then I'm going to need a bookmark ... that way I never lose you."

Paige couldn't help it; she let out a loud laugh. She wondered if it was the first time she'd laughed in a month—it sure felt like it, anyway.

"Lance ... that's *awful*."

She had to give it to him, though: his confident grin was endearing. He wasn't afraid of rejection in the slightest. The guy was just having fun. His attitude was infectious.

"As long as you're still smiling, I don't care," he said. "You're perfect when you smile, you know that? But I bet you get that a lot."

"'*When*' I smile?" she repeated, unsure if she'd been complimented or insulted.

"From across the bar, it didn't look like you were having such a great time." Lance gave a cocky shrug. "So I came over to brighten your day."

Paige rolled her eyes. "Gee ... thanks."

"Can I buy you a drink?"

Before Paige could say *thanks but no thanks*, Emily piped up on her behalf. "Yes, you absolutely can buy her a drink!"

"... This is my friend, Emily, by the way," Paige said while she shot side-eyed daggers at Emily.

Emily and Lance shook hands and exchanged pleasantries.

"I *love* your suit, by the way," Emily said. She grabbed his sleeve. "God, it's so soft! What's this made out of?"

Lance flashed his piano-key-teeth. "Thanks. It's cashmere."

"Cashmere! Wow!" Relishing the role of matchmaker, Emily elbowed Paige's side. "Feel his jacket, Paige."

Hesitantly, Paige touched her hand to his arm. But the fine cashmere was so sleek and soft and smooth, she couldn't help but run her fingers up and down his arm. The hard, chiseled muscles that lurked underneath only complemented the luxurious fabric.

"That *is* soft," Paige said quietly.

Having worked her magic, Emily slid off her stool and excused herself. Paige gave her one last look before she pranced off.

Nice try, Emily, but it's still not gonna happen.

With Emily gone, Lance stood closer to Paige. He commanded the bartender's attention. As he reached for his wallet, his round, meaty shoulder gently brushed against hers.

"Just so you know, I'm not going to sleep with you," Paige said abruptly.

"Brutal honesty. I love it." Lance laughed and passed Paige her drink. "So where are you from?"

"Lived in Tennessee my whole life," Paige answered in her slight, sing-song southern drawl.

Lance smiled. "I like your accent."

"Thanks. And you don't have one. So where are you from?"

"I grew up in upstate New York, but I've lived all over. Right now I live in Boston."

"And what brings you to Nashville?"

"Business," he said with a wink.

Paige knew that wink was an invite to ask what he did for a living. But based on the quality of his suit, it was obvious that this guy made a killing at whatever it was he did. She figured he didn't need to have his ego stroked any more—so she didn't take the bait.

"Neat," Paige said simply, sipping at her drink.

"Yeah, I'm pretty much a modern-day superhero," Lance added, shifting his body weight.

It's killing this guy that I won't ask him what he does, isn't it? she thought to herself.

"Wow, a superhero, that's really great," she teased. "So do you wear underwear on top of your outfit?"

He laughed sarcastically and leaned closer to her ear. "No. That'd be weird. Actually, since you asked, I'm not wearing underwear."

"I didn't ask," Paige rambled, at a loss for words, "and besides, I don't believe you."

But her eyes stole an instinctive glimpse at his crotch. The thick bulge that ran down his thigh told her that he was telling the truth ... and that he was hung, too. Because *of course* a guy that handsome and well-to-do would have a big dick. Regardless, the sight of him put a tense knot in her throat. She quickly forced herself to look away, but the damage had been done—Lance had caught her looking.

"Don't believe me, then." With a devilish spark in his eye, he shrugged and sipped his whiskey. "You can find out later if I'm telling the truth or not."

"*Lance!*"

She smacked his chest with the back of her hand—but his

chest was so rock-hard, she might as well have smacked a brick wall. It didn't faze him at all.

"I think I liked you better when I thought you were a cheesy guy with bad pickup lines," she said while she pressed her smarting hand between her thighs. "Because now you're just being aggressive and weird."

He gave a shrug, and the accusation rolled off him like water from a duck's back. "You're really beautiful, Paige. You know that?"

She lowered her head. "You're just flattering me ..."

"No. Seriously. You are." Gently, he touched his massive hand to Paige's chin and raised her gaze to his. It was all-too-easy to get lost in his big green eyes—and even easier to forget that only a few minutes ago she could feel nothing but an ailing heart. But all she could see now, staring back at her, was the desire burning in this handsome stranger's eyes. He wanted her, and he wanted her badly, and the very *idea* of his lust made her grow weak in the knees. She knew she had to look away, but she couldn't, and then Lance steadied her jaw and moved in for a kiss.

She was surprised. She shouldn't have been—it was *obvious* this guy would try something exactly like that—but she was. Too stunned to move away, Paige didn't try to stop him. Their lips touched, and Lance kissed her deeper.

It was *nice*, wasn't it? Kissing a total stranger—rather, kissing a *new* set of lips. His lips moved with hers in a new way; his kisses didn't feel empty or scripted or fake. They were lips that hadn't betrayed her. Lips that wouldn't ever get the *chance* to betray her ... because this guy meant nothing to her.

He was just a total stranger. A hot guy from Boston. Some young, entitled, rich guy with an ego. A guy who didn't mean anything, who couldn't *ever* mean anything, because she'd never see him again. He was a guy who could make her forget about her idiot ex-boyfriend and her backstabbing roommate ... at least for a little while.

Maybe Emily's right? Maybe this is what I need.

Paige was surprised by how eagerly she kissed him back and how much of herself she gave to him. They kissed deeper, hotter, right there in the middle of the bar, knowing people were watching—and soon she felt his bulge pressing against her thigh as he lengthened in his trousers.

In the drunken darkness of the bar, she reached an eager hand between his legs and touched him. Now she knew it for sure; he'd told the truth earlier. Only a thin layer of baby-soft cashmere stood between her hand and his rock-hard manhood.

Cashmere and cock.

That was a dangerous combo.

She tightened her fingers around his throbbing desire while they kissed, hungrier, needier, conveniently forgetting for just a moment that she was practically stroking a stranger in public.

Paige cracked an eyelid and peeked over Lance's shoulder. Sure enough, every last one of his buddies stared, slack-jawed and open-mouthed, a hint of blush on their chiseled manly faces.

She pulled away from Lance and hid behind his massive torso.

"Your friends are watching," she said.

"So's yours," he said, gesturing over her shoulder.

She turned around and saw Emily. Caught, Emily panicked and pretended to look elsewhere.

"You wanna go somewhere else? Another bar?" Lance asked. "Or ... we could skip all that and go back to my hotel."

Paige couldn't believe that she'd even consider doing something like that, with a guy she didn't know, a guy she wasn't sure she'd even like if she knew him properly. But ...

"Where are you staying?" she asked, biting her lip.

"Across the street."

"The Heritage?" she asked with a tipsy giggle. "You're staying at the Heritage?"

It was the most expensive hotel in downtown Nashville.

"Well, yeah. Where else do you think I'd stay?"

"I have no idea …!"

I know nothing about you! she thought to herself.

He pulled her closer, until she was snug against his body, and Paige felt his pulsing cock against her leg. God, he was even bigger and harder now.

"So what do you say?" he asked, his breath hot and seductive on the lobe of her ear.

She stammered, "I—I swear I never do this."

But his cock, so warm and hard against her body, beckoned for her touch. She ran her hand down his bulge again, wanting to feel *exactly* how long he was. At the end of his many inches, she found something foreign and unexpected—a small, hard ring.

"Wait, what is this?" she asked, tugging and pulling at the object.

Lance's eyes fluttered with barely contained pleasure.

"That would be my piercing," he said with a gasp.

"You … you have a piercing?"

He nodded.

For some reason, that was the last push a good girl like her needed to go for the bad boy like him.

She downed the rest of her drink and hopped off her stool.

"Let's go."

… to be continued!

BOOKS BY JUNE WINTERS

Dallas Devils:

Date with a Devil (Book 1)

Comeback (Book 2)

Bad Teammate (Book 3)

Keeper (Book 4)

Just Friends (Book 5)

Best Man (Book 6)

Boston Brawlers:

Forbidden Puck (Book 1)

Ice Daddy (Book 2)

Crush (Book 3)

Colorado Blizzard:

Hooked (Book 1)

Grudge Puck (Book 2)